# I Should

# Have Said

# Something

By

## KIM BOYKIN

For my brilliant, beautiful son, Austin Boykin.

You're a miracle!

# TABLE OF CONTENTS

# Chapter One

**W**hen the snotty barista pushed the wrong drink across the counter, he had a smirk on his face that said he knew I was a take-what-you-get kind of woman. Any normal person would have asked for a do-over and taken advantage of the mom-and-pop coffee shop's guarantee *to make it right, or it's free*. But I was never good at saying what I wanted, which is how you end up with the wrong drink, the wrong life.

So, I slinked out the door with some kind of vile chai-tea-whatever because, most of all, I didn't want to visit my parents in the assisted living facility across the street. That sounds terrible; it is terrible. But I love them so much, it hurts to know that they won't live forever, that when one of them goes, the other will likely follow from a broken heart. At fifty-five, I'm keenly aware of how lucky I am to have both my parents. But I've avoided the Sunny Side Seniors Community, or more specifically, the Memory Care unit where my father lived since I started doing things like putting the hammer in the refrigerator and losing my car at the mall twice on the same day.

It was easier to accept losing myself somewhere in a less-than-shiny thirty-two-year marriage, but losing my mind? Not knowing my kids' faces the way my dad hasn't known mine for the last couple of years. Knowing my kids will feel that kernel of pain in their chests like I do when Dad tells the nice stranger, that would be me, about his only daughter, my oldest sister Julia. And on some days, Julia doesn't even make the cut.

Mom has pretended not to notice my avoidance and brings Dad to her apartment, so I can see him. It's easier that way. She did the same thing for Dad, back when he used to get upset about all his forgetting, and smoothed away his little hiccups the same way she made her fitted sheets look like Martha Stewart lived in her laundry room. And did it so well, most people were shocked when they learned Dad had to go to Memory Care. It was as embarrassing as it was terrifying when she noticed my gaffes and tried to do the same for me.

Most days, I can forget anything, everything, but I can't forget that my mind is likely ripe with Dad's disease. I haven't seen a doctor unless you count WebMD. Staying out of Memory Care, where everyone except the certified nursing assistants has lost their minds to dementia or Alzheimer's, had made things better, much better, until yesterday when I forgot my husband's birthday.

Granted, things between Rhys and me have been tense since he joined me in early retirement six months ago. The kids had good excuses for not calling until after ten pm. Emma was fresh out of law school doing grunt work on a big case here in Charleston. Jordan was on location in the Catskills with spotty cell reception. They called within seconds of each other, and when the last call ended, Rhys shrugged with that little half-smile that used to melt me to the bone.

"Don't sweat it, Maise. It's fine."

I apologized and couldn't stop until I realized my tone was the same as Dad's when he apologized because he didn't know who Rhys was.

But my retired detective husband never missed a thing. He knew I had bad genes and was likely diseased. He knew I'd forgotten a lot of things lately. Stupid little things that added up and reminded me I was the same age as my dad's baby sister when she was diagnosed with early-onset Alzheimer's, which was nothing like Dad's brand that was thankfully as easy-going as he is. What Rhys didn't know was I forgot his birthday because I didn't love him anymore.

Before today, I never would have considered taking a chainsaw to our family tree to mark myself and Rhys as the only people from our families ever to divorce. I would have gone to my grave living a life I didn't want with a man I didn't love if that barista hadn't given me the wrong drink, if Mom hadn't summoned me to help her find the pair of earrings Dad gave her to celebrate my birth.

I pushed through the doors of the Sunny Side Adult Care facility and made my way down the hall to Mom's apartment. Her place was a tiny replica of the Charleston single house on Wentworth Street where my sisters and I grew up, just two blocks north of Broad. It was so charming that Sunny Side had used it in some of their advertisements. I announced myself three times before she finally heard me and put a note in my phone so I wouldn't forget to search for the hearing aids she was forever losing.

I kissed her hello and started looking for the teardrop pearl pair in the usual hiding places, digging my hand between the mattress and the box spring and running it around the edges, opening and closing drawers, and, lastly, picking through the peacock blue trashcan beside her bed.

I stopped short when I recognized a piece of crumpled paper as a stray from the ancient pink notebook Mom took to her creative writing class. She had no idea the cute, retired professor who taught

4

the class had a crush on her. Every day the two of them sat at the same table in the Memory Care dining room, him with his blank-eyed wife who hadn't known him for years, and Mom with the only man she'd ever loved.

The poor guy had been trying to send Mom messages for months with writing assignments like: *Write a love story and then rewrite it, changing the hero or the hero, I'm* pretty sure he meant for one of those to be heroine, *to a completely different person. Perhaps someone in this room.* But the assignment in the trashcan was just a simple list, and it made me wonder if he'd given up on love like I had.

I'm not sure what bothered me more, that my eighty-five-year-old mother, who'd lived the perfect life with the perfect man, had a bucket list that might go unfulfilled or that she threw it away. Regardless, I shoved the list into the waistband of my yoga pants and kept searching for the earrings.

"So, how's Rhys?" Mom blurted, head cocked to the side, almost pleading for me to say *he's wonderful. We're wonderful.* She'd done that a lot lately because she knew something was wrong. Still, it was hard to discuss the state of my marriage with someone who'd lived the majority of her life in a nearly perfect one.

"He's f ine," I assured. Her look demanded more, and she exercised her special talent of getting what she wanted without actually saying it, a trick she taught me--the not-saying part. I just keep waiting for the-getting-what-I-want part to kick in.

"Rhys is at the gym again."

The last word sounded bitter, but I was grateful he was committed to washboard abs at sixty, which took a lot of time and effort.

This was when Mom always pressed for more information or offered marital advice from atop the pedestal where she and Dad have resided since she was eighteen, but losing those earrings must have really been niggling her.

"Good for him." She nodded at the stylish mid-calf winter white sweater dress laid out on the bed. "Help me on with my dress, sugar?" I slipped the dress off of the hanger, relieved she'd redirected herself. But every time our dance altered, it made me a little more paranoid. Did she worry about having the *big A* like I did?

Or worse, did she already have it?

"Well, you be sure and give him *our* love." Her words were saccharine as she held her arms out for me to help get her dress on without disturbing her hairdo, but the inflection was clear. *Our love* included *my* love.

The dress floated down Mom's slender frame and kissed the tops of her stylish, flat cognac boots. She completed the look with a funky, Vogue-worthy brown belt and checked her look in the full-length mirror before glancing at me for approval.

"You look beautiful, Mom. Don't worry about the earrings; I'll find them," I said. "You should get down to Memory Care; it's almost lunchtime."

"I know you'll find them. You always do." She pawed through her jewelry box until she found a dangly pair she bought at Forever 21, not that she'd ever own up to setting foot in the store. "In the meantime, I'll just wear these costume things." She put them on, fluffed her silver shoulder-length bob, and blotted her painted lips on a tissue before heading for the door. "Should I have a place set for you?"

"Thanks, but I have an appointment." I turned away so she couldn't see the lie stain my cheeks.

"All right then, sweet girl, I love you." The door closed behind her, and the dark cloud that always came with being the youngest of Dad's three daughters playing Alzheimer's roulette was banished by a kind of victory that was both good and bad. The earrings, along with Mom's hearing aids were in plain sight in a little jewelry dish where both of us had looked at least ten times. If Mom was still in the apartment, she would have praised the fairies for putting them there, but all I could do was doubt myself.

I flopped face down on the bed, the crumpled bucket list digging into my skin. I fished it out of my pants. There were only five items on Mom's list. I smoothed the paper out on the bed and smiled at the first four she'd checked off. One, marry a wonderful man. Two, have beautiful children. Three, have lots of grandchildren. Four, help Daddy, she always called my father Daddy, learn to love black people and gay people, and anyone who wasn't Southern and white.

To her credit, she'd done that, and with a little help from Alzheimer's, my father forgot he was a bigot and loved everybody now. But the last item on Mom's list got to me because it was the one thing she wanted that was just for her and nobody else. Sure, she got the good marriage with a great guy, except for the bigot thing, but their marriage was always more about making her husband happy and keeping him that way, a refrain that sounded uncomfortably familiar.

"See the redwoods before I die." The last word caught in my throat. My mother was never going to die. At least, that was what the six-year-old inside me said. But she was eighty-five. Even with the benefit of having Dad in Memory Care, she'd slowed down considerably this past year. Worse, she'd thrown her bucket list away like it wasn't possible to have everything she wanted. Of course, any sane person would tell her she was right. But what if they were wrong? What if you really can have everything you want, or it's possible to create a life that feels that way?

What would *my* list look like? What were my *redwoods*?

I got the perfect kids and would probably get the grandkids one day, but the marital union that felt more like a business arrangement with occasional sex wasn't what I wanted. What if I never got what I wanted? Did I even know what that was? The answer came from somewhere in the hollow of my gut that began to fill with hope and resolve and brought me back to the coffee shop and the barista who was staring me down.

"This isn't what I ordered." I all but squeezed my eyes shut in anticipation of some cataclysmic event swallowing me whole, but nothing happened. His pierced eyebrow raised, full lips and razor-sharp Picassoesque cheekbones set in a defiant look that would usually have sent me scurrying away with the lukewarm chai tea, but not today. "It's not what I want."

The words poured out like a jailbreak as I told him precisely how to make my drink. Iced, double shots of chocolate and espresso but WITH whipped cream this time, double chocolate syrup on top. The barista snapped to with a thin smile like his bitchiness was all part of a test, and I'd obliterated the curve. Minutes later, he popped a straw in my drink and slid it across the bar.

Molecules of sugar connected with dark roast coffee and chocolate and did a frantic victory dance to honor my great awakening. How could I live another moment worrying about offending the people I loved when I was shortchanging myself? But could I blight my and Rhys' divorce-free family trees? Mom was slipping a little, or on some days, a lot. Would the end of my marriage send her careening over the edge? If I had to keep pretending I was happily married, I would eventually send myself careening over the edge.

"Get you something else?" The sheer possibility of the barista's words stole my breath.

"Yes." I sucked the entire drink down to the milky ice cubes. "I want a divorce."

# Chapter Two

**N**ever in a million years would I have thought that a godlike man like Rhys would have picked me out of a crowd, but he did. Fresh out of the University of South Carolina, I was beyond stressed, thanks to my first teaching job, and had gone straight to Bertha's Kitchen in North Charleston for comfort. I ordered the high priestess of soul food's okra soup and cornbread and probably would have spotted him if I hadn't been mooning over plates full of legendary fried chicken, mashed potatoes, and collard greens that passed by my table.

Rhys said I had a deer-in-the-headlights look, and he was probably right.

I'd just finished orientation for my new job at Mary Ford Elementary in North Charleston and was terrified. The school and the teachers were nice enough, but the stories they told about many of the impoverished children who would be in my charge, about some of the parents who didn't seem to care about their children's education, made me wonder if I was even capable of doing the job.

Pat Conroy's *The Water Is Wide* had always been my Bible, the whole reason I'd gone into teaching and chosen nearby Mary Ford Elementary over the cushier, albeit less paying job with the private school, Porter-Gaud. I'd wanted to immerse myself in making a difference in the lives of my students like Pat did until I saw the pitifully low test scores of my incoming third graders and was forced to admit I was no Pat Conroy. I was a twenty-two-year-old ball of doubt and frustration without the first clue as to how to bridge the cavern between where my students tested and where the state said they should be.

Rhys said I bumped into him on my way out of the restaurant. To this day, I don't remember that moment. With a face like his, he was used to that trick, but I didn't look up, just murmured, "sorry," and went straight to my car.

The early August heat was stifling, but I didn't turn on the car. I just sat there baking, trying to convince myself I was capable of doing the job, when someone knocked on the window. I looked up at the most stunningly beautiful man I'd ever seen, smiling because he'd finally gotten the reaction he was accustomed to. "You okay, ma'am?"

Sweat trailed through my mascara and stung my eyes. "I'm fine, officer," I swiped at my sockets that were officially raccooned.

"You're cute," he said with a smile that made me forget about The Water Is Wide and low test scores. "Might want to crank up your car and turn the air on."

I did, and when I looked up again, he was writing out a ticket. I did a double-take to see I was parked illegally. He jerked his chin at the sign and then pointed at the appropriate lines on his ticket book. "Your name and phone number here."

"I'm really sorry, officer." My hands shook as I jotted down my information. "I started my first real job today, and, well, I'm a little overwhelmed. Honestly, I didn't even see the sign." Which was a six-foot square with giant red letters that said. *No Parking. Deliveries Only.* He glanced up from writing in his notebook and grinned before ripping off the top copy and handing it to me.

"Call me." I looked down to see his name and phone number next to mine. "And if you don't, Maisie Jenkins, I'll call you."

I don't know why out of all the dazzling beauties Charleston is famous for, Rhys Carver chose me. But he made it clear on our first date when he made my head swim with our first kiss and breathed, "I'm gonna marry you, Maisie Jenkins." I remember laughing at the absurdity of a guy like him making that declaration to an average girl like me, and then he kissed me until I believed him.

Less than a year later, I looked into Rhys Carver's gorgeous face, crying so hard I could barely get out the sacred promise to love, honor and cherish because forever seemed completely doable back then.

But the rush of courage I'd felt at the coffee shop vanished the second I pushed through the mudroom door, and the man who had meticulously planned every aspect of our lives for the past thirty years was looking at me with his detective's face that didn't retire when he did a few months ago.

"Hey." He gave me a cursory peck on the cheek and then studied me for a few seconds before cutting right to the chase. "Something up?"

"No." My hands shook as I struggled to get the domed lid off of the coffee cup; the remnants of my drink sprayed the laundry room sink. He rinsed them away before snapping the lid back on the cup and throwing it in the recycle bin. "I went over to Mom's to help her find her earrings and got coffee."

A speck of chocolate and whipped cream on my finger prodded me to add, *I don't love you. I'm not even sure I like you, and I don't want to spend the rest of my life with you.* I washed my hands and wiped away the thought.

"Hmm," he said, like he was still solving crimes.

"Nothing's up. I'm fine." I hung my coat on one of the hooks by the door to the garage and tossed my sunglasses in my bag.

He followed me into the kitchen. I opened the refrigerator door and pretended to sort out dinner in hopes he would retreat to his man cave. Instead, he picked up the ledger off of the kitchen counter and scanned the neat rows of numbers. "Did you write the coffee in?"

"No, I didn't write my coffee into the ledger," I snapped. "But I want to take Mom on this trip to California--I mean I'd like to--- If that's okay with you." The lump in my throat slid to my belly, where all the truths I'd swallowed back resided.

"Why?" His eyes narrowed.

"Mom's not getting any younger, Rhys. She needs this trip." I was going to hell for chickening out but lying and using my mother as an excuse would get me an all-access pass.

"Sounds expensive." Rhys' go-to line to put a stop to anything that didn't jibe with what he wanted. "Something's up, Maise. This just isn't like you."

*Of course, it's not like me because I never say what I want.*

"*Damnit,*" I barked. The shock on his face was like a mind-altering, life-altering drug. "I need a break from—from--."

14

"From what?" He regained his composure quickly, and a lifetime of interrogating Charleston's finest criminals kicked in. "Where is this coming from, Maisie? We don't swear at each other. We never yell."

"This is so stupid. I'm a grown woman who is going to take her grown mother, possibly her sisters, to California. I don't have to *ask* you for permission; money isn't an issue. And don't you dare say it is. I'm going, and that's final."

"You can't--."

"Don't you tell me what I can or cannot do, Rhys Carver."

Maybe I couldn't ask this man, no *tell* him I wanted a divorce, but I could do this trip and figure things out. "God! I can't believe you told me *no* like I'm a child." And how many times had I let him do that over the past thirty-two years? I swiped Mom's number on my phone. The voice in the back of my mind that used to be so small was huge and angry. *Why did you ask for his permission? Why can't you tell him what you really want?*

The call connected. I turned my back on him like a pissy teenager demanding privacy. "Mom. Hey, it's me. You know that trip you always wanted to go on? The one to see the redwoods? Well, we're doing it."

"Come on, Maise." Rhys was the good cop now, cajoling me with that silky plea that got me into bed every single time and made me feel guilty later for liking sex so much. "First, you called it a trip, then you called it a break. But the way you said it—it sounded like you meant a break from me." His words had the same effect as his gifted hands. My body responded, knowing where he would eventually take us and eager to get there until he said, "Baby, you can't take that trip."

*"Can't?"* I spun around to glare at him.

After all these years, I should have been immune to my husband's good looks, but he was muscly and fit and made George Clooney look like Jabba the Hutt. And how was that even fair when half of my teacher's pension was spent on anti-aging miracle creams and supplements so that maybe, on one of my best days, I would look like I belonged to him?

"Babe." The wanting in his whiskey eyes weakened me considerably until he opened his mouth again. "I know that isn't what you want."

But Rhys didn't know what I wanted; he didn't pay enough attention to even be in the general vicinity of knowing. "This isn't about you, Rhys." Over half my life had been lived based on what he wanted, what he thought was best, which was just as much on me because I went along with it. "Not everything is about you," I whispered on the off-chance Mom had her hearing aids in. "I'm going to see the damn redwoods, and that's final."

"Redwoods?" Mom sighed. "Oh, honey, that was just some silly something I jotted down in class."

"Mom, you need this trip." I need this trip. "So, California--,"

"Sounds like this is more than just some trip." Rhys was right. I needed some distance between him and me.

"This feels like you're leaving us. Is that really what you want?" His eyes pled for the answer he wanted to hear. At that moment, I could have probably asked him for anything, including a divorce, and he would have given it to me, and I hated him for that. I hated myself even more because I didn't know what to do with this thing that was between us or that that wasn't between us anymore because we were different people now. "I deserve an answer, Maise."

That was the moment when I should have told him I stopped loving him a long time ago, that I was becoming myself. A new and different me who couldn't exist another minute with a king-of-the-castle husband. But the rush of caffeine and sass that had burned through my body like a monster hot flash was smoldering with a high probability of tears. "*God,* Rhys, just leave me alone!"

"Sugar, I can hardly hear you," Mom's voice rescued me. "You know, the lady who moved in next door to me? She has that new iPhone and the volume works like a dream every time."

My husband moved in close. Practiced hands kneaded my shoulders. His breath on the back of my neck sent chills down my thighs.

"Baby, I know things haven't been great since I retired. And I get that you're making some kind of stand here, but you can't just leave." I know *can't* was Rhys's way of saying he didn't want me to go, which would have been sweet. Except he was big and intimidating and still used that in everyday life like he did when he was a beat cop.

I jerked away from him. "I didn't realize you wanted a new phone, Mom. I'll go online and order one for you when we ring off."

"Talk to me, Maisie." He kissed the back of my neck and waited for a beat for me to melt into a puddle. When that didn't happen, he said, "Screw it. I'll be in the den when you get off the phone."

The moment he left the room, all the oxygen that had been gobbled up by things unsaid whooshed back in. I'd tried to take advantage of my recent forgetfulness and forget things between Rhys and me had deteriorated. I've tried to forget that after thirty years of marriage, he still doesn't know me and doesn't have a clue how lonely I feel when we're in the same room together. I've tried to forget that I've wasted years of precious time, his and mine, by not asking for an end to this marriage that was never perfect. I never expected it to be, and I don't think Rhys did either. It was better when it was new, and then we just kept contributing to it, separately, kind of like an IRA. Both of us committed to keeping it going, but for a long time, neither of us had contributed. We worked. We raised kids. We grew apart.

So why couldn't I just tell him that?

It would be easier if the plane to California crashed. But that would take Mom and Willa and Julia out too, and that wouldn't be fair. Or if Rhys could drop dead because apparently, I'm just like my mother when it comes to saying what I want, and Rhys and I will be celebrating our 50th anniversary with our kids and grandkids and Mom because she's never going to die, and I'll still feel the same way about my husband.

I swiped at my tears. Rhys wasn't a bad person, and neither am I for wanting a divorce.

"A new iPhone sounds lovely, Maisie. Any color will do, but I'm not so sure about this trip."

"No, Mom. You, me, Willa, and Julia, if she can get away." Fat chance of that happening. "We're going, and it will be fantastic."

"Oh, honey." The emotion was thick in her voice. "It's sweet of you, really it is, but I can't just run off to California. Your daddy——."

"Has great CNAs to take care of him. That's what you pay them to do. I promise you, Dad will be fine, and it'll be good for you to take a trip with your girls. It'll be good for all of us."

"Maisie, darlin', if you saw my list, you know I've been blessed, so blessed, a bunch of old trees just aren't that important."

Tears threatened, and my nose stung so hard I could barely get the words out. "They are, Mom." And for reasons I couldn't explain, those redwoods I'd never seen were important to me too.

Rhys banged around in the den to remind me he was waiting to finish our conversation. "So, we're going," I said. "I'll touch base with Willa and Julia to coordinate schedules and get back to you soon with dates."

"All right," she sighed. "I love you, sweet girl, and don't forget my phone. One of those thirteens if they've got it."

I ended the call and fired up my laptop to order Mom's phone. The one she wanted cost ten times more than the one-hundred-dollar price tag that always made Rhys cringe. I didn't need a new phone, but Verizon reminded me I was due for an upgrade. I changed the quantity to two, clicked the Buy button, and headed for the den to upgrade my life. But Rhys was already dead.

# Chapter Three

I didn't mean to wish my husband dead, but he was sprawled out on the floor in front of his recliner, the remote under his cheek, his glassy eyes staring at the television that was on the Travel Channel.

*"Rhys!"*

My body quaked. I dropped to my knees.

"Wake up, *Rhys.*" My fingers trembled as they danced over his neck, checking for a pulse. Nothing. I pumped his chest hard and then remembered it was possible to break his ribs as cleanly and easily as I had wanted to break us.

"Goddamnit, Rhys." I breathed into his mouth and got excited when a puff of air came out of his nose, but it was my own breath. "Shit." I pinched his nostrils and breathed again. Still no response.

I punched 911 into my phone and put the call on speaker, so I could continue CPR.

His body was limp and lifeless, and why was this happening to him, the health nut? He was never the jelly donut kind of cop. He ordered salad when I ordered fries and coffee when I got cake. He worked out seven days a week and had even taken up CrossFit recently. One of the few post-early-retirement things I was grateful for because it got him out of the house for a couple of hours every day.

"911. What is your emergency?" I opened my mouth to speak, but nothing came

out. "What is your emergency?"

"My husband had a heart attack." I felt the stabbing pain of past tense, the hollowness of a million regrets.

"Okay, ma'am. Is he breathing?"

I leaned over to feel the breath that had sent chills down my body just minutes ago. "No."

"An ambulance is a few minutes away. Can you confirm your address for me?"

Wait. Wasn't this what I wanted? But how would I ever explain to the kids that I wished their beloved father dead?

"Ma'am, your address." I don't know if I whispered or screamed the words or if they were just one more thing that would go unsaid like always with Rhys and me. "What's your name?"

"Maisie."

"Okay, Maisie. I'm going to stay on the phone with you until the EMTs get there. Do you know CPR?"

I nodded and began to beat the crap out of Rhys' chest.

"Hang in there, Maisie. The ambulance is three minutes away."

His lips were warm. God, he was a good kisser. There were times when we first met that we kissed for hours. He'd steal my breath, and I'd steal his, back and forth, until we were drunk from the sheer intimacy of the exchange. A body could exist off breath-sharing, breath-stealing kisses like those, a dying relationship could resuscitate. When was the last time Rhys and I kissed, really kissed? Years? The answer was more likely a decade or so ago.

"Keep going, ma'am," the dispatcher said. "You're doing fine."

Hands stacked over his heart, I pumped wildly and tried to remember the CPR class Willa and I took ten years ago for Mom and Dad, just in case. But the class was long and boring, so Willa and I skipped the last part of it to get coffee. The instructor had said the rhythm was easy to remember because it matched a Bee Gees song. But the Bee Gees sang a lot of songs, and the only one I could think of was *How Can You Mend a Broken Heart.*

The world dissolved into a wall of tears as I sputtered, "I can think of younger days." I pitched the song too high, even for the Bee Gees. "When living for my life was--. La La la la--." I couldn't remember all the words, and it was such a sad, slow song. "How can you mend this broken *man?*" This man I didn't love. This man I wanted to divorce. "And let him live again." I didn't want him to die.

"Ma'am?" The dispatcher shouted. "It's Staying Alive." I nodded. Of course, the pumping and the breathing were all about staying alive, but Rhys was dead. I knew he was, but I just couldn't stop singing. "Please help me mend my broken heart. *And let me live againnn.*"

"No." The dispatcher screamed. "The CPR song is 'Staying Alive.'"

With my eyes closed, I could see Rhys' face on John Travolta's lanky body in *Saturday Night Fever,* bopping down a New York street in those tight pants, checking his reflection in every shop window. It was too much, so I concentrated on the rhythm instead of the words because I knew they said something about the wings of heaven. A piece of me felt good, relieved. *Just let him go.*

But his life flashed before my eyes, our wedding day, clips of him with the kids. He was such a good dad to our babies; I couldn't let him die; Jordan and Emma would be devastated.

"Ah, ha, ha, ha stayin' alive. Ah, ha ha ha, stayin' alive." I pumped, but he didn't stir. I slapped him hard. "Goddamn it, Rhys. Wake up."

"Keep working on him, ma'am," the dispatcher said, but Rhys was gone. There were other dispatchers in the background who had more important emergencies than mine.

Sirens blared. The ambulance was close. How many times, just after we were first married, had I been paralyzed by that sound because I couldn't get used to being a cop's wife?

"Life going nowhere, somebody help me." I gritted the words out through tears because it's impossible to sing a pop song from the '70's when the man you once loved was dying. "Somebody--help me--yeah." But Rhys *is* invincible. *Was* invincible, and after what seemed like forever, the sirens went blessedly silent.

His eyes were shut. I didn't see them close, but the way I'd been slapping him around and heaving into his mouth, I shouldn't have been surprised. How long had he been sick, and I didn't know it because I was too busy trying to get up the nerve to ask for a divorce? I grabbed his face and screamed. "*Wake up.*"

His neck was like jelly, the beginning of jowls that proved my Dick Clark husband had aged way more gracefully than me, and I could not stop thinking about him in the past tense. What was his

25

last thought? How long had his brain been without oxygen? Was he dead? Because if he was, this marriage was really over, and I never got the chance to tell my husband of thirty-two years what I wanted.

"*God damn you, Rhys.*" My fist slammed into his chest, and my shoulder dislocated like it always did at the most inopportune times. White-hot pain scorched a path down my arm and zinged up my neck before circling my head like the stars in that cartoon with the coyote. But I didn't want to be the coyote. I wanted to be the roadrunner who always won and got what she wanted.

I tried to stay conscious, but Rhys was gone, and I was drifting farther away from him than ever.

# Chapter Four

The hospital room smelled like rancid beef stew, but it didn't keep my stomach from growling.

The scent mingled with a disinfectant that was not supposed to smell like a disinfectant but did. The harsh light made opening my eyes seem like a bad idea. A commercial for a miracle drug blared in another room, Tom Selleck talking about erectile dysfunction before the announcer listed all the complications that could arise. Headache, heartburn, diarrhea, hearing loss. "You may be at risk for a stroke or heart attack."

Heart attack. Rhys never needed Tom's miracle drug for Friday sex. Or maybe he used it all the time, and I just didn't know.

I tried to open my eyes, but my own drugs made that impossible. God, I hadn't been that relaxed in years. It was good. So so good, like the way I used to sleep before I had kids or before Mom sent Dad to the grocery for bread, and he ended up two states away in Florida.

Whatever they gave me, I was definitely getting my sister, Willa, some for her birthday. She was tired all the time, and sometimes I worried she had some rare, incurable form of cancer or something like fibromyalgia that didn't seem so bad but definitely was. But that wasn't why she was so worn out. Even though Mom and Dad had been at Sunny Side for almost a year, neither of us had fully recovered from the dark time between now and that trip to the Piggly Wiggly that ended when some lady running carpool T-boned Dad's car.

Someone called my name, trying to draw me out of my drug-induced cocoon. I ignored them the way I did when Rhys wanted sex and pretended to sleep.

Wow. Rhys. He was really dead. That was horrible, so horrible. But it didn't seem so bad with the drugs. I'd need a lot of drugs for the funeral. God, I wasn't looking forward to that. Everybody loved

Rhys, except me. But I didn't want him to die, although that was part of the gig if you're alive, and I was alive. The annoying machine keeping pace with my heartbeat said so.

Would mourners be able to look at me and tell I didn't love him anymore? I'd been to enough funerals over the years to know how I was supposed to act when death made a surprise visit. I wasn't sure I could pull off the angsty grieving widow, and that wouldn't play well with the kids, with Rhys' family. But Mom would cry enough for both of us, Willa too, because she could see one of those Budweiser commercials with the puppies and the Clydesdales and cry for a week. My sister Julia would be stoic or absent, maybe both.

The drugs were like therapy with painkillers that made me want to never wake up. You never saw that advertised on TV between Tom's ED commercial and the ad with the woman who wore pink tights and played the part of Diarrhea. But if I died, the kids would lose both their parents. Shit. The kids.

How could I tell Jordan his father was gone? And Emma? She was such a daddy's girl. She'd be crushed. All the more reason to stay strong. Maybe I could be stoic like Julia was when her husband died. God, she was beautiful at the funeral, always so put together. She'd probably melt like Elphaba's sister if you poured her into a pair of jeans and a T-shirt.

I lived in jeans and yoga pants. The last time I wore a little black dress was at Rhys's retirement party. It was kind of cute, but not so cute you couldn't wear it to a funeral. Would anyone notice if I wore the same dress? Probably not. They'd be too busy morning Rhys because everything is *always* about him.

"Mom?" Emma. My girl, Not just Rhys's. The one who knew what she wanted and spoke her mind, even when I wished she'd just shut it sometimes. "Mom, I love you. Please wake up." Her voice was sweet, like the first time I heard her cry. My lips turned up, and the muscles around my closed eyes flexed and crinkled.

Even with my brow raised to my hairline, my eyes wouldn't open. "Just keep talking to her, honey. She'll come around." I didn't know that voice, but someone took my hand, and I would know that warmth anywhere because I gave it to my daughter when I brought her into the world.

"I'm right here, Mom." She kissed my palm.

Staying in such a lovely cocoon was a chickenshit thing to do. She was smiling at me when I opened my eyes, her face so hopeful. Her hand clasped in mine, and this was the bond that would sustain us until the end of my days.

"Blaby." Talking was a lot harder than I thought it would be.

In a way, Rhys' death was a blessing. That's what Mom would call it because it would kill Emma if he'd lived and we'd gotten divorced.

The nurse left to give us some privacy. "Emma. Sweetheart, your dad-."

She held our clasped hands in front of my face, and *whoa*, a big freaking diamond was on her finger. Cameron must have proposed. She met him the year before she started law school and had waited three years for this rock. H*oly cow*. "You're engaged."

She blushed and held her hand out in that proud way all newly affianced girls do. "Tonight, after work. Cam called me into his office, shut the door, and--."

"Oh, God, please don't tell me about sexy-time."

"*Mom*." Her giggle was sweet. "It wasn't like that. Cam went all traditional, and got down on one knee. It was so romantic. He was going to ask you and Dad for permission, ex post facto of course. But when we got to your house, the ambulances were leaving."

Ambulances. "Honey, about your dad--."

"The hospital is crazy tonight, Mom. Literally, people lined up out the door. Cam has a friend who works in the ER and went to find out more about Dad. God, Mom, both of you scared the crap out of me." She squeezed my hand hard and cried like someone had opened a faucet. "But you and Dad are okay," she gushed through happy tears. "And I'm getting married. Everything's going to be okay."

"Emma." It was my job to tell her before some well-meaning doctor came in to tell me what I already knew. "Honey, your father is dead."

Her gorgeous face that looked so much like Rhys' crumpled.

"I'm sorry," I blubbered. So sorry Willa and I went for coffee instead of learning how to really do CPR.

Sorry I couldn't save him any more than I could save our marriage. "I'm so sorry."

The truth knocked Emma out of the chair and onto her knees. "*NO.*" She sobbed and crawled into my bed like she did when she was little. "No, Mommy. Please."

Before I could wrap my good arm around her, she was levitated up and away from me. Cam pulled her onto his lap and held her so beautifully, so possessively, like he would happily kill anyone who hurt her, including me. Especially me, but seeing him protect Emma like that made me love him a lot.

Emma raised her head from Cam's chest and looked at me. The pain in her eyes would always be there, less as the years went by, but when she walked down the aisle, when her and Jordan were swaying during the fatherless daughter dance, Rhys's absence would suffocate her.

"Honey, I tried to save him, I did, but-."

Cam cupped Emma's face and pressed his forehead against hers. "Baby, your dad is big and strong. He's okay; I promise you he's going to be okay."

He shouldn't have lied to her, but wasn't that how all marriages started out? Two people making promises they're not sure they will keep, can keep? But was it a lie if you believed it? Because I did promise to honor and cherish Rhys, but not obey because I lived through the feminist movement. Would things have worked out better if I had promised to obey? It would have been great for Rhys, but he was dead.

"But Mom said--."

He put his fingers over her lips. He would call the firm for both of them to take time off; he'd probably call Jordan if I asked him to, but that was my job.

Before I could say anything, Willa bustled into the room, threw down her oversized Brahmin bag, and hugged Emma before looking at me like she knew I killed Rhys with ineptitude.

"Good God, Maisie." I yelped when she squeezed my hand. "Sorry," she soothed. "It's just I thought—, she swiped at tears," the worst.

"Emma called when she saw not one but two ambulances leaving your house." Willa took a deep breath. "I jumped in the car and got here as fast as I could. The nurse says they're taking you down to surgery in a few minutes for that damn shoulder of yours. I haven't told Mom yet, but I called Jordan."

The memory of a portly Indian man standing by my bedside explaining something with an iPad and some nurse asking me to sign on the dotted line had seemed dreamlike but had apparently been real. "Thanks for calling him."

"I talked to him, too," Cam said. "He's on standby at JFK and should be here late tonight."

My poor fatherless son, alone at the airport. Maybe he had a nice guy with him. Not that he would ever tell me about anyone he's dating because I got a manly gay son who keeps his feelings to himself.

Jordan's coming out had surprised me a little, but it really confused Rhys. Apparently, there had been an incident he'd never told me about when Jordan was a senior in high school. Rhys went to get Jordan up for Saturday swim practice, and a girl was in his bed. Rhys never mentioned it until Jordan sat us down during Christmas break his freshman year to tell us he was gay.

"But I saw you in bed with a girl," Rhys said slowly, "a naked girl."

"That was a last-ditch effort to--," Jordan hung his head but didn't finish his sentence.

"Honey. A last-ditch effort for what?" I asked.

"To not be gay because I didn't want to disappoint either of you." Fat teardrops plopped onto the leg of his jeans. "That's what it feels like I'm doing now."

Rhys tipped Jordan's chin up. "Son, look at me" The shame in Jordan's eyes broke my heart. "You, being who you are, could never disappoint your mother, and it sure as hell could never disappoint me. I'm proud of you for having the courage to tell us, damn proud. It doesn't matter to us who you love because we love you, and nothing's ever going to change that."

I was proud of Jordan, but I don't think I'd ever been prouder of Rhys than I was that day. It even gave our marriage a shot in the arm. But, unfortunately, the shot only lasted a little longer than the drugs for my shoulder that was wearing off.

"I couldn't get any information from anyone in the ER, but your dad is tough Em." Cam's shirt was wet where she'd snotted on him, but he didn't mind one bit. Yep. I definitely loved this guy. "He's going to be fine." Except for the lying, but he could work on that.

Willa pulled a chair to my bedside. Just being in the same room with her felt better. "I called Julia. She sends her best."

"Of course she does." I never thought I was the kind of person who'd cut a family member out of my life, much less a sister, but I had decided to make an exception for Dr. Julia Watson. "Bet she won't even come to the funeral."

Willa gave me a hard look because we only said what we really thought about our eldest sister when no one else was around. But good God, we were talking about my husband's funeral. Sure, he would have been my ex-husband if he had lived, but still.

Emma started up again with great big hiccupping sobs.

"Baby, your mom doesn't mean that," Cam said and glared at me.

I looked to Willa for a little support because, *hello*, I was not the bad guy here. I was wounded and widowed. But Willa's heart was breaking for Emma, and I loved that she loved my kids as much as I did. If it had been me in the morgue, instead of Rhys, Willa would be the stand-in mother-of-the-bride at Emma's wedding and Jordan's if he ever settled down. She would mother my grandchildren and great-grandchildren.

"Everything's fine, honey." She rubbed Emma's shoulder. "And if it's not, you can be damn sure I'm going to make it that way because you're my favorite niece." Emma laughed, and my heart was lighter.

Maybe I should have just shut up and let everyone believe everything really was going to be okay. *No.* I shook my head. The muscles revolted like they were simultaneously being yanked in every unnatural direction. "Help," I whispered to Willa because I needed her to make Emma understand Rhys was gone.

Willa nodded at me. She stooped so that she was looking up at Emma. Sensing what was coming, Cam held her a little tighter and kissed the top of her head to soften the blow. Willa's tear-filled azure blue eyes steeled Emma for the sad truth.

"Your dad is alive."

# Chapter Five

Somewhere between the time I crushed Emma with misinformation and the time I was put on the gurney for surgery, Willa announced Rhys was being prepped for a quadruple bypass.

The man who exercised every day until he negated his calorie intake, which didn't take long because he rarely ate anything fun, with a heart attack? My shoulder throbbed at the memory of my fist slamming into his chest, which had apparently saved him. Everyone, from the EMTs to Rhys's sister, who'd never liked me, was giving me credit for his resurrection.

"There's my hero." Jordan made his entrance into the room. Uncommonly gorgeous, like most gay men, he had Rhys' build but had my eyes and heart-shaped face. With a few days of stubble, Jordan could easily pass as a perfectly coiffed mountain man and was dressed like one too. He kissed the top of my head and handed me a cup of coffee. "Drink this. You look like shit."

I would never have talked to my mother like that in a million years. But I loved that my son and I could and did say anything to each other and hoped that wouldn't change after I finally had the divorce talk with Rhys and, eventually, the kids.

"Hey, baby. Thanks for coming."

"You should be thanking me." His coffee cup almost hid his smirk. "Aunt Willa and Emma brought Grandma by earlier. Gram said, considering what you'd been through, you looked lovely but that you might want to put on a dab of lipstick when you woke up and maybe some *rouge*. I suggested they go out for breakfast and come back when you're awake."

"Even if you weren't my only son, you'd still be my favorite son." The coffee was not the hospital crap out of a coin-operated machine; it wasn't even Starbucks. My handsome coffee snob had sought only the best beans for his ailing mother and probably threatened some poor barista's life to perfect the blend. "You," I took a sip and moaned, "look like you stepped out of a Patagonia ad."

He flashed the grin that paid his rent. "Actually, I did step out of that Patagonia ad I told you I was shooting. It was nice to get out of the city for a few days, but that was over a month ago. I've had a couple of auditions since then, haven't booked anything, but that's the business." Cockiness didn't quite conceal his worry. Jordan didn't live paycheck to paycheck because he hadn't had a steady one since he quit his marketing job to go for his dream of being a working actor. "I'm getting used to it, that and being poor. But hey, they let me keep the clothes after the shoot, so there's that."

"You look amazing. I can't wait to see the ads." I really shouldn't feed his gargantuan ego. "Did you bulk up for the shoot?"

"A little bit." Jordan might look like he could scale Annapurna and live off the wilderness for days, but he wouldn't even be caught dead glamping. "So?" He paused and waited for me to say something.

I rolled my eyes. "So, I love you, and thank you for coming?"

"Not the answer I'm looking for." He reminded me I needed to exfoliate but said it in a sing-songy voice like that would cushion the blow. And it did a little.

The Indian doctor came into the room and checked Jordan out. He was round and flirty with his British accent but apparently not

Jordan's type. Actually, I wasn't sure what my son's type was because he'd never brought anyone home to do the meet-the-parents thing.

The doctor examined the incision and then another place with a smaller bandage over it, like maybe it took him a couple of tries to slice into the right spot.

"That's where your bone came through your skin when you dislocated, but it's doing quite nicely. I'm thinking you can go home tomorrow." He shook Jordan's hand, said it was a pleasure meeting him, and left.

"So?" my son repeated like I was an actor who'd forgotten her line.

"*So what?*" Honestly, it was a good thing he was adorable and brought me coffee.

"You and Dad are getting a divorce?" Coffee spewed across the industrially bleached sheets while Jordan casually sipped his drink until I could breathe again. "Wanna talk about it?"

I hadn't told him about the divorce; I hadn't told anybody about the divorce, not even Willa. "What are you talking about?" I wiped my mouth with the back of my hand and tried to sit up a little straighter.

"You were mumbling about it in your sleep. Apparently, you're really looking forward to traveling more. Oh, and something about missing sex on Fridays, which I really did not need to know."

This was a joke. Had to be. He was smirking, scrolling through his phone like a divorce was no big deal. "Good one," I said and took a long draw from my drink. "Funny."

"Don't worry, Emma and Grandma didn't hear. Maybe Aunt Willa did, but my guess is she already knew because you never make a decision without consulting the sacred sisters." Sacred *sister* because Julia had been derelict in her sisterly duties for over a year.

But I haven't talked in my sleep, not since Willa and I were kids and shared a bedroom. Or maybe I recited the Declaration of Independence nightly, and Rhys just never mentioned it. Either way, Jordan knew. *He knew.* And all I could think about was his little face when he came home from kindergarten crying and asked if Rhys and I were going to get 'vorced because all of his classmates' parents were divorced.

By the time we convinced Jordan we were not going to divorce, he came home from school after Christmas break and demanded to know why he didn't get 4 Christmases like Lizzy Bays did, thanks to her divorced parents and grandparents.

"Honey, I'm sorry, but--," I didn't know what to say to my son, who should *not* be the first person to know. I'd thought I'd get up the nerve to tell Rhys, and then the two of us would sit the kids down and tell them together, but that ship had sailed.

"Mom, it's okay. And don't worry about Emma; she wasn't in the room when you started rambling. I'm not going to lie, she'll go nuts when you tell her, but she will get over it."

Will she? She's getting ready to marry and start her own family.

"It happens," he said like the end of a thirty-two-year-old marriage was akin to getting rid of a car that wasn't worth the astronomical repair bill. "You and Dad had a good long run, but nothing lasts forever." His words stung. I raised him to believe in forever. I thought I believed in it too. I was supposed to love Rhys until one of us died, but I couldn't even manage that.

"Your father sort of died--before I could--you know, tell him. But now he's not dead, so I should tell him. I *will* tell him." Jordan nodded, a slight smile of encouragement. "Are you sure you're okay with this?"

"I am if it makes you happy." He threw his empty coffee cup into the trash. "Question is, are you okay with it?"

The whole near-death thing was enough to shake anybody up, but when the dust settled, nothing had really changed. I cared about Rhys. I always would. I was grateful to him for my kids. I was grateful I didn't kill him because I didn't know how to do CPR. But, if he insisted on being alive, I wanted him to be happy. I just didn't want to be married to him anymore. "I am sorry, baby, but I need to do this."

"There's no need to be sorry, Mom. I love you both." He sat on my bed and figured out a way to hug me that didn't kill me. "And, bonus, I'll finally have that extra Christmas I always wanted."

The sun filtered in through the windows of the lounge area on the cardiac floor. It was nice outside, one of those startling blue-sky days in the middle of February when Charleston gives winter her dainty middle finger. Rhys and I used to take the boat out on days like today, back when we had a boat. We sold it not long after Jordan left for college. With both kids gone, the house had felt empty. I'd felt empty, and looking back, I think Rhys did too.

If we'd had the kind of marriage we'd promised each other so long ago, we would have looked at our newly empty nest as an opportunity to love more, enjoy each other more, and have sex wherever we wanted whenever we wanted. Instead, we lived his and hers kinds of lives and watched our union die a slow death. But now it was time to proclaim it dead and set both of us free.

Brave words from a woman who was trembling so hard, the orderly who wheeled me to Rhys' room asked if I had chills.

We were never one of those couples to wear matching anything, so it was odd to see Rhys dressed in the same drab hospital gown, the same non-skid neon green footies as me. A hot blonde nurse attempted to act professional, but her flirty grin gave her away.

"On a scale of one to ten, Mr. Carver, how is your pain today?"

An equally pretty blonde in different colored scrubs, maybe some kind of bombshell in training, was waiting her turn to crush on my husband. To his credit, Rhys' eyes were on his ringless hands folded across washboard abs that had been his pet project for the last six months.

My thumb swept across the cold, naked crease on my finger where my wedding rings had been. Since the day Rhys slipped them on my finger, other than removing them for two childbirths and a hysterectomy, I had never taken them off. But he took his ring off all the time to work around the house, whenever he worked out at the gym or played golf.

The nurses finished up and turned in a choreographed move that would have stopped Rhys' just–fixed heart if he'd been looking. The one who'd asked about his pain flashed her best smile in my direction. But when her eyes met mine, she blushed hard, like I'd caught her giving my husband a naughty sponge bath. Before I could say anything, the orderly rapped on the door and pushed my chair into the room. "Somebody's got company," he sang, sure this was a reunion of a happy couple.

"Hey." Rhys drew the word out like he was genuinely glad to see me. "Come on in." The hot nurses scurried away when the orderly pushed me close to the bed. Rhys reached for my good hand, but that seemed to hurt, so he just smiled. "Aren't we a pair," he laughed.

"We are." The lie felt like a dart to my chest.

"Emma filled me in on every possible detail of your shoulder, the bone jutting through your skin. I'm pretty sure between the two of us, you had it the worst. Are you really okay?"

His face looked almost as perfect as Jordan's, only he never had to use outrageously priced skincare products. Damn him. His color was amazing, an indication of just how sick he was before the heart attack.

I shrugged. "The doctor said it wasn't going to hurt much, but they're all a bunch of liars."

Wasn't that what Rhys and I were? Two people who lied to each other, who pretended that what we had was good enough until death parted us?

He smiled and winced when he shifted around in his bed. "Was it worse than your appendectomy?"

I'd almost forgotten about the time, a couple of months after we started dating when I nearly died thanks to a ruptured appendix. Up until that time, Dad was also prejudiced against men who wanted to date his youngest daughter, but that all changed when he saw Rhys with me in the hospital.

Rhys brought me flowers every day and brownies. He sweet-talked the nurses into letting him warm in the break room microwave. He topped them with praline pecans and ice cream, the good kind. Not that crap the hospital served in paper containers with those little tongue depressor spoons. He slept in that horrible chair beside my bed until the night nurse made her last visit, then closed the door and crawled into bed with me. With his arms around me and my head pillowed on his chest, I'd never felt so safe, so adored.

Mom proclaimed him to be good husband material, and my sisters gave Rhys the thumbs up. Not that it mattered; I was so crazy about him that I married him three months after I got out of the hospital.

"Maisie? You kind of checked out on me for a minute." His voice stopped my careening down Memory Lane. "Baby?" My heart rate spiked at the sound of his voice, the way it used to jolt when we were dating or that first ring of the phone when I knew, without the benefit of Caller ID, it was *him*.

I commanded my heart to beat slower because this felt more like the beginning of something between us than the end. "Maise?" he whispered.

This man was my husband. My Friday lover. He'd been my best friend until I decided he wasn't. Maybe I was wrong about the joint culpability for our dead marriage. Maybe the sticky truth about the end of us was that I was the one who fell out of love. I was the one who had been so eager to put an end to us.

The need to fix our marriage slammed into me. Being a take-what-you-get kind of woman, I'd never had to fight for anything in my life. I wasn't even sure I knew how, and I sure as hell didn't know how to fight for us. Other than a garden-variety rough patch somewhere in our first year of marriage that culminated into one awful night Rhys didn't come home, we'd never had to fight for our marriage.

Even then, he'd walked through the door remorseful, looking like hell. He'd taken me in his arms and promised to do better, to be better, and I'd promised him right back.

And things were good. Changes had been slow and imperceptible. The kids were born. Growing up, they were in everything from travel league basketball and swimming to community theatre. For ten, maybe fifteen years, Rhys and I were so attached to our schedules we didn't schedule time for each other. By the time the kids went away to college, I knew our love wasn't what we'd promised it would be, but while we were raising kids, it seemed good enough. Looking back, it was that acceptance that did us in, clinging to the everydayness of our lives instead of each other. No wonder I'd felt so alone in our marriage.

"Rhys--," Thirty-two years of history said, *love him.* Thirty years-two of history said, *find my way back to the man I'd once adored, to the times when things were good, and love wasn't a chore* "I—."

"Babe," he interrupted. "I've been thinking about that trip, the one to California. I want you to go." I didn't want to *go* anywhere. I wanted to fall in love with my husband again. I wanted to make things right. "It'll be good for you."

*He loved me.* He'd unclenched his fist and thrown the hundred-dollar rule out the window, and he was right. The trip would be good for me. I'd have a great time with mom and my sisters, and then, I'd come home and tend to my marriage. *Our* marriage. And if I really did have Alzheimer's, Rhys would be there for me.

I would know his face the way Dad always knows Mom's. And he would comfort our kids when they hurt so Goddamn much because I don't know them. The way I do when Dad takes my hand in his and smiles at me, so sheepish, so embarrassed he doesn't know who I am. When he gets that look, he breaks my heart every single time and says, "I don't know who you are, but I know you belong to me."

I belonged to Rhys Carver.

Tears spilled down my face. I *belong* to him. Sure, I'd fallen out of love, but couldn't I just as easily fall back in? I didn't know what he wanted for the rest of his days, but I was ready to say what *I* wanted from this marriage, what I needed from him.

My darling husband's misty blue eyes said he'd missed the good parts of us. The tears in his eyes said he'd been hurting too. He smiled the way he did when we were new. Maybe not quite like that, but back when our marriage was salvageable. And God, I wanted to save it. Had to save it. And I wouldn't have to do it alone because he wanted this too. He wanted *us*.

"I love you, Rhys." It would take some time, but if I just kept saying it, it would be true. Our anniversary wouldn't be a day of dread and regret. I'd stand proudly in front of the anniversary rack at the Hallmark Store and choose that card that said *I'd do it all over again. It was worth it. WE are worth it, a*nd it would be true.

"Maisie?" His deep rumbly voice unleashed big fat goosebumps over my body. "Baby." Just that one word used to make me crazy for him.

Before I could think about how much it would hurt to get out of the wheelchair, I was in his bed the way he'd climbed into mine all those years ago. I kissed his temple and made a silent vow to be a better partner, a better lover, a better wife.

Completely overwhelmed with emotion, he looked away. "I want--." His voice was as clear and determined as it was on our wedding day. "I want a divorce."

# Chapter Six

**R**hys had barely finished the words that sent me reeling when Emma bustled into the room with three Starbucks coffees. "There you are! My two happy and, most importantly, healthy parents."

Well, she got the healthy part right.

She planted a kiss on her dad's cheek and then mine without the first inkling that I was ready to explode.

Reconciliation? A new life with Rhys Carver? What was I thinking?

Even with our daughter there, the only thing that kept me from strangling Rhys with his IV tube was a big bag from Sugar's Bakeshop peeking out of Emma's giant purse. I would have bet my divorce settlement she had a half dozen brownies in there, and I needed chocolate almost as much as I needed answers. So, how did all of this get so turned around? I was going to be the one asking for a divorce. Until he keeled over from--from what? A stupid argument? And just how long had he been thinking about getting rid of me?

I gave that man three squares a day. I did the laundry and the cleaning before the actual cleaning lady who came every other week. I watched his stupid TV shows, his sports, and the same movies over and over again, but did he watch mine? No, and believe me, My Cousin Vinnie is as un-funny after the fiftieth time as it is the five hundredth. I had sex every Friday whether I wanted to or not. Okay, most of the time, I wanted to because I liked sex.

I deferred to this man's every wish. And he wanted a divorce?

"On what grounds?" I hissed while Emma rambled obliviously about whom she'd chosen to be her bridesmaids.

Rhys gave me the same we'll talk later look we'd exchanged over the years when the subject of our discussion wasn't kid friendly.

"Screw that."

"What did you say, Mom?"

"Honey, your dad and I were just talking --."

"I know you were, but me first. I'll be really fast." Emma sat down on the bed and gushed about wedding plans while my mouth gaped open at our daughter's inability to take a hint and Rhys' nonchalance over what had just happened.

"Sounds expensive," he said and looked at me for support. "Don't you think so, babe?"

"Come on, Dad, you know it's meant to be when Middleton Place has a cancelation for this summer. And I've dreamed of having my wedding there since I was six." Emma sat down on the bed and took Rhys' hand. "Please, Daddy."

"Honey, your mom and I love you, and we're happy for you and Cam, but Middleton Place? Our pockets just aren't that deep."

In truth, Rhys was right. Even though we'd saved for the happy occasion, a stripped-down wedding at the famed Charleston Plantation for a scant one hundred guests would set us back over sixty grand.

"I want the fairytale wedding you and Mom had." Emma put my hand in Rhys's and then held them together. The tips of his fingers were like ice, and the pulse in the V between her thumb and index finger beat like a hummingbird's wings. "I know it costs more than it did way back then. That's what I wanted to tell you. Cam and I are paying for the whole thing. All you have to do is show up and look beautiful."

"Emma, I get that you want the fairytale," he said. "I just don't think it's such a great idea for you and Cam to spend that kind of money just starting out." He looked at me like he hadn't just asked for a divorce. "What do you think, babe?"

I think if you call me babe again, I'm definitely going to strangle you.

He jerked his hand away like he'd heard my thoughts and pulled the sheet up to his chin.

"Dad, it's not just me," Emma scoffed, "Cam wants this wedding too, and we can afford it. So, stop worrying."

She'd finally gotten the gold ring with Cam attached to it, and I was truly happy for her. As angry as I was at Rhys, I didn't want our impending divorce to kill our daughter's enthusiasm. I raised her to believe in love and marriage, and even though it was clear things weren't going to work out for Rhys and me, I still wanted Emma to get the happily ever after she deserved.

"Maisie?" Rhys cajoled. "Honey, you wanna help me out here?"

It was obvious I wouldn't have to kill Rhys. Just the thought of Emma and Cam dropping a small fortune on a Middleton Place wedding was sending him to an early grave. But it was their money, their party.

Before I could weigh in, Emma had already begun her closing arguments. "It is a Charleston wedding, Dad. Besides, I work my butt off and have been saving even before I met Cam. He's got all the money from his college savings plan he never had to use because he had merit scholarships. We already have a house and everything else we need. So, we've got more than enough money to pay for the wedding. Not to mention that it's my day to be a princess, and every girl wants that. Right, Mom?" Emma's tone was the same as when she was fifteen and begged me to talk her dad into letting her go to senior prom.

"Maisie," Rhys countered and gave me a hard look that said, come on, but there was no contest for my allegiance.

"Emma, honey, go get some lunch and give your father and me some time to talk. By the time you get back, I promise, everything will be just fine."

Emma kissed us both on the cheek, and Rhys watched her go.

"You think this is a good idea?" When I didn't answer, he looked at me. "Come on, we have to talk about this." I tortured him with good old-fashioned guilt and silence until he looked like he'd rather be waterboarded by CIA amateurs. "Do you really think it's not flat-out crazy to let the kids spend that kind of money on a wedding?"

"Do you really think we're going to discuss Emma's wedding?" I growled.

He said nothing. The machine monitoring his heart rate tapped out an annoying rhythm that said his heart didn't beat for me anymore.

"Okay then." He blew out a deep breath. "Are you happy, Maisie?" His eyes looked tired. And, for once, thank God, he looked his age. Maybe even older. "Are you happy?"

How long had it been since I was happy? Truly happy? As bad as my memory was, it should've been harder to remember, but I knew the exact day, the exact moment. December 24th, two years ago at Mom and Dad's sixty-fifth-anniversary party. The moment my parents cut their cake, the whole world fell away, and it was just the two of them. I was so happy they loved each other so much, so proud I was their daughter. And when they did that corny thing where they linked arms and fed each other cake, I was so happy I cried.

"Happy with us?" I spat. "No. But how long have you been so unhappy that you suddenly want out?" My last word had more bite than I'd intended, but I was furious with him. Furious with myself for even thinking I wanted to stay married to this man for another minute.

He did not look like the picture of health like he did when the orderly wheeled me into the room. He looked regretful and uncomfortable, as he damn well should, and maybe even a little green.

"Look at me and tell me when you decided I wasn't enough for you?" I bit out.

I don't know why the answer mattered to me. Our marriage was unofficially over. Both of us had failed this union. Both of us had wasted a huge chunk of our lives on fools' gold, and nobody was coming out of this a winner.

"You're right," he said.

The heart monitor beat out a dizzying rhythm and set off an alarm. He watched his chest rise and fall and opened his mouth, but nothing came out. For one honest moment, he looked at me and then said something I couldn't make out over the noise of the machines. A half dozen nurses sprinted into the room.

# Chapter Seven

**W**hen someone dies unexpectedly, everyone comes out of the woodwork to see the corpse for themselves and pay their respects. Most of Rhys' comrades in blue turned out along with most of the kids he'd coached in basketball for fifteen years. Some of them had kids of their own now. Everyone from Rhys' roommate from one semester of his freshman year of college to his wheelchair-bound eighty-nine-year-old kindergarten teacher was lined up to see the corpse I couldn't look at.

If it had been up to me, there would be no open casket. But, after three decades of attending funerals together, Rhys and I had played the "when I die" game enough that I knew that was what he wanted. And didn't that say something about the guy who lived his whole life so obnoxiously good-looking that his final act on earth would be making throngs of mourners take one last look at his pretty face and hate him just a little bit for being so beautiful?

I know it wasn't his fault that he was born smoking hot, but living with the man had made me self-conscious about every line on my face, every extra pound. If I heard one more person say, "He never aged" or "He looks fantastic," I was going to slam the casket shut.

Emma refused to leave her father's side and acted the way a loving daughter or a grieving widow should, alternating between crying hysterically and sitting quiet as a stone in the folding chair Cam put at the head of the coffin. When people offered their condolences, she nodded, tearfully met their eyes, and whispered her thanks while I circulated the room to get away from the corpse. First clockwise, then counterclockwise, then a loopy spiral stroll down the center aisle that was supposed to resemble a church. Wash, rinse, repeat, never stopping for more than a few seconds to greet someone who loved Rhys, adored him.

Each embrace was slightly more suffocating than the last, every single sorrowful word like a gunshot that made me flinch. Forty-five minutes into the marathon viewing that was scheduled to last for four hours, my bum shoulder throbbed in time with the good one that screamed from perpetually cringing. Between the pain in my shoulder and the dull body buzz from anger, I couldn't endure another hug.

My good hand jutted out of my navel like a shark's fin to offer wimpy shakes, but mostly to keep the huggers at bay.

"I'm so sorry about Rhys." The barrel-chested man ignored my hand and, with the skill of a world-class tango dancer, yanked me into his arms. Pain scorched a path to my brain and collided with the comforting scents of the cherry pipe tobacco my grandfather used to smoke and Rhys' blue Listerine.

I laid my head on his chest, my good hand gripping his lapel. "Thank you for coming," I meant it and lingered a little too long. He pulled away first with an awkward smile and pity in his eyes. Mourners with sad thin smiles shuffled along the slow-moving line to the casket. I silently forgave a sorrowful-looking young woman who shook my hand and said, "You must be Rhys's mother. "

She had mile-long legs, and her little black dress was more appropriate for clubbing than visiting the dead. I don't know why I told her yes, but she burst into tears and confessed Rhys coached her older sister's basketball team. She'd always had the hots for him. And why would you tell a bereft mother that much less his wife?

The line to see the body stretched down the center aisle and out the door of the funeral home. It was impossible to breathe, but I kept moving because it seemed to help tamp down the urge to run, even though there was no way I would ever abandon my kids. So, I was back at twelve o'clock, beside the casket to kiss Emma's cheek, and tell her I loved her. There was no need to ask if she needed anything, if she was okay. She needed her daddy, and she wouldn't be anything remotely resembling okay for a very long time.

The flowers we told everyone not to send were beautiful. I admired them, along with the woman in front of me. She had J. Lo's ass, long dangly earrings, and was wearing the same dress I tried on at a cute little boutique on King Street but didn't buy because it was way over Rhys' hundred-dollar limit. While I still couldn't look at him, there was a guilty comfort in knowing I'd never have to listen to him bitch over my buying a nice dress or anything else for that matter.

Cam coaxed Emma into drinking some water. I was so grateful for him. He hadn't left her side since she found out about her father. If Cam was holding Emma together, Willa was the glue that bound all of us together. She brought Mom and Dad tonight and sat them in folding chairs near the front of the room, but not so close so that they were right up on the casket. Every fifteen minutes or so, Dad suddenly got the idea that he was at his sister Regina's viewing.

Dad hasn't known who I am for over a year now. Rhys never knew who I was. I wasn't even sure I did, but I needed my dad to look at me just one more time and say, "There's my girl, Maisie."

So, I waited until Mom ducked into the restroom and took the opportunity to sit in her chair beside Dad and held his hand while he cried for his sister, who never drew her first breath. Him being there was Mom's idea. She'd wanted him with the family, or maybe she wanted him with her because a surprise death will make you paranoid, make you believe if you can keep your loved ones close, you can keep them alive. But having Dad at the viewing was a terrible place for him. Too many memories and funerals jumbled together in his mind.

Mom shouldn't have told him about Rhys. All of us should have just let Dad live in his world where nobody aged or died. But his mind was stuck on Regina. Such a pretty name, and she'd died a thousand deaths in less than an hour. "Daddy?" The word was like comfort food to me. ""Regina's not in the casket." His blank stare pierced my heart. "It's my husband, Rhys."

His grief-stricken face rankled. "That pretty boy? I never liked him or his pretty boy name. Rhys." My heart swelled with pride that he'd had one of those rare moments of clarity, but I was dying for him to remember me. To sing "A Bicycle Built for Two," like he used to when I was little, substituting Maisie for Daisy.

"Why, hello there." His blank face was back, and he was gone again. "I'm James Carver. Forgive me, but I don't remember things too good these days, darling. Now, tell me who you are."

I am your baby girl. Your face used to light up every time I walked into the room. When I was little, I promised to marry you. You accepted my proposal and put my feet on the tops of your shoes, and we danced to old-timey music. Then you'd pick me up and hold me close. You promised you would love me forever, and now you don't even know who I am.

"You'll have to forgive me, dear. I'm awful good at forgetting." His eyes pleaded. "Do I know you?"

"I'm Daisy." My smile wobbled. "My name is Daisy."

"That's right." He slapped his thigh. "Such a lovely family reunion, don't you think? I'm so hungry. What time do you think we'll eat? Don't tell my wife, but Aunt Halley'," who died when he was a child, "makes the best fried chicken, good enough to bring tears to a glass eye."

Mom was headed toward me, her smile tentative until she could see for herself that Dad was all right.

"You're right, James." I put my good arm around him and laid my head on his shoulder. "It is a lovely reunion."

"Everything okay?" Mom asked.

"'Course it is. I was just talking to--." His blank apologetic smile felt like a punch in the stomach. "To this fine young woman here. We were wondering when they're putting out the spread."

"Soon, James." I kissed him on the cheek and went back to pacing.

Jordan was off to one side of the viewing room with a handful of friends who had flown in from New York and California. He told me not to get excited; they were all just friends. He excused himself from the group when I passed by to check on me. The last couple of times I'd passed by during my intricate walk-through, he'd said some variation of you should sit down. Translation: You're freaking me out with this circular, zig-zaggy thing, and you need to stop.

I felt bad that Jordan was the only person alive who knew I wanted a divorce. There was no need to tell him that in the end, I'd waffled, and it was his father who wanted out.

Once Switzerland, Jordan was all Team Mom and didn't even tell me I looked like shit from not sleeping. His Bumble and Bumble friend, Kai, flew in last night from San Francisco, so my hair looked great. He swore he channeled Jackie Kennedy when he worked. It was kind of hard to picture Jackie decked out in her every day Gucci, styling hair, but I loved the idea and appreciated his solemn oath to help me find my inner Jackie before the funeral tomorrow.

Quite the feat considering I hadn't slept for more than a couple of hours over the last three days. Every time I drifted off, I was back in that damn hospital room, and Rhys was either asking me if I was happy or asking me for a divorce. Then I'd jackknife up in his recliner I had to sleep in with a mother of a hot flash, my heart pounding in time to my throbbing shoulder, my eyes feeling like they were going to explode if I didn't cry. Something I hadn't been able to do since I told the kids Rhys was really dead this time.

My stomach growled when I hugged Emma. She'd avoided me during the viewing, or more aptly, I'd avoided her since she insisted on never leaving her father's side. She collapsed in my arms, and I held on tight. Her desperate embrace burned down to my bones, but there were still no tears.

What was wrong with me? My daughter was in agony, and I was dry-eyed and starving.

Thanks to Jordan, my doctor knew I couldn't sleep or cry and had called twice to offer me the customary funeral drugs to get me through the next few days. Old school prescriptions like Valium, Xanax, Librium, or Klonopin. Both times, the conversation was the same; he asked me how I was, and I said I was fine before he had a chance to finish his sentence, but he wasn't buying it.

"Perhaps you are, Maisie, but this is one of those times you need to be especially kind to yourself. I could prescribe something to take the edge off over the next few days and help you rest."

Was there a new wonder drug to combat my anger for Rhys? A magic pill to ease the tightness in my chest because I'd wished him dead? An elixir to erase the bottomed-out feeling in my gut that reminded me Rhys' last words, or at least the last words I heard, were, I want a divorce?

I probably would need something for the funeral. People forgive drugged, red-eyed widows for almost anything, but mourners had begun to notice my dry eyes and my inappropriate laughter that was a little too loud and lasted a few beats too long. Rhys's sister, Becca, who never liked me, pulled me aside a couple of times to ask if I was okay and not in an I'm-worried-about-you-kind-of-way. She was understandably wrecked over her brother's death. Her tween-age girls were equally broken because you could add favorite uncle to the long list of Rhys's attributes.

There was an inordinate number of gorgeous women in the crowd that I didn't recognize. An hour or so into the viewing, the hot blonde nurse from the hospital entered the room but didn't stop to sign the guest book. She was tall, really tall, with thighs that were so far apart they didn't recognize each other. Dressed in turquoise scrubs, she stood out amongst the decked-out mourners. She was willowy except for her muscular arms and had a face that left me slack-jawed by her beauty. She glanced around the room until she spotted me and headed my way.

I sucked in my stomach and stood as tall as my five-foot-four-inch frame would go and laughed at the dark chocolate comedy of her being everything Rhys wanted, everything I was not, except for the blond part.

Before she could get to me, a CrossFit couple sauntered up and took turns putting their arms around me. The guy was beautiful, one of those men who probably wasn't as a kid but grew into his looks nicely. I rubbed my cheek against his buff chest until his wife wasn't smiling anymore.

"Thank you for coming." I hugged her again, and she seemed to forgive me.

"We adored Rhys," the woman said because she was part of a *we*.

Whether Rhys had lived or died, there would have been no we, no us.

The man nodded in agreement, his neck so fascinatingly corded I wanted to ask him to do it again. "He was such a good dude." The man sandwiched my hand between his roughed, calloused ones that were like Rhys's, like all CrossFit junkies'. That alone should have made me cry because I loved those hands, calloused or not, and what they could do to me on Friday mornings.

"Thank you for coming," I said, and really meant it.

The man put his hand on the small of his wife's back and slid her into the line to view the body. The blonde nurse stepped up and shook my good hand. She glanced down at her scrubs and then around the room at the mourners all decked out for the big occasion, every one of them Charlestonian to the bone. A restaurant or a dinner party can claim to be easy breezy casual, but Charleston was a city of beautiful people who loved to overdress without looking overdressed.

By some cruel trick, the nurse and I were standing by the coffin. She looked down at Rhys, and her face went from apologetic to sorrowful. Her brown bedroom eyes turned to whiskey gems, glistening with tears. Emma recognized the nurse who hugged her and Cam, and then there was a long awkward moment when the nurse didn't hug me.

"Mrs. Carver." She hitched up the shoulder strap of her bag and tried to sound professional.

Her voice was the same one that had asked Rhys, "On a scale from one to ten, what is your pain level?" Only it wasn't flirty like it was then. Who was this woman? Why was she here? And why was I aching for her to ask me the same question so that I could tell her, I was a ten. I was a goddamn ten.

"I was one of Rhys' nurses in the hospital." My skin crawled when her calloused hand shook mine. Definitely a CrossFitter. "I'm so sorry for your loss." Her voice cracked on the last word, and she swiped at her tears. Even in her scrubs, she was the stuff nurse fantasies are made of; the hollows of her collarbone could have starred in their own porno.

Was she the reason Rhys had asked for a divorce? My stomach lurched from one too many realizations. I didn't want to know why she was acting the way she was over a man I hoped she barely knew. But her grief was so pure, so real, all I could do was parrot her words.

She looked confused that I'd breached bereavement protocol and said she was sorry again before tugging on the hem of her scrubs. "I'd better get to work." She gave me her best stiff, upper-lip smile. The tracks of teardrops went down her neck and plopped onto her scrubs.

This woman had cried ugly over my husband and then had the nerve to whisper, "Thank you." I followed her halfway down the center aisle with the romantic notion that I would confront her right here in the middle of the viewing, but I was too Charlestonian for such a display. So, I thanked her for coming and watched her go.

# Chapter Eight

"Too much thanking goes on at these things." My body stiffened at the sound of my prodigal sister's voice. I turned to face Julia and her thin unapologetic smile. She didn't try to hug me, just triaged me like I was one of her patients with a busted heart. Grief—check. Anger—check. Raw from betrayal, from Rhys, from her.

She looked me dead in the eyes. "Come on. You need to get out of here."

Julia's words were reason enough to forgive her for abandoning Willa and me when Dad was in the neuro ICU because nobody, not even Willa, had had the courage or the grace to offer me an escape from this shitshow. I followed Julia out of the hall, sure we were headed for the bathroom. Instead, she took one hallway and then another to the back of the building before pushing the Exit door open.

The orange-purple sunset sky backlit a long carport with three ancient shiny black hearses. The contrast was too sharp, like one of those paintings on black velvet of Elvis or Jesus or sometimes both.

The hearses didn't look anything like the sleek modern one parked out front that would take Rhys to the cemetery tomorrow. When the doors closed behind us, I gulped at the air. Oxygen filled my lungs, and a feeling I barely recognized coursed through my body. Thanks to my big sister, who had always been twice as savvy as Tarzan's Jane, I was safe from cannibals and quicksand and judgy mourners. She pulled me onto a bench and lit up a cigarette.

Since when did she smoke? She took a long draw and held the smoke in long enough for me to realize she was smoking what Dad called a funny cigarette.

"Good God, Julia. You're smoking pot?"

She nodded in mid-toke. Perfection from head to toe, she was dressed in tapered pants, a fitted silk blouse, a gorgeous knee-length duster, all winter white. She offered me the joint, and I took it without the slightest idea of how to smoke it. It took four or five tries before I could hold the smoke in long enough to feel anything, and, boy, was it nice.

"Wow," I said. "Wow." She nodded and smiled as she took another toke. "I didn't think you could get high the first time."

"You've never smoked pot?" She was genuinely surprised, and if Meryl Streep was ever kidnapped by aliens, Julia could double for her and win the Oscar. "I don't believe that."

"Never. But I could get used to this." I reached for the joint.

"This is really powerful stuff," the perfect doctor said, and I wondered what else I didn't know about my pothead sister. "One more puff, and I'm cutting you off." She laughed, and it was such a lovely sound.

Time was syrupy sweet. I had the incredible compulsion to make jazz hands or spirit fingers, but I couldn't decide which was more appropriate for the viewing.

"I'm still mad at you for not coming last year when Dad was in the hospital, but I was right. You'll show up for a funeral." I was filled with THC and pride that I hadn't swallowed back the truth.

She drew hard on the joint, the tip flaring bright enough to burst into flames. "When did you get to be so smart?"

"Is that how it is now? Somebody has to die for you to make an appearance. They told us Dad was going to die. I begged you to come home. Mom needed you; we all did." More truth bubbled up. "I needed you."

She did her unapologetic, know-it-all doctor thing and adjusted my sling a bit. "I told you to get that acromioclavicular joint fixed years ago. It's rare for the bone to puncture the skin; maybe you should enter a sweepstake or buy a lottery ticket." She handed me the joint again. I took another long toke and was back to mellow. I fought to hold the smoke in my lungs and lost, making me half cough, half laugh as it poured out in thick gray waves.

"I killed Rhys," I wheezed.

She laughed and took the joint from me. "Might not want to talk like that with all those cops around, sweetie."

"Well, I got the ball rolling with the heart attack. Then there was this trip to see the redwoods Mom always wanted to go on. Anyway, I told Rhys I was taking her on the trip, and he died. The first time. Then he had the surgery, and--." He wanted to leave me so much he didn't even bother to stick around for the divorce.

"No, darling." She shook her head and exhaled. The smoke caressed her features, and I will always feel less beautiful in Julia's presence, less smart. Just—less.

She handed the joint back to me. "Rhys was like a walking time bomb, Maise. He had a saccular cerebral aneurysm and could have just as easily keeled over at the gym or eating a bowl of cereal. His number was up. It happens." She was so nonchalant about death. Had being a doctor made her that way, or was it losing the love of her life five years ago?

I tried to exhale all cool like my big sister, but the smoke did not caress me. It crawled back up my nose and refused to come out until I hacked up a lung. Julia slapped me on the back until I was finally able to speak. "I was so mad at you. SO mad, but I'm glad you're here now." I laid my head on her shoulder.

She leaned her head against mine. I could feel her wanting to say something, needing to say something that wasn't funny or smart, but she said nothing. A breeze kicked up off the Charleston Harbor, and for the first time in my life, my big sister swallowed back her truth.

"We should probably go back inside, Maise."

Everything was swimmy when she pulled me up. Sand crunched between my half-price designer stilettos and the concrete sidewalk. Moss on ancient live oak trees danced like Looney Tune characters in the stiff breeze.

"Careful. You might be a little woozy, especially in those heels." For once, I towered over her, sort of. We were really more eye-to-eye when she looked down at my feet and laughed. "Jesus, who dressed you? Jordan?"

My head felt like it had a small roller coaster inside, and now I knew the true meaning of the words good shit because Julia's shit was fantastic. So maybe it wouldn't be so horrible to go back inside where my dead husband was.

"He did. Jordan, not Jesus." I giggled. "I can't feel my feet, but that's okay because I don't want to feel anything."

She looked at me again like she was going to tell me whatever was so important a few minutes ago but said nothing. So, like any good, stoned sister, I volunteered to fill the silence. "Thank you for sharing your pot," I whispered the last word. "That's the nicest thing anyone has done for me since Rhys croaked.

"Not croaked. God, Julia, please don't let me say stupid shit when I go back in there." I took her face in my hands, and the tears that wouldn't come threatened. "Help me be okay."

"You're not okay, Maise, not even close. You will be, but not for a long time." She sighed and pushed my hair behind my ear the way she did when I was little, and she was trying to gently explain why I couldn't go on dates with her and her boyfriends.

She pulled a small perfume bottle from her Hermes bag and spritzed us. The stuff smelled divine. I teetered again, and she cupped my elbow to support my body, to support the little girl inside me that was stuck in a lovely time warp where her big sister was here when she was needed most.

Her smile was forced, and if my heart wasn't already broken, it would have been from the sadness in her eyes.

"I've got you, Maisie."

The anger I'd held onto for the better part of a year turned to dust and took to the breeze. My big sister was here now. And that was enough.

# Chapter Nine

The exit sign wasn't really flashing or calling my name, but it might as well have been. When I passed Jordan and his circle of friends, he pulled me into their shiny gay bubble. Even with a dead husband and so many unanswered questions, being surrounded by a dozen drop-dead gorgeous, impeccably dressed men, groomed within an inch of their lives, was breathtaking.

In my presence, the bubble was gayer, and brighter because nobody loves moms, especially really good moms, more than gay men. "This lasts four hours?" Jordan sounded like a whiny twelve-year-old.

I giggled a little too loud. Becca's head whipped around again, and she looked like she wanted to kill me. I told myself she was just mad at Rhys for dying, but her death stare said she wished I'd been the one who hadn't made it out of the hospital.

"Suck it up, buttercup." I started to adjust his tie, but it was perfect, and even had the little dimple Rhys taught him how to make.

My son crooked his finger under my chin and inspected my pupils. "My God. You're high?"

The cops trading stories about Rhys in the back of the room went silent. Then, Julia appeared and inserted herself into the bubble. Being perfect and always knowing what to do and where to be, except when Dad was in the hospital, she hugged my son to shut him up.

"Hello, sweetheart. I'm so sorry about your dad."

He pulled away and looked at her black dinnerplate-sized pupils. "You're shitting me."

Julia blushed and shushed him again before pushing my hair behind my ear. "Mom and Dad are tired. I'm going to take them back to Sunny Side. Are you still feeling okay?"

My head was swimmy, but I was so hungry, and that whole munchies thing stoners talk about must be true. Or maybe it was still the anger and the sadness that made me want to stuff myself.

"I'm still high." I was never good at whispering.

All conversation stopped; heads turned and looked at me. The lovely protective bubble closed a little tighter, and the rest of the mourners returned to their doldrums.

"We can leave." Jordan's hushed voice said he wanted to get out of there too.

I looked over his shoulder at the judgy mourners and Emma, who was still entrenched by her father's side. She wouldn't leave, even if I played the mom card and sent her home to get some rest. She wouldn't leave until the funeral home threw her out. Cam rubbed her shoulders. She'd clung to him in a way that made me envious but happy, so happy they had each other, and God, I hoped it would last. I hoped she would never feel rejected and betrayed by the man who slept beside her for decades.

Another sour look from Becca made me duck for cover. "Ignore them. All of them." Ronald, the adorable ginger with the cute bow tie, gave the gawkers a razor-sharp look and then smiled at me. "You're queen for a day. You can do anything you want."

I nodded like the bobble-headed CrossFit guy and whispered, "Honey? 'Member when you lived at home?" My sweet boy smiled at my sing-songy voice. "Where did you go out to eat when you got stoned?"

The entire brotherhood in blue stared at me. Becca hissed something to her husband as he rushed their kids out of the room. Thank God Emma was too far away and grief-stricken to hear me. Mom and Dad were so obliviously happy Julia was leading them out the door; if they heard me, they didn't care.

Jordan grabbed my good arm. "Let's get out of here."

I made Jordan drive us twenty miles to the Waffle House in Summerville to make sure I wouldn't see anyone on the off chance that some of the mourners wanted breakfast for dinner. Jordan was such a foodie, I would never have thought he'd be caught dead in one, but Waffle House was where he used to go when he was up to his teenage shenanigans. And why was shenanigans one of those great words nobody uses anymore?

What shenanigans had Rhys been up to that made him ask for a divorce? Was he in love with that nurse or the bevy of hot mourners I didn't recognize? Did I really what to know? No, I needed to get sad. I needed to look like the most distraught widow the Holy City had ever seen to make up for getting high at the viewing and leaving forty-five minutes before it was over.

The waitress came, and I ordered the right side of the menu. Jamar, the cute Broadway gay, joined the party and plopped a Burger King crown from the restaurant next door on my head. In his big Broadway voice, he crooned that I could have everything my way, and his eyes were so warm and sparkly that I believed him.

"Bitch." And this was one of those times when it was an honor to be called a bitch. "Eff that queen for a day shit, Mrs. C. You are queen. Period."

Everyone cheered, and I thanked him, but I shouldn't have even been there. I should have manned up——. Hell no, womaned up and acted like a proper widow; I should have been with my grieving daughter. Shit. Emma.

I sent her a quick text and got an answer almost immediately. This is Cam. Emma's fine, really tired. I put her to bed. She was out in 3 seconds. You okay?

Thanks, I'm fine, which sounded like I was barely hanging on by a thread when I was really having a rollicking good time. Tomorrow's going to be rough. Get some rest and call me if either of you needs anything.

Ginger Ronald assured me Emma had said she was glad when he told her Jordan and the guys were taking me home. Maybe he was just saying that to make me feel better, but maybe not. Emma was just so much better than me at grieving her dad. Maybe that was why she was okay with my hasty exit.

But leaving was a huge relief like the moment the doctor told us Dad was going to live. While I felt bad about leaving Emma, she wouldn't have wanted to be here at Waffle House having fun. But, at that moment, I would have given anything to see her happy. Snorting like a sonic boom when she belly laughed would always set everybody off again, including her, and more snorting.

My thoughts were interrupted by drumming on the tabletops, much like that scene in My Best Friend's Wedding where Rupert Everett and the whole restaurant break into song, only it was gayer and louder. Jordan's friends didn't stop at "Say a Little Prayer for Me;" they took requests. Even the cooks and the waitresses were singing, and the ones that weren't were laughing or smiling and forget Disney Land. Waffle House was the happiest place on earth.

A cheer went up when one of the guys started an Alicia Keys tune. The chorus was deafening, "This girl is on fire."

"You okay?" I wished the question Jordan shouted over the music was casual, but he wanted the truth.

I would rather set myself on fire than sit in that church tomorrow and hear all the wonderful things about my wonderful husband who didn't love me, who was probably having an affair with a blonde bombshell with calloused CrossFit hands.

"Talk to me, Mom."

I shook my head. "I don't know if I can do this, Jordan. Maybe you should just have the funeral without me."

One of the guys snatched the catsup bottle microphone off the table and belted, "Nobody knows that she's a lonely girl, and it's a lonely world." And ain't that the truth.

"You really don't know, do you?" My face flushed, and my heart slammed against the walls of my chest. Did Jordan know Rhys' secret? "You're the reason I work my ass off for the impossible chance that one day, I'll make it as a working actor. You're why I can sit in a diner in South Carolina with a dozen gays and sing at the top of my lungs. You, not Dad. I loved him, I did, and I hate that he's gone, but he never saw you for the miracle you are.

"I wish you would see that. I wish you would own it."

My eyes throbbed with tears while the boys continued an endless repertoire of show tunes and songs I actually knew from the 60s and 70s. And how did my twenty-something-year-old son know the words better than me?

My face was still hot from Jordan's words when my gargantuan meal came. I ate and sang and snorted, but the restaurant was too noisy for anybody to hear except maybe Jordan. For the first time in three days, my boy looked happy, so happy I prayed the moment was big and bright enough to swallow tomorrow whole because the funeral was going to be way worse than the viewing. Throngs of mourners would listen to Jordan say goodbye to his beloved father and deliver the eloquent eulogy he'd written, and I would bury the man I thought I knew along with his secrets.

The manager stopped by our table. She was short and Hispanic and dressed in a too-tight uniform that looked like it belonged to someone else. She talked with her hands that were nicked up from hard work and joked that we were so good for business she should hire us. "Happy Birthday, Mommy," she said, mistaking my paper tiara for a birthday hat.

"Thank you." I didn't tell her I was queen because my husband was dead. She comped my meal and even ordered the kitchen to make me a hot fudge sundae that wasn't on the menu.

In the middle of Lady GaGa's "Born This Way," the CrossFit couple from the viewing walked in. They looked around the room to see where the party was and spotted me.

My crown fell off in my lap, but I couldn't put it back on. It was wrong for me to sit there and pretend there was no funeral tomorrow; I just didn't realize how wrong it was until Mr. and Mrs. CrossFit scowled at me.

The song ended, and the cook called out "Born to Run" in the thickest Jersey accent I'd ever heard.

"Bitch. Please," Jamar called back. "We do not do Springsteen."

Everyone laughed, even the CrossFit guy but not his wife. He put his glasses on to peruse the menu as Jamar beat out a different tune on the tabletop. The woman squinted hard at me like she could make me burn in hell for my un widow-like display. Everyone joined in the song I didn't recognize until Jordan said, "Strike a pose." His friends did that same echo thing like the Queen of Pop did in the video.

My boy hadn't made it to Broadway yet, but he was primed and ready to sing the shit out of Madonna's Vogue. "Look around; everywhere you turn is heartache. It's everywhere that you go. You try everything you can to escape the pain of life that you know."

The waitress poured the CrossFit couple's water; the husband sent her away so they could have more time to look at the menu, but his wife's eyes were still angry slits directed at me. She finally looked back at her husband and cracked up because he was singing, voguing.

I put my crown back on and tried to hang on to that last bit of swimmy feeling that had saved me from a fourth full hour at the viewing. It made me feel happy and gay in a non-sexual context.

The CrossFit woman's squinty death stare was so hard that I thought her head might explode. But I couldn't blame her for hating me for my healthy appetite, for laughing and singing, for not being distraught over Rhys' death. Her husband said something to her, and I hoped he told her not to judge me until she'd walked a mile in the peep toes that were killing my feet. She nodded and rummaged through her purse until she found a pair of Coke bottle thick glasses and put them on. When she looked at me, the most beautiful smile split her face. She joined in the chorus and struck a pose.

# Chapter Ten

The party moved from Waffle house to my living room, where a half dozen bottles of wine and more food awaited us. The refrigerator that had contained the bulk of Rhys's health food was filled to overflowing with Southern funeral staples like honeyed ham, potato salad, fried chicken, collard greens,

Lowcountry shrimp and grits, cold dips, and ones that were yummy hot, and three different kinds of breakfast casseroles.

Jordan and his friends parked themselves in Rhys' man cave and cranked up the sound system. They were midway through a Beyonce' set when I walked into the room with a charcuterie board made from a Whole Foods goody bag one of the neighbors had dropped by. Most of them were singing Irreplaceable at the top of their lungs. They were having an infectious good time, but I was suddenly immune.

If Rhys had lived, everything in the room would have been boxed up and ready to go when he got out of the hospital. Or maybe strewn across the lawn, courtesy of the girl on fire. It would have been an act of self-defense because I couldn't live through him picking through things he wanted to keep, the push-pull of wanting to live my life without him, yet not wanting to end up in the discard pile.

Ginger Roland danced over and took the tray from me, his horrible singing almost drowned out by the other guys. "So since I'm not your everything, how about I'll be nothing." Once upon a time, I was Rhys' everything until I was nothing. "Baby, I won't shed a tear for you...Cause the truth of the matter is replacing you was so easy." Rhys would have replaced me in a heartbeat. I was a hundred percent sure of it, and from the looks of it, maybe he already had.

According to The Book of Beyoncé, all it would take for me to replace him was to claim my diva sass, my new life. Did I have that in me at fifty-five? A dozen pairs of eyes watched me for an impending meltdown while I pretended to listen to the music and made a Scarlet O'Hara promise to myself that tomorrow would just be another day. Or technically, today, since the funeral would be in about nine and a half hours.

Jamar was stretched out on the floor in the very spot I'd attempted CPR on Rhys. For whatever reason, God or the fates had looked at Rhys and me and said, We'll leave the menopausal and possibly Alzheimer's ridden one and take the health nut.

One of the guys got up from Rhys' recliner to get more food. Jordan snagged the comfy seat before anyone else could, genetically predisposed to throw his long leg over the arm of the chair the way his father used to do. The playlist dissolved to Broadway, and Bette Midler belted Hello, Dolly. The Bumble and Bumble guy cracked Jamar up with a joke.

A hard cocktail of fear and adrenalin coursed through me when he rolled onto his back and quaked with laughter, the way Rhys' body had quaked when I'd tried to save him.

I needed to get out of the man cave, or I was going to start breaking things. I stood up too fast. I could see a bespectacled Rhys at his desk, pouring over ledgers like he was assessing me, avoiding my eyes when he asked for a divorce.

A half dozen hands reached out to steady me. I laughed off my wobbliness and deflected the boys' concern, hoping they'd think it was the wine or the pot that had worn off hours ago. "I'm fine, but

I should probably head up to bed. You all stay up as long as you like."

"You sure you're okay, Mom?" Jordan nudged one of the guys out of the way and was by my side. It was sweet and comforting but mostly annoying that his first thought was to cup my elbow like he did my eighty-five-year-old mother's.

"Yeah, baby. I'm fine. Just tired, that's all." His dark blue eyes were full of concern. "I'm really okay. Enjoy your time with your friends."

"You sure?" I took a few surprisingly steady steps and smiled at him over my shoulder. See. Except I wasn't okay.

I stood at the bottom of the stairs for close to an hour, kneading the banister Rhys painted just last week. I was kneading the newel cap, or more technically, the wooden ball thingy on top of the banister post. Rhys taught me about newel caps, and if I went up those stairs, if I pretended to sleep like I had the last three nights since he died, I'd have to bury him tomorrow.

Matt, the cute Asian boy, was looking for the powder room. I pretended I wasn't frozen in place and pointed him in the right direction. He nodded and asked if I was okay. "Yes." I flashed my most appreciative smile because I couldn't bear to say thank you to another soul. "You can't miss the powder room; it's down the hall, just off the kitchen."

The moment he disappeared around the corner, my brain ordered my body to take the first step, but I couldn't budge. My sweaty palm had rubbed some of the cheap white paint off of the newel cap. There was a spot on one of the spindles Rhys missed and a few small specks of new paint on the oak risers because he ran out of masking tape and didn't want to buy anymore.

God, he was cheap and way more handsome than he was handy.

The large rectangular mirror opposite the stairs was askew. I'd never seen him leave the house without giving his great body a once over and then running his hands through his hair until he was satisfied with perfection.

I caught my own reflection in the mirror, wobbly chin, eyes that couldn't cry for Rhys, for myself. I ran my hand through my short, bottle-blond hair. I was fifty-five years old and looked my age, maybe a few years older, thanks to a lack of sleep. Had being married to a man who never aged, aged me? What would it feel like to get dressed every day without feeling like a mismatched shoe next to him? When had the nagging loop that said I wasn't enough for him begun to play? When would it stop, and how had I lived like that for so long? The answer was clear. I hadn't lived, not really, and as easy as it would be to blame that on my dead husband, it was on me.

A cheer went up when Bette Midler was abruptly switched to Diana Ross's' I'm Coming Out. As the great debate raged in the man cave over Broadway legends versus mega pop divas, the watery smile of the diva staring back at me said, But my dear, you are more than enough.

She was pretty in ways I'd never noticed. Her eyes were tired and sad but bright and smart. She had great cheekbones. Her face was a perfect heart shape. When her shoulders weren't up to her ears from trying to look like she belonged to Rhys Carver, she had a long graceful neck.

In my heart of hearts, I was sure Rhys had never tried to make me feel unworthy. Still, I'd gotten so many of those astonished, he's with her?, looks over the years, I'd taken on the unworthiness, and I was the only one who could fix me. "This girl is on fire," I promised the diva before climbing the stairs.

Our family history lined the hallway, a hodgepodge of five by seven and eight by ten pictures of the kids growing up, more recent ones of their college days and graduations, last Christmas. There was only one photo of just Rhys and me. It was taken about ten years ago at an oyster roast on Sullivans Island. I couldn't remember the last time we took a selfie or asked someone to take a picture of us, and it had nothing to do with Alzheimer's.

The boards in front of the hall bath and our bedroom creaked under my weight, which had always annoyed me. Something Rhys had said would cost a fortune to fix. After that, he went out and bought a new set of golf clubs that did cost a fortune. He thought the new clubs would make him a fantastic golfer because he was good at sports and wanted to play more when he retired. He'd used the new clubs exactly once before switching to CrossFit because having a great golf game was about as easy as having a great marriage.

I opened my bedroom door at the end of the hall. Willa's trademark scent of Meadows and Rain Fabreeze stung my nose. She and I had hardly talked since Rhys died, but she'd been here every day, like a fairy, appearing when the kids and I were taking care of funeral stuff or just out. She'd cleaned, made notes of the endless parade of platters and bowls friends dropped by, and somehow fit everything into the fridge.

The king-size bed was freshly made and looked odd without Rhys propped up on his pillows and mine, scrolling through his phone before we turned out the lights. My throat tightened at the thought of eventually sleeping in that bed alone. I would miss his big body, those moments of muscle memory during a dead sleep when I'd wake up melted against his chest, my leg thrown over his hip. In those first sleepy moments of each new day, pretending I still loved him was easy. In the fleeting haze, sometimes I wished I still did.

His wing-backed recliner, which didn't look like a recliner, sat opposite my chaise. The latest Harlan Cobin book he'd been reading was lying open on a small round accent table between our chairs and face down. I could almost hear the spine cracking but had ignored it the past three nights because Rhys had put it there. I snapped the novel shut and discovered Willa had Fabreezed the hell out of that too.

The Meadows and Rain smelled nothing like Rhys' convoluted scent of body wash and shampoo, conditioner, and hair products.

I opened my closet to get the robe I was relegated to sleeping in until my shoulder was better. The hamper that had been full of my husband's sweaty gym clothes was empty, thanks to Willa. He had almost as many shoes as I did; they were lined up with precision. My fingers trailed across the sports coats he used to wear to work and stopped at a suede one that was so out of date it should have ended up in the giveaway pile years ago.

Why did the thought that I would have ended up in the giveaway pile bother me so much? I was the girl on fire. I didn't love him anymore. Yet I had a feral need to know when he stopped loving me and why.

I turned out the closet light, closed the door, and then stubbed my toe for the millionth time on the massive dresser I never wanted. Pain swallowed my foot in one toothy bite, streaking a path straight to my heart.

Everything hurt. The sing-along downstairs camouflaged the guttural sound that poured out of me. One swipe of my arm sent everything flying over the dresser and across the room. I used my good hand and dug my hip into the beast, trying to move it where it should have been in the first place. It wouldn't budge.

The giant plastic hospital bag with Rhys' clothes, his cell phone, and the contents of his wallet was strewn over the room, his wedding ring by my foot. "Goddamn you, Rhys," I growled and pushed harder. Clawed feet dug into the hardwood, making deep scars across the floor, but this thing would never hurt me again.

Like one of those birdlike women who come upon an accident and is able to lift a car to rescue someone, I rescued myself and shoved the massive dresser all the way across the room. Exhausted, vibrating with anger, I slid down the wall and onto the floor. Pre-eruption and after meeting the porno-worthy nurse, I would have been afraid to look in Rhys' phone, his wallet, but not now.

I plugged the charger into the dead phone and picked up his gold wedding band. It was wide and plain and nicked up in places, but the inscription was still there: M+R=Forever.

Forever had been exhausting. Forever had nearly stolen my soul. His phone arose from the dead and pinged like a pinball machine with missed calls and texts. I grabbed it and entered his passcode, 1963, his birth year, and scrolled through the texts. Most were sent postmortem, mostly from younger cops who left messages like RIP, buddy. Love you, bro, or CrossFit junkies wishing him heavenly WODs and AMRAPs.

I hated acronyms, especially when I didn't know what they meant. What the hell was an ATG or a H2H in CrossFit speak? I used his phone to Google WOD and found it meant Work Out Day. When he'd had his first heart attack, he'd missed his WOD because we were arguing about the trip to California. No, the girl on fire corrected. He was arguing for control.

An auto text said he'd missed an appointment at noon on the same day. There was a phone number to call and reschedule. I started to delete the message when it occurred to me Rhys never made appointments. He didn't even go to the doctor unless work forced him to for his annual physical. Even then, he had me schedule his appointments like a personal secretary.

So, where was my husband going the first time he died?

I rang the number and waited for the machine to pick up. "Welcome to The Grief Counseling Center." The greeting continued, but I was too dumbfounded to get the rest of the message. I called the number again. "Welcome to The Grief Counseling Center. If this is an emergency, go to your nearest emergency room. Otherwise, please leave a message." I didn't leave a message but called a third time because that couldn't be right. My husband was seeing a grief counselor?

I turned his wallet inside out. His driver's license and credit cards were scattered. Among them were six appointment cards from past dates with a grief counselor named Misty Mars.

She sounded like a stripper therapist, and I definitely remembered wondering why he left home those days in his workout clothes and came back in khakis and a polo. Why was the man who avoided gym showers at all costs and any kind of probing, medical or otherwise, seeing a grief therapist? Had he spent the last six weeks getting pointers on how to get rid of me?

The world shook. An earthquake. The house creaked and moaned like it was opening its jaws to swallow me whole, and then Jordan was there holding me. My body vibrated with the velocity of an Apollo astronaut reentering the earth's atmosphere.

"I've got you," Jordan sputtered and wrapped his arms around me. I moaned and sobbed with the empty wallet clutched to my chest. I cried for Rhys, for the love and the secrets that died with him. I'd married him believing love was simple and pure, but it's not. Love is slippery, so slippery. Something you have to hold tight with both hands, with your whole heart. Because when you let it go, when you even begin to think about the possibility of letting love go, it's already gone. And you can never get it back.

# Chapter Eleven

The thing about non-funeral crying jags is that when they end, you've had a good cry and feel better. So while I felt a lot like I did when I was pregnant and my water finally broke, I knew I wouldn't truly feel better until the burial was over.

On the other strange and juxtaposed hand, I felt like Cinderella. I was up before six for Jordan's Bumble and Bumble friend to color and style my hair and was at the nail salon with Jamar and Jordan for mani-pedis by nine. Three of the boys who acted like personal stylists and one who actually was a stylist dressed and fussed over me. I giggled when the whole lot of them threw up their hands because I refused to wear the peep toes from last night.

"Doesn't Grandma always say a woman has to go through a lot of pain to be beautiful?" Jordan asked in a last-ditch effort.

"Yeah, well, Grandma doesn't have to wear those things. Besides, my Easy Spirits look fine."

"Not even when you pretend they do." He sighed. "But it's going to be a long ass day, so okay."

I looked down at my shoes and wiggled my toes. "Another good reason to wear them."

He checked my face like I used to check his when he was little, turning it from side to side before he looked me dead in the eyes and said softly, "There's no ditching this one, Mom."

Oh, how I wish he'd been wrong.

I was at the front of the line with a hundred and fifty or so members of the Carver and Jenkins clans waiting to file in for the service, but Julia was not among us. I kept looking over my shoulder, hoping she would push through the massive double doors and make her way to me before the service began, but that didn't happen. The last time I glanced at the door, Willa caught my eye and pulled me aside. "Hey," she whispered. "I'm so sorry Jullia's not here, Maise. I don't know what the hell is wrong with her, but the rest of us are here for you."

"Thanks," I whispered back. I'd overheard Jordan talking to Willa this morning. He'd told her he was worried because I wasn't sleeping, that I'd finally cried, but only once. "Thanks for everything you've done."

"I've hardly seen you since the hospital. How are you holding up?"

"I'm okay," I lied.

"I'm so sorry, Maise. If I could bring him back, I would." She kissed my forehead. "But I know Rhys would have wanted--."

"I don't give a shit about what Rhys would have wanted," I hissed.

"Honey. You don't mean that."

"He wanted a divorce, Will," I spat loud enough to be overheard, but everyone was too busy catching up since the last wedding or funeral we'd all attended. Willa motioned to the funeral director to give us a minute before she yanked me into a Sunday school room and closed the door. "It was the last thing he said to me. He wanted a divorce."

"That bastard." She shook her head, and I felt marginally better she was as blindsided as me by Rhys' last wish. "I knew you weren't happy, but if anyone was going to do the asking, I thought it would be you. Was he cheating?"

"Did you see all those gorgeous women at the viewing? I didn't know any of them, but they sure as hell seemed to know Rhys."

The funeral director opened the door, and I slammed it shut. "I can't sit in that church with our flaky sister noticeably absent from my almost ex-husband's funeral and listen to how wonderful he was. I just can't."

"I know you don't want to do this, but you're going to walk down that aisle with your head held high, knowing you saved Rhys Carver's sorry ass and you survived, Maisie. You survived."

"Now what? What comes after survival?"

"Life, my darling sister." She held me close. I felt safe and relieved that someone other than me and Jordan knew the truth about the divorce. "Now, let's bury that bastard."

The music Jordan picked spilled out of the sanctuary and into the vestibule of the North Charleston mega-church we'd rented out for the occasion. Songs he knew his father loved that were never meant for a pipe organ like "Stairway to Heaven," "Free Bird," and "Hotel California." The organist's eyes widened when Jordan handed her the playlist, but she was sweet and said she'd wing it.

Al Green's "Let's Stay Together" dissolved seamlessly into "You Can't Always Get What You Want," while all my texts to Julia went unanswered. The calls went straight to voicemail, and her mailbox was full. Maybe she was hurt, or worse, dead. Maybe she had to rush back to Richmond to perform an emergency surgery. But she had a practice full of doctors who would gladly stand in for her.

Where the hell are you? I texted and put the phone in my lap.

The sanctuary was packed with over a thousand people. An Eagles tune ended, and John Mellencamp's "Little Pink Houses" played. Sandwiched between my kids, second pew from the front, Emma's head lolled between my shoulder and Cam's; Jordan held my hand so tight it hurt. The dark screen of my cellphone stared up at me.

I needed Julia. After last night, I shouldn't have had to spell that out for her.

The music ended, and the pastor, who didn't know our family but somehow knew Rhys proclaimed this a celebration of his life. He extolled my husband's many virtues, at least the ones that could be mentioned in church. I craned my head to look at the massive Hogwarts-style doors at the back of the sanctuary, willing them to open. For Julia to stride down the aisle to where we were sitting and wedged herself between Emma and me, bolstering us all. But she was a no-show.

A hoard of specially selected mourners lined up to add to the impossibly good and perfect picture of Rhys, the pastor eloquently painted. Emma and Jordan were last in line. He fidgeted with his notecards, bending them this way and that, putting his arm around Emma from time to time when one of the eulogizers hit a particular nerve. Even though he memorized reams of lines for a living,

Jordan handwrote his long speech onto notecards this morning because he wanted to do his father proud.

A lovely young woman with mahogany skin took her place at the podium. My heart sang when my phone vibrated with a text, but it wasn't from Julia. The airfare alert I'd set up for our trip to California announced a too-good-to-be-true deal that included a stay at a fancy resort near the heart of redwood country near Santa Cruz. Another text alert teased with an offer from Zappos for the eleven hundred-dollar shoes I looked at for grins a few weeks ago but didn't have the nerve to try on. They were on sale, twenty percent off.

"Rhys Carver," the woman at the podium sighed. She said she'd met him through her job as director of the local Boy's and Girls' Clubs. She laughed and cried while she told her story about, "The man who was generous to a fault." A tiny sweet smirk crossed Jordan's face; Emma smiled for the first time in days. "Rhys was always so giving," she paused for everyone except me to agree. "Why, there wasn't a more generous soul on God's earth."

The next few speakers took the generosity theme and ran with it. Apparently, Rhys was generous to all of them, but for thirty years, he'd made me write down any purchase over five dollars in a ledger and set a hundred-dollar threshold I dared not cross. His control of our money and my aversion to crossing him had made me one of those just-looking kind of ladies. Yet, after the pretty young cop who was speaking had had a particularly bad day, she'd happened to see Rhys downtown and poured her heart out to him. Then, to make her feel better, he'd taken her to lunch at the Charleston Grill, the restaurant we went to once on our anniversary, and never went back after the waiter brought the check.

My phone buzzed again, but it wasn't Julia. Apparently, I'd left a trail of virtual breadcrumbs. Nordstrom and Neiman Marcus had gotten wind of Zappos' offer. They, too, had 20% off sales. "Rhys was the kind of guy who would give you the shirt off his back," the pretty cop said.

Mom put her hand on my good shoulder from the pew behind me because this was definitely not the Rhys she knew, either. She squeezed it as if to say, You and I both know these people are full of shit.

Not to be outdone by the other retailers, Zappo's email alert offered an extra five percent off if I ordered within the next two hours. I tapped the link and ordered the shoes. Rhys Carver, be damned.

The travel deal popped up again as if to say, What about me? I swiped the buy button for me, Mom, and Willa to fly into San Jose in two months; they practically threw in the rental car for free. Even though I was on an impromptu shopping spree if Julia couldn't get her ass to my husband's funeral, I sure as hell wasn't buying her a plane ticket.

Purchases confirmed, I turned my attention back to the open mic, which was Emma's idea. Judging from the line that stretched halfway down the center aisle, it would go on forever. If FDR were here, he'd admonish them all with, "Be sincere." And I would add, "Be brief, tell us something we haven't heard ad nauseam, and be seated."

Honestly, how many different ways could you glorify Rhys Carver? Apparently, there were only four, five, tops, because these people kept saying the same thing over and over again. He was a good friend. He was kind and generous with his time, his talents, and his/our money. The more eulogizers, like the half dozen gorgeous women I didn't know but recognized from the viewing, gushed about his generosity, the angrier I got that my husband had reserved the best parts of himself for everyone but me.

Finally. Finally, the last speaker said his piece. Arm in arm, Jordan took the podium with Emma. For a few seconds, her swollen eyes danced with laughter at something Jordan whispered to her. Then she let go of him and took a small step back. With Jordan's perfect posture, he was a little taller than his dad. He glanced at his notecards before shoving them in his pocket, swallowed hard, and then mouthed, I love you, Mom.

"I had a long speech prepared, but it didn't say anything that hasn't already been said about Rhys Carver except that he was a great dad." His voice cracked on the last word. Emma rubbed Jordan's arm while he waxed eloquently about Rhys and got a laugh when he talked about how creepy it was when all of his and Emma's middle school and high school girlfriends crushed on their dad.

The more Jordan talked, the more I was acutely aware of how small I was on the bench reserved bench for the kids and me, how

103

alone I would be when he returned to New York when Emma went back to work and threw herself into planning the wedding. But after thirty-two years of being married to Rhys, I knew that feeling well.

The pastor offered a closing prayer, and the organist began her version of "Free Bird." The congregation rose, and the family started the procession down the aisle. The eulogizers had been seated together, the prettiest of the lot with their own pew. They were beautiful and tearful, clinging together, whispering words of comfort to each other, but the hot blonde nurse was absent.

The kids ducked into the limo first. Before I could follow. One of Emma's friends from law school nudged me out of the way to stick her head in the car to say she had to get back to work and was sorry she couldn't stay for the burial. I glanced around at the throngs of mourners, hoping to see Julia, but she wasn't there. I took my phone out of my clutch and tapped out one last text to my sister. I am done with you. I erased the sentence, but the girl on fire retyped it in all caps with a few expletives and hit the Send button.

A couple of decades ago, Rhys parents got some kind of buy one, get one deal when they bought their cemetery plots and gave us ours that year for Christmas. His mom had been so excited she'd found the perfect gift for us that was practically free. Our plots were next to theirs and just a few blocks from our house, so whoever went first, I'm pretty sure they expected me to precede Rhys in death, would have a leisurely stroll to the cemetery.

The place hadn't changed much since that Christmas morning his parents took us to see the plots Nana Carver had decorated with giant red bows like the ones in the Lexus commercials. A pile of dirt where Rhys' grave had been dug was on my side of our deathbed. A tiny button that could have been hundreds of years old or fresh from a Dickie's work shirt was lying next to the heap. I wasn't going to tempt fate by going out and buying another plot for myself, but there was no way I was going to spend eternity lying next to Rhys.

The pastor must have read my thoughts about being brief. He uttered a few words about God and grief, the promise of a day without pain or suffering, and then nodded at the funeral director. Stoic and dry-eyed, Emma nearly squeezed my hand off as the casket inched into the grave. Jordan swiped at his tears and bowed his head, unable to watch.

The three of us rose when the funeral director took the fancy shovel off its stand so we could take part in the age-old tradition of throwing dirt on the coffin. Jordan took the lead, the heel of his dress shoes pressing the shovel into the middle of the pile. He broke down for a few seconds before he threw the dirt onto the coffin and then took his seat.

"Ashes to ashes," the pastor said and handed the shovel to Emma. Somewhere between the church and the cemetery, she'd put away the pitiful little girl who'd lost her daddy a few days ago and seemed stronger, steadier. She tossed Rhys' Atlanta Braves hat into the grave, followed it with dirt, and sat down between her brother and Cam.

The pastor nodded at me. "Dust to Dust."

I threw my own offering into the mix, Rhys' wedding band and mine. The shovel hissed when my Easy Spirit jabbed it into the soft dirt. A healthy portion of sand thudded onto the coffin, and then another and another. I couldn't stop. Chest heaving, sweat rolling down my legs on a crisp February day, I dug with my good arm until Jordan relieved me of the shovel.

A sliver of sunlight peeked under the tent to warm my tear-streaked face, but the tears had nothing to do with Rhys. He was gone, buried alongside my excuse for how easily I had accepted a life I didn't want. The weight of owning the rest of my life was full of beautiful and terrifying possibilities. I had no idea what I was doing or where this new life would take me, but it was mine.

# Chapter Twelve

J ust after midnight, the cell phone on my nightstand jolted me awake. My heart skidded out of control when I saw my early-to-bed-early-to-rise mother's picture on the caller ID.

I dispensed with hello and cut to the chase. "Mom? Are you okay? Is Dad okay?"

"Hello, sweet girl. Yes, we're all fine. Sorry to call so late." Her tone was the same as it was when Danny Dobler broke my heart in the third grade or when Rhys didn't come home that one horrible night decades ago. "How are you?"

"I'm fine, Mom."

"So, you've said so in your texts."

"It's late. You scared the crap out of me."

"Glad you finally answered the phone. If I was still driving, I'd have been over there by now to see with my own eyes, but Willa said you needed time to yourself."

"I'm okay," I repeated, like that might somehow convince her. "Are you angry?"

"Yes, a little. I'm your mother. It's my duty to fuss over you, especially when you're hurt, and I know you're hurting. I can feel it down in my bones."

"So, Willa told you." The last thing I wanted her to know was that Rhys wanted to end our marriage.

"Told me what?"

"Never mind. It's nothing."

"It's hardly nothing if it kept you from calling your mother back for over a week since your husband's funeral."

There was no reason to tell her about Rhys. She'd always adored him, although if she got a couple of sherries in her and it was just the two of us, she would let words slip like tightwad and cheapskate. There was no question she would be on my side if I told her about the divorce he wanted and the probability of his infidelity? But she had enough on her plate with Dad and worrying about me.

"You don't have to tell me anything if you don't want to, Maisie, but I do need to hear from you now and again, to know you're okay." She was right. I'd called Emma several times a day for that very reason; come to think of it, she'd sounded miffed at me too. "No matter. I am calling because I saw you bought that trip to California during Rhys' service. I'm sure you did it to spite him, and the way he controlled your money, I don't blame you. But I'm just wondering if a trip like that is too soon for you."

"No, Mom, I think this trip is exactly what we all need." Except for Julia, the girl on fire added, we are done with her. But telling Mom would either break her heart, or she'd do that thing she did when we were little and make us stand nose to nose, toes to toes, and stay that way until both of you say you're sorry, that you love each other. Even if we almost never meant it at the time.

"I'm so relieved you think so. I hadn't heard a peep out of Julia since the viewing, so I called her just now and got her on board with the trip. She's looking for airfares as we speak. The suite you got has a foldout and is plenty big for the four of us. You girls can take turns on the couch like that first time we all drove to New York City and crammed into that tiny little hotel room. It will be fun." She waited for me to agree. "Darling? Are you there? Hello?"

"I'm here, Mom." She waited for me to fill the long silence. "But I don't want Julia to go."

"All things considered, including her not showing up at Rhys' sendoff, you are sisters." Her voice was terse. "There's no condoning what Julia did; I was disappointed in her too. But you started this trip thing to honor my bucket list. If I re-wrote that list this very minute, I'd put the reparation of your and Julia's sisterhood straight at the top."

"But Julia started this!"

"Good Lord, Masie, you're not a child. Julia did a terrible thing to you. I don't know why any more than you do; I'd like to believe she couldn't watch you put your husband in the ground because she's never gotten over losing John.

"I don't know the why of what's going on between you two because neither of you will talk about it to me. You won't even talk to each other. So, I took matters into my own hands. Julia is going to California with the rest of us. The two of you will lay down your swords. And so help me; if it kills us all, you will have a good time."

I felt small after Mom blessed me out. In the grand scheme of the sisterhood, was I being petty? But was I ready to forgive Julia? On the other hand, I had never heard my mother so agitated, and believe me, raising three daughters who'd fought over everything at one time or another, she'd had plenty of opportunities to eclipse that mark.

"Fine." She waited as long as it took for me to say more. "Your trip. Your rules."

"Thank you, darling." Her mom-in-charge voice gentled considerably. "This trip is going to be good for us, but it's going to be especially good for you, Maisie. Rhys ran the show your entire marriage; that was just the kind of man he was, but it's your turn now. To grow, to blossom, to make your life what you want it to be."

Coming of age at fifty-five is like trying to ride a bike for the first time. I had this wonderful thing underneath me, inside me, surrounding me that made the world look even bigger than it had from astride my banana seat bicycle. So big it made me want to take my shaky legs from astride the thrill machine and plant both feet firmly on the ground. But doing what I wanted to do when I wanted to do it was as glorious as that first ride around the infield of the red dirt baseball field near my childhood home.

Instead of automatically thinking WWRD, what would Rhys do, or going along with whatever he said, I had to stop and think about what I wanted. An invite to a teacher friend's second wedding asked that I decide between chicken or salmon. I'd prepared and eaten both two or three times a week for years because they were healthy, and Rhys liked them. I'd always eaten what was put in front of me, but being asked to choose between the two made me realize I really didn't like either, so I checked the vegetarian box in a smaller print at the bottom right corner of the invite. Not that I was a vegetarian, but I could be if I was allowed fresh seafood or a burger every once in a while.

Even with my newfound independence, I still felt a little lopsided by Rhys' absence. The day after the come-to-Jesus conversation with Mom, my check engine light reminded me Rhys had been in charge of car maintenance. Seeing the flashing red light was creepy, like he was voicing his doubts from beyond the grave that I was capable of getting this new life right.

I took the car to the same place he did; the mechanic didn't know Mr. Carver was dead. It was strange to hear them talk about Rhys in the present tense as they pointed out what Mr. Carver usually had them do, which was the minimum. With one hundred and ten thousand miles on the thing, there was a multitude of things Rhys had put off that needed to be done now or in a couple thousand miles. The guy behind the counter looked slightly rattled when I told him to do it all. He suggested I call Rhys and ask his permission.

I waved him off. "All of it, and put some new tires on while you're at it."

Emboldened by my take-charge afternoon at the auto repair shop and a few glasses of wine with dinner, I ventured into Rhys' man cave and sat behind his desk. I opened the middle drawer and pulled out the color-coded checkbooks he kept there, blue for household expenses, mahogany for savings, and green for investments.

It had been forever since I'd written a check of any sort, and it had been months since I'd looked at banking or investment statements. The balances in the blue and mahogany ones were about what I'd thought they would be. I couldn't remember when I'd last seen a statement for the green one. It had more money than I expected, which was understandable since the market had been good.

I tossed the checkbooks onto the desk and pulled out a stack of concert ticket stubs he'd held onto over the years. There were tons from the '80s, back when we drove to Columbia or Atlanta to see shows that didn't come to Charleston, significantly fewer for the '90s and only three in the 2000s. A paper clip held tickets to six different Stevie Nicks shows; he'd always had a thing for her.

There were stacks of old photos in the drawer, duplicates of the ones I'd pressed neatly into albums from Halloweens, Christmases, the kids' sporting events, and birthdays. I pulled them out and sifted through them, remembering almost every moment, despite my diseased mind, because I'd been the one behind the camera. The last handful of photos yielded a black checkbook stuffed in the back of the drawer.

I knew Rhys' commandments for the other checkbooks. Thou shalt only pay for household expenses out of the blue checkbook.

Thou shalt never write a check from investment or savings; only he could do that. But what about the secret checkbook, and why was he hiding it from me?

My heart plummeted when I opened the crisp pages to find the deposit ledger for a Chase investment account in his name only, his account login information printed at the top of the page in cobalt blue ink. There were two deposits from just after his parents' deaths seventeen years ago totaling a little over four hundred thousand dollars. I'd had no idea how much money he'd inherited from their estate. After their long bouts with cancer, I didn't think it would be much and just assumed whatever he'd gotten, he'd put in our investment account.

My thumb traced six withdrawals in varying amounts just south of ten thousand dollars from 2001 to 2006. There was nothing for twelve years and then another withdrawal for a whopping thirty thousand dollars. Who did he give the money to? What was the money for? Were there more secret accounts?

I threw back the rest of my wine and dumped the contents of the drawer onto the desk. Thankfully, there were no more little black books. But what did this one mean? Aside from the fact he'd given almost a hundred thousand dollars to someone, why hadn't he told me about the inheritance? Was it an inheritance, or was he a dirty cop? No, and if he was, he sure as hell wouldn't have waltzed into the Chase Bank on Meeting Street and opened an account. No. The dates were right for the money to have come from his parent's estate, but they would have considered it our money.

I fired up his laptop and used the information Rhys had scribbled in the front of the checkbook to open the account and clicked on the Statements tab. The only ones available were from the past twelve months. The Request a Statement tab taunted me. Did I really want to know what my husband was up to? Could I walk away from this without knowing? There were just over three hundred thousand dollars in a secret account where there had once been four. There'd been no withdrawals for twelve years, and then suddenly a final withdrawal for a whopping thirty thousand two years ago?

I squeezed my eyes shut and tried to remember what was going on during that time. Emma was a freshman at the University of South Carolina and was on her second round of braces, all covered with scholarships and insurance. Jordan was visiting colleges that had offered him a full ride, but he was more interested in his part as Danny Zuko in his high school's production of Grease. I'd changed schools that year, tired of the long commute to Mary Ford Elementary in North Charleston. So, what was Rhys up to?

I typed in the date of the first withdrawal and the date of the last into the search engine and slugged back the rest of my wine as the tiny roulette wheel on the screen whirled in search of answers. Moments later, I had the answer or would have it in five to seven business days via the United States Post Office. I paid twenty dollars to expedite the report and hoped it would be two days instead of three.

Before I closed the laptop, a Google ad popped up for mail-order brides. I stood up too fast, Rhys' little black book clutched to my chest. The worry and the wine made my head spin. Did a mail-order bride cost ninety grand? I held on to walls and doorways as I made my way to the foot of the stairs. The imperfections on the steps I'd mooned over the night before the funeral were glaring and ugly. A rush job by someone I didn't know, someone who didn't care.

The mirror he couldn't pass without stopping to adore was slightly askew. A guttural sound came from nowhere, from everywhere. Body vibrating with rage, I reared back and heaved the checkbook at his goddamn mirror, at Rhys. The book splintered, register pages scattered. And in their midst was a bright shiny debit card.

# Chapter Thirteen

Three days later, a fat Chase envelope arrived with no answers. The checks had not been made payable to a mystery woman or women; Rhys had made them out to cash. I told myself I didn't care what he was up to. He was dead, and if he was having an affair, it was done. Was I curious about which one of the tearful hot babes from the funeral it was, the tragically beautiful nurse? Yes. But digging around in his life was bad for me.

Besides, I was drunk on freedom and focused on WWMD, what would Maisie do, or want or need. It felt delicious to say yes to myself, and Rhys wasn't there to say, "not today," which really meant "never." If I wanted something, I said yes to amazing food at restaurants Rhys would have taken one look at the prices on the menu and walked. I said yes to fewer mirrors and a more sensible arrangement of the furniture.

I fell in love with clothes again, or more aptly, my body, which was almost the same as before he died but was strangely pleasing to me. I loved my curves, the wonders of yoga pants guaranteed to lift one's ass spectacularly, and since when had I cared about what my ass looked like? It didn't matter. Change was coming, mostly from inside me, but outside, I was blossoming. Or, more aptly, I was learning to appreciate the flower I'd always been.

I'd grown so accustomed to Rhys' snoring that it took me a while to get used to sleeping without it, but when I did, I awoke feeling amazing. My body clock still had me up every morning at seven-thirty on the dot, and today was no different. In my sleepy haze, I could have sworn Rhys had nudged my backside for sex, but then it was Friday, albeit the thirteenth, the day I started new things, a new diet, a new skincare regime, a new life. And what did that say about our Friday sex? Was I subconsciously trying to reboot our marriage over and over again?

I had not made the short walk to the cemetery to visit Rhys' grave since the burial. Jordan had gone a couple of times before he went back to New York. He'd said he wanted to go alone. I think that was more for me than for him. Emma had probably gone several times, but after the discovery of Rhys' little black checkbook, I couldn't set foot near his grave, not when just thinking about him or who I might find there mourning him made me ill.

Otherwise, I was okay. It would have been nice to have Julia to help me navigate widowhood the way she had. She'd made it look easy and graceful, but then John hadn't left her wondering who he was or if she'd ever really known him in the first place.

Even though I felt like I didn't need Julia, the first thing I did when I woke up every morning was check my phone for a call or text from her. There was nothing. Part of me wanted to believe her ditching me the day of the funeral was a calculated kindness to distract me during the third act of the funeral festivities, but it wasn't. The loyal, giving, protective big sister I'd known since birth had disappeared into the brilliant doctor who didn't give two shits about her family.

Of course, Mom and Dad didn't seem to know this, and Willa was still basking in the afterglow of Julia's flash visit for the viewing. But forgiving Julia was impossible. Then again, I couldn't forget she'd saved me that day any more than I could forget about Rhys's little black checkbook. And Mom expected me to suck it up like

Julia hadn't abandoned the whole family again, like she hadn't abandoned me.

Still, my heart leaped every time my cell phone rang. Sure, it was her calling to explain, to apologize, and then say, "Sisters?" like she always did after she'd had a row with Willa or me. Then I'd parrot her response, and we would be right as rain. But the caller ID confirmed there would be no apology, no affirmation of the sisterhood; it was Cam, who rarely called, and never so early in the morning.

"Hey," I tried to sound normal, but I could hardly breathe. "Is Emma okay?" Because after someone dies, it switches on that paranoid spot in your brain that buys into that whole death comes in threes bullshit.

"Maisie." Cam's voice was tentative, but he got right to it. "I'm worried about Emma. She visits Rhys daily, but you probably know

since you're at the cemetery often." The guilt blooming in my belly was the approximate size of a beach ball and growing. "I get that she's grieving, but she's not eating. She's not sleeping. Nothing I do seems to help. Can you please talk to her?"

"Yes, of course." I'd called and texted Emma several times a day since the funeral and asked her if she was okay or if she wanted to get together. Was there anything I could do for her? She'd sounded okay and promised she was fine. Sure, her words had become more clipped the last few days, but that's how she was when she was slammed at work. "Cam, I know this must be hard

120

for you, but Emma was close to her dad." So much closer than me. "Her behavior sounds normal."

"Is it?" The long silence was unnerving. "Look, I know you've had a rough go of it; we all have. That's why I didn't want to worry you, but it gets worse.

"Emma and I rarely see each other at work, so yesterday I swung by her cube, but she wasn't there. One of her colleagues told me she's been on bereavement leave since Rhys died and will be for four more weeks. Every morning since the burial, she's gotten up, pretending to go to work when she's been at the cemetery. I went to her and told her I was worried about her, but we ended up in a huge fight, and she stormed off.

"When I couldn't find her, I doubled back, and the caretaker confirmed she's there every day until he closes the gates. I don't know what to do, Maisie."

Emma had been keeping vigil over Rhys' grave? No wonder my conversations with her had been lopsided and clipped. While she was grieving her father's death, I'd slept with the lights on whenever I felt like it, watched Jimmy Fallon most every night, and gloried in the toilet seat always being down. I'd trawled Wayfare and Overstock for things for the house. Yesterday, I ordered Alexa along with a few things from Amazon because you just can't beat free shipping. I'd been to the mall twice, once to try out that La Mer face cream Jordan 'wears by, then the next 'day to get the whole skincare regime. It cost a fortune, but my face looked better than my Dick Clark husband's did before he died.

And the whole time I was immersing myself in retail therapy, feeling better, looking spectacular, my daughter had been deceiving her fiancé, surrounding herself with dead wreaths and flower arrangements, and probably lying prostrate on her father's grave.

"So, you'll talk to her?" he asked.

The thing about flawless, younger-looking skin is that you can't undo it in a hot minute, which isn't fair because, with enough stress, a woman can go to bed looking forty and wake up looking sixty. Unfortunately, your daughter knowing you've been whooping it up since her father's death wasn't enough to reestablish hard lines, dark circles, and balloon pores. Even eating like crazy, I'd lost ten pounds. It was like Rhys died, and the weight I could never lose just started falling off, so I'd joined a new gym to firm up. I even hired Katherine, my personal trainer, who said she'll make my teacher's arms disappear after I was done rehabbing my shoulder.

"Maisie?"

"Yes, I'll talk to her this morning. Thanks for letting me know."

I rolled out of bed, grateful my new haircut made a horrible bedhead. I threw on my baggiest jeans and eased into an oversized College of Charleston zip-front hoodie before slathering on my old skin products in hopes that my old skin would suddenly appear. But I looked brighter, happier, and not at all like a grieving widow.

My phone pinged with a text from Amazon; the new patio set I bought was back-ordered. I threw on my beat-up gardening shoes, and stuck the Visine in my pocket that had become a staple for whenever I saw someone who expected me to look bereft. I didn't think of Julia or Rhys and his secrets. I rifled through his wallet, took what I needed, and hurried to the cemetery.

Rhys' parents weren't kidding about the gravesite being an easy walk from our home. I entered through the ornate iron gate, and there she was, dressed in her King Street finery, sitting on a Burberry wool picnic blanket, eyes closed, back pressed against the side of the freshly carved headstone. The briefcase Rhys and I gave her when she graduated from law school was beside whatever grossly expensive purse she'd chosen to complete the ruse.

Since the funeral, I'd asked her a million times if she needed me, and a million times, she'd said no. Emma had always been fiercely independent and always hated my hovering. So, when Rhys died, I gave her the space she asked for. I didn't feel like I was shirking my mom duties as Emma's only parent because she'd always been so strong, always said what she wanted, what she needed. And I'd believed her because I needed her to be okay.

She opened her eyes but didn't smile, much less look at me. "Hey, honey." She said nothing. Her long, manicured finger traced the deckled edge of the headstone. A lone hawk circled in the stark blue sky as two cars passed by, headed in opposite directions like Rhys and me, like Emma and me. "Cam called me this morning and said you'd be here."

"He shouldn't have done that," she said, still not looking at me.

I fidgeted with the Grief Counseling Center business card in my pocket. I felt a bit like those people in the kiosks at the mall who always want to curl your hair or straighten it or give you cream made from Dead Sea animals that nobody wants. She flinched hard when I moved closer. Definitely not the time to whip out Misty Marr's card and suggest we make therapy a mother-daughter thing like we did when she was into ceramics or those places where everyone drinks wine and paints the same picture.

"Cam loves you, honey; he's so worried about you. I'm worried about you too." She said nothing. "Emma, I get that you're grieving, but being here all the time just isn't good for you."

"Seriously?" She barked, eyes narrowed. "You're going to lecture me on grief when you haven't been here once since Daddy died?"

"Honey, everybody grieves in their own way." The mall. The gym. Online shopping that was like a drug, seeping into my veins until I was glassy-eyed from BOGOs and free shipping. "Cam's worried because you didn't tell him about the bereavement leave, and you lied to him about work."

"I did not lie," she spat.

"Maybe it's not an out-and-out lie, but you made it appear you were going to work every day when you were coming here. That's not the truth; that's not a good foundation for your relationship."

"And you'd know all about good relationships, wouldn't you?" She glared until she couldn't stand the sight of me and looked away. "I. Am. Not. Okay. You should not be okay, but apparently, you are. So okay, you don't bother to show up at your husband's grave, at my father's grave, and I want to know why."

I looked down at the gray sandy mound covering Rhys and the indentions in the soft dirt where Emma had sat. And maybe she had lain prostrate, but I couldn't know for sure because I hadn't been there.

My daughter, who has loved to argue since she could speak, railed on about my absence. My silence only stoked her fury, distracting her from the fact that her daddy was never coming back. But I didn't want Rhys back. He left me in every way possible. I would never tell her about the divorce, or the secret money, with tens of thousands of dollars missing. Shattering her illusions about her father would be cruel and pointless because she'd never believe me.

Grief had marked her beautiful face with hard lines no potion could cure. She was gaunt and so much thinner than she had been two weeks ago. Her eyes looked bruised and swollen like she was trying to give that Twilight girl a run for her money, and how could one person cry so many tears?

I could. If I lost her, if I lost Jordan, my tears would fill Charleston Harbor. But Emma's eyes were dry now, and there was a bit of color in her cheeks. "Well?" she snapped.

When I reached for her, she wrapped her arms around her bent legs and rocked with hot anger. "I'm here now, Emma. I--."

"In the hospital, you kept telling me Dad was dead when he wasn't." Judge and jury, there was no stopping her. "Then, when he really did die, you hardly cried, Mom. You didn't act like you were glad he was dead, but you acted—."

"Angry? I am angry at your dad, Emma. But that's not an unusual reaction to death, honey."

"Your husband of over thirty years died," she growled. "You skipped over shock and sadness and went straight to anger, and I want to know why."

"Emma, your Dad and I were together for a long time. But sticking it out for a few decades doesn't make a great marriage. It doesn't even make a good one. Your father--."

"Don't you dare blame this on him," she seethed. "Why did you leave the viewing early? What did Daddy do that would make him not worth one goddamn tear? Did he hit you?"

"No," I stammered. "Never. Honey, marriage is --."

"Were you cheating on him? Are you cheating on him?"

"No. Emma, marriage is complicated."

"Bullshit."

The fire inside had crystalized her tears. She was in her comfort zone, the dogged defense attorney, arguing for her beloved father, and it felt like she'd plunged her fist clean through my heart. But how do you grieve a husband who had a secret life, a husband who didn't want you anymore? How do you grieve a man you didn't know? And he didn't know me, couldn't see me evolving so damn slowly, but changing, growing.

The two of us limped through life as the twenty-somethings who married too young without knowing ourselves, much less each other. Thirty-two years later, all we had to show for it was a broken union neither of us had the courage or a clue to fix. The damage of living that way for too many years had been done. I'd suffered. Rhys had suffered. Maybe that was the explanation for the missing money. He was trying to fill the hole I didn't or couldn't.

Emma's seething blue eyes demanded answers. As much as her anger hurt, it had made a tiny stitch in my broken heart and had sent her sailing over the gulf between denial and anger. In some inexplicably small way, my daughter had begun to heal.

Gratitude knocked me to my knees. Stubborn tears that were never there when I needed them wouldn't stop. Still furious, she opened her clenched fist just enough for me to see her perfect nude manicure, caked with dirt. "I'm sorry, Emma. I'm so sorry."

My child, who was never quick to forgive, launched herself at me and clung to me like she did when she was small. I wasn't forgiven, not by a long shot. There would be plenty more days when Emma would be mad at me for being alive when her father wasn't. But the sun filtered through near-naked branches of live oaks that would soon be glossy and green, offering hope for life, hope for us.

# *Chapter Fourteen*

On the walk home, I basked in that little thrill that comes with kissing a boo-boo or doing the mom thing right and maybe helping my daughter take baby steps toward the life she had before it was upended. While Emma didn't hug me, she laid her head in my lap and held tight to my hand until she pulled her phone out of her bag to call Cam and apologize. The tremor in her shaky voice said she needed him far more than she needed me.

Ten minutes later, a BMW screeched to a halt at the curb, and Cam sprinted toward her. She scrambled out of my lap and into his arms. The relief and the love that radiated from them were so glorious I sobbed until the hot kissing began.

An icy February gust chased me toward the cemetery gate, sending my hands into my pockets. I took the business card from the Grief Counseling Center out and turned it over to find something written on the back, not Rhys' handwriting. There was a neat, straight line with the ends marked points A and B. Underneath was scrawled, "How we want grief to work." Beside the nice straight line was a scribble with so many lines it looked like a tangled ball of yarn; the caption read, "How grief really works." Trade out grief for sex or forgiveness or sisterhood, and the analogy still held.

Maybe Rhys' stripper therapist was more qualified than I thought, but it wasn't like I needed to go to therapy. Sure, it took me a while to visit his grave. Still, I did it, and it didn't suck. Not that it was particularly good, and I might never have gone were it not for Emma, but that small gesture had begun to unravel the tangled mess between her and me and gave me hope that she would be okay, that we would be okay.

Gorgeous mahogany oak leaves skittered around vibrant whisper gray new headstones and ancient faded charcoal-colored ones that marked abbreviated lives, Beloved and Dearest ones who'd died much younger than Rhys. The tannin-soaked

Lowcountry sand peppered with tiny bits of oyster shells and oak bark crunched under my feet as I walked victoriously into the land of the living. My breath quickened with the sheer simplicity and joy of being alive. I jogged a couple of steps until my shoulder screamed and then walked as briskly as the crisp winter wind promising mock spring days ahead.

My neighbor, Mrs. Kinsey, shuffled toward me with her walker, her head craned down at the sidewalk tree roots had pushed up like mismatched puzzle pieces. In her early seventies, she was dressed for winter in Minnesota. Every day, rain or shine, she made her way to the cemetery for fresh air and exercise and to visit her husband, who died ten years ago.

"Morning, Mrs. Kinsey," I said a little too brightly.

She stopped, so I did too. "Well, hello, Maisie. Why I haven't seen you since the burial. Rhys' passing was quite a shock. How are you? Fine, I hope."

I was grateful her cataracts didn't let her see just how fine I was. "I'm doing well, and you?"

"Wonderful. And your kids? I've been so worried about Emma." She took a tissue from her coat pocket and dabbed at her dry eyes. "I started to call you about her but decided it wasn't necessary. A good mother knows when her children are hurting."

Mrs. Kinsey might have been a sweet old lady, but she was gunning for a direct hit to my conscious. "The kids are good. As a matter of fact, I just saw Emma at the cemetery a few minutes ago."

"Oh." Her lips stayed in a circle for eternity. "You did? Here? At this cemetery? How interesting." Apparently, Emma wasn't the only one who had noticed my absence. "Maisie dear, if you don't mind, I'd like to give you a little widow-to-widow advice." Her tone was grandmotherly and matched her unusually genuine smile. "Deal with your shit. Before you lose it again, like you did at the burial, deal with your shit."

My mouth gaped open as she resumed her trek. I speed walked toward my house, hating Mrs. Kinsey, who was not a sweet old anything, much less a lady.

Who did she think she was? She didn't know me. She didn't know my grief or how I was dealing with it. Her husband did her the courtesy of dying instantly in a car accident. He didn't pack up their communal baggage like Rhys did and then leave it for her to sort through by herself. Deal with my shit? I was dealing with my shit quite nicely, thank you very much.

A rogue branch on the thick camellia hedge grabbed my hair as I stormed around the corner to find my street blocked by a perfect storm of delivery trucks. I untangled it while Elvis, my UPS guy, unloaded my packages and joked with Sam, my USPS guy, about seeing him at my house again. I finger-combed a twig out of my hair and stood unnoticed at the foot of the driveway when The FedEx guy tried to get in on the fun. "Man, this chick has either

131

won the lottery or stolen a bunch of credit cards. Look at this pile of boxes, and it's like this every day."

"Hey," Elvis barked. "A little respect. Her husband died a few weeks ago."

"Yeah." The FedEx guy put the last box on top of the others stacked against the garage door to protect them from the winter rain we were supposed to get later in the day. He gave Elvis and the packages that obscured half of the double garage door a smug look. "If you ask me, she's gone completely crazy."

"Crazy?" All three men turned, surprised to see the widowed Mrs. Carver with balled fists on her hips, chest heaving, ready for a fight.

"I didn't mean anything by it," the FedEx guy stuttered as I stormed toward him.

"He was just being an idiot, Mrs. C," Elvis offered.

"Dude. He deserves whatever he gets," the USPS guy said before he got in his Jeep and sped away; Elvis left too. When the FedEx guy made a move toward his truck, I blocked him. Toe to toe, he was maybe three inches taller than me, but with my anger, I towered over him.

"What's your name," I growled.

"Ralph," he said desperately. "It's Ralph."

"You don't know me, Ralph."

"No, ma'am." He tried to sidestep me, but I body-checked him and stayed in his face. "No, ma'am, I don't."

"You don't get to judge me."

"I wasn't judging you. I just meant --"

"You wanna see crazy, Ralph?"

"No. Please no. I was making a little joke, that's all, and I'm sorry." I yanked open the first package I laid my hands on. Fancy bobby-pin-looking things went one way. Marbles on a string went the other. I pulled a hot pink vibrator out of the box and jabbed it under his chin like a knife.

Eyes full of terror, he tried to bolt, but the rechargeable battery came to life and stopped him in his tracks. "Please don't hurt me," he whimpered. "I got a wife."

I gripped the handle harder, pushing buttons that made the shaft of the pink penis gyrate. "How long have you been married, Ralph?"

"Ten years. Eleven." Inch by inch, he backpedaled toward his truck. "I don't know."

"Do you think your wife is happy, Ralph? Does she like being married to you?"

"Yes. I--I think so. I don't know."

"You think, or you know?" He backed off the curb, trembling, eyes darting in every direction, trying to figure out how to escape crazy little ole me.

"I don't know," he whined. "Maybe."

The pink penis whirled under his chin and tipped his face up to look at mine. "Well, take a good look, Ralph, because this is what a woman looks like when she's not happy."

His hand reached the open doorway of his truck, and in an athletic move that surprised both of us, he leaped into the driver's seat and cranked up the beast.

"Crazy bitch," he screamed after he'd shoved the truck in gear and was halfway down the block.

I watched him drive away, twenty miles per hour speed limit be damned, then picked up the bobby-pin-looking-things and string of glass marbles and tossed them into the box with my hot pink weapon. As I tapped out the security code on the garage door keypad, I felt victorious until the door opened slowly, and Ralph's words rang true.

With mine and Rhys' cars under the carport out back, the solid wall of pasteboard boxes touched the ceiling in most places, hundreds of brown containers, most of which had never been opened. In the hours prior to their same-day arrival, there was something comforting about pressing the Buy button, something soothing about brown cardboard bargains filling Rhys' most cherished space. The floor that was usually clean enough to eat on was littered with oak leaves he would have raked up before they hit the ground. I'd moved everything out of the garage except for his sacred riding lawn mower, Bess. And I would have moved her too if I could have gotten her started.

After his stranglehold on our money, buying whatever was in those boxes with Rhys' secret credit card had felt good and well deserved. While my diseased cerebellum knew each fuck-you purchase was an attempt to wall him out of my life, there was no ignoring the Great Wall of Amazon before me that confirmed Ralph was right. I was crazy, but I could fix this. I would fix this.

I grabbed an armload of smaller boxes off of the new stack and asked Siri to dial the number for the Grief Counseling Center. A woman with a voice that was much too cheery for a place that dealt with grief answered and asked how she could help me. I turned my back on the brown cardboard and closed the garage door. "I'd like to make an appointment."

"Do you have a particular therapist you'd like to see?"

"No." I unlocked the front door and put the boxes on the floor in the foyer. On rainy days, there was the slight smell of bacon from Rhys' Atkin's Diet days. We'd argued over wallpaper for the foyer. I grew up in a Charleston single house with period everything and soundly voted for no wallpaper. However, Rhys was surprisingly attached to a brown-on-brown damask pattern I hated. And here it was twenty years later.

"The first new client appointment is six weeks from today, May 15, with Karen Ferguson," the woman chirped. "She's fantastic. You'll love her."

My thumbnail slid under a spot on the wallpaper where Rhys had committed the cardinal sin of overlapping seams. "Nothing sooner?"

"Well, I do have a cancelation for today in a little over an hour with Misty Marrs. "

I pulled at the sliver of paper. The sheet loosened and tore away in one piece from the bottom of the wall, clear up to the vaulted ceiling. I should have waited for Karen or any of the nine therapists whose names were crammed onto the business card besides Rhys' stripper therapist. My fingernail loosened the corner of another sheet; it pulled away as cleanly as the other.

"Misty's excellent. Usually, her first appointments are an hour and a half, but if you really need to see someone, I know she'd be happy to talk to you." When I didn't jump at the chance, she said, "I get it. You'd be surprised how many people don't leave their houses on Friday the 13th." Then, she clicked away on her computer. "There's a couple of openings in the Monday night grief group. That would be a great place for you to start."

The naked drywall begged for color, but the walls were too tall for me to attempt the job.

"Most of our members have been in the group for years. If you want to see Karen, you could start there until your appointment."

"Grief Group?" And be in a room full of Mrs. Kinsey's? No way. I'd just stop ordering stuff; that would be easy enough, and I'd send back the mountain of boxes. I didn't need to buy a whole bunch of new stuff to feel better. But I was curious about Misty. Even if she was halfway ethical, there was no way she'd take her former patient's wife as a client, but it wasn't like Rhys could sue her for violating his privacy. Besides, I would be there to work on myself. "I'm not sure the group is for me, but I will take the appointment today."

"Perfect, I have you down at two o'clock, but I do hope you'll try the grief group. The more, the merrier," the woman said. "Now, let's get your information."

"My name is Maisie," I said without thinking. "Jenkins," I added hastily. Not a complete lie since it was my last name for 23 years. I ended the call and ripped the rest of the wallpaper off of the foyer walls.

A few years ago, I replaced the cheap builder-grade chandelier with one that had tiers of luminous natural shells that softly diffused the light with a romantic glow and made the ugly brown walls bearable. With the paper gone, the space looked bigger and brighter. A lively yellow coat of paint would make it more inviting. A petal pink would be beautiful and chic.

The doorbell rang. I opened the door to see the DHL deliveryman I'd only seen a few times during my recent shopping spree.

"Morning, ma'am. Sign here." He pointed to a spot on his electronic pad. I glanced at what I knew was a small Tiffany's box under his arm.

Good God. I couldn't spend the rest of my life trying to give myself the things Rhys never gave me. But the recent barrage of those TV commercials where he went to Jarods for Valentine's because every kiss begins with K reminded me that other than my rings, Rhys had not once in thirty years of marriage given me one piece of jewelry. So, last night, I'd grabbed his secret credit card, and I went to Tiffany's, virtually, of course, and bought a diamond bracelet.

Granted, the twenty-thousand-dollar price tag gave me pause, but considering it was the equivalent of buying a Starbucks every day for thirty years, it didn't seem so extravagant.

"Sign right here." He handed me the stylus and pointed to a line on his tablet.

"Do I have to?" It was the most beautiful bracelet I'd ever seen, four gold bangles with a diamond-encrusted one in the middle. But I was going to do better, be better.

"Beg your pardon?"

This wasn't how the dance normally went when there was a box from Tiffany inside a pasteboard one. "Do I have to accept the package?"

"Nah, lady." His laugh was almost flirty. "You don't have to do anything you don't want."

Heart jackhammering, my back slid down the closed door as his truck rumbled away. I sorted the boxes I'd brought in from the garage into two piles: things to return like the As Seen On TV Huggle, a combination sleeping bag and hoodie that would definitely make me look like a giant sperm, and things I absolutely had to have, like the new black bra I needed after losing some weight. Inside the last nondescript package was an impossibly blue box that opened easily to reveal a mass of tiny glittering diamonds. Four overlapping eighteen-karat yellow gold bands slipped onto my wrist, gently shifting shape as they glided with my body.

The product description on the Tiffany website promised the bracelets would create the gentle music of a beautiful life, and that's what I wanted more than anything. Not the diamonds, although they were really nice. From here on out, what I wanted most was a beautiful life.

# Chapter Fifteen

I was dressed like I was going to see my dead husband's mistress instead of his therapist, complete with full makeup and hair coiffed into a style that said sexy chic bedhead. The mirror confirmed my new dress was cute, a little Donna Morgan black and red printed shift from one of the few boxes I'd actually opened during my shopping spree. But, slipping into the peep toes that had persecuted my poor feet at the viewing, I was definitely overdressed. Still, the girl on fire said there was no way I was going to visit Misty Mars in my usual yoga pants, T-shirt, and tennis shoes.

Thanks to a wreck on the Cooper River Bridge, I arrived ten minutes late. The waiting room was empty. A sign on the desk said the receptionist was out to lunch. Beside one of the tufted turquoise wingback chairs was a note from Misty on pink paper with fuchsia swirls that said for me to fill out the intake form and she would be right with me. I stared at the form that asked questions that should have sent me packing, my name, my spouse's name, my address, insurance information, and so many answers that connected me to Rhys.

"Maisie?" I jumped out of my skin and felt like Misty had caught me in a compromising position with her husband if she had one. "Such a pretty name and unusual; I've only known one other Maisie or known of her." My face blushed hard. She introduced herself and told me the receptionist would get my insurance info after my appointment. "My office is upstairs."

She led me down the small hallway of the brick three-bedroom, possibly two-bathroom, re-purposed mid-century home in which the living room served as the waiting room. The floors were the original narrow oak slats with nicks and scars buffed to a high shine. What used to be the dining room was now a conference center with French doors and thin sheers that barely disguised a long table.

Misty took the stairs, palming a white Newell cap identical to mine. The stairway was narrow and dark compared to the reception area. The risers groaned under the weight of all the secrets carried up these stairs by the family who lived here when the place was their home, by the worried well who trod them five days a week. Misty looked back over her shoulder and gave me a reassuring smile that could be construed as a come-hither look if some poor client romanced the thought around enough.

Even in her sensible navy-blue sheath, she was the stuff fantasies are made of with her killer body and blond hair that fell in soft waves down her back. Rhys loved long hair, but I'd always worn mine short. It was easier, and I thought it suited me until Jordan's friend suggested growing it a little longer would soften my features. When he noticed my red face, he assured me I would be more of a knockout than I already was. But trailing behind Misty, with her backside a little more than a foot from my face, I was just a fifty-five-year-old, fighting wrinkles and teacher's arms, and the prominent smiley face on my belly from gravity and childbirth.

As much as I tried to stop thinking about Rhys, I couldn't help but imagine him following Misty and her muscled calves up the stairs, the hollows of the backs of her knees, the hem of her not-too-short or not-too-long dress teasing him.

The renovators had split each of the three bedrooms into two offices. Misty led me into her half of the master suite, complete with an attached bath. A small fountain on an end table sang. Boxes of tissues were spread strategically about the office, along with shelves full of self-help books. An interesting mixture of Lowcountry African American art and Native American articles adorned the cream-colored walls. A small Navaho-looking tapestry played surprisingly well alongside a series of tiny sweetgrass baskets. Jonathan Green's print of an ebony woman in a billowy yellow dress hung beside a dream catcher with feathers that matched the scarf on the ebony woman's hat.

I sat down on the nubby blue oversized settee that was too big to be a loveseat and too small to be a proper couch. The chair directly across from the settee was clearly Misty's. The end table beside me had one of those half bottles of water on a sweetgrass coaster.

I'd never been to a therapist before and really didn't know what to expect. Did they all have a knack for putting people at ease and turning them into open books? Misty hadn't asked me a single question, and I was bursting to tell her about the girl on fire who comes and goes and learn what I needed to do to get her to stay.

She took a long draw from some kind of thick, green, healthy-looking drink. "Sorry for drinking my lunch. It's been such a busy day."

"No worries," I said, eager to tell her about the naughty delicious rush that ended seconds after I hit the Buy button and left me feeling empty in a way that could never be filled. If she could help me sort through my diseased mind and find the moment my marriage went from good to lonely or help me understand why I lived that way for so long, this wouldn't take more than one visit, two tops.

Even with her movie star looks, I suspected her ethics were as intact as any good therapist's. So why was I even here if I couldn't be honest with her? Because Rhys was here, the girl on fire said. He sat where you're sitting for a total of six hours, and he'd had such a thing for that therapist on The Sopranos.

At one point, while binge-watching the series, he had the gall to say, "Tony should just ditch Carmela and go with Dr. Malfi."

I'd said, "Nobody in their right mind would ditch Carmella." She was brilliant and beautiful and the Superglue of the Soprano family, but a few episodes later, Rhys cheered when Tony did just that. Was Misty his Dr. Malfi? Did he keep coming back because he'd wanted to start something with her? Had he fallen for her so hard that he asked for a divorce? What other reason would have kept him coming back? I waited for answers, but Misty couldn't read my mind any more than I could read hers, so I said nothing.

Seven minutes of silence and a tabletop fountain that was meant to be relaxing only made me want to pee.

"What brings you here today?" Misty balanced a fresh legal pad on crossed legs.

I spent fifty-four thousand dollars in a week.

"I'm good," I answered too quickly, and we both knew it was a lie. "Mostly good."

Misty nodded but studied me like one of those snake-handling researchers who calculated the precise moment and angle to grab the viper and milk the venom out. I brushed my hair from my eyes, the four diamond-studded bangles separated and came together as advertised, but their music was hideous.

She scribbled some notes on the pad and laid her pen down, content to wait me out. Her eyes were smart and kind, but her silence was unbearable. "I lost --." My dad to Alzheimer's, my husband to heart disease and maybe infidelity, and Julia. I lost Julia. God, I was so sick of losing, of not knowing how to fill the hole nonstop self-care and retail therapy hadn't put a dent in.

I'd actually Googled this perpetual bottomed-out feeling before my last shopping session. I didn't read all two hundred and eighty-four million articles. But one easy fix in the bulk of what I read suggested gratitude was the key to everything, including happiness. I was grateful for the love and support of Jordan, and Emma, who wasn't exactly on Team Mom but hopefully would be soon. I was thankful for Willa and Mom, and--. "My sister." There was a long silence. "I lost my sister, Julia, and, before that-," my husband, "my dad."

"Are either of them still living?" She smiled at my puzzled look. "Sometimes people come here because they've lost someone but not to death."

Was that why Rhys was here? Did he feel the loss of our dying marriage, or had he lost the nurse or one of the other tearful beauties I didn't know existed before the funeral?

"My dad, to Alzheimer's," which felt more like a death than Rhys' actual death. Julia's exit from my life wasn't as clear cut; I couldn't point to a date or moment she started pulling away from the family, from me. A year? At least a year. "And my sister's not dead, but she's been gone a long time."

Misty nodded and propped her feet on a lovely needlepoint footstool. Her dress was short but not unprofessionally so. Her knees were together and slanted to the side. She was no Sharon Stone, but Basic Instinct was Rhys' all-time favorite movie. It came out a few years after we married. The panty-less interrogation scene had been so hot we drove directly to our apartment.

The interrogation room, which doubled as our kitchen, living room, and dining room, wasn't as sparse as the one in the movie. My dress was sufficiently short. Sharon's blatant sexuality inspired me to take my panties off on the drive from the theater. By the time we pulled into his parking lot, Rhys was crazy with want and reached for me. I ignored his advance, opened the car door, and headed for the apartment. In moments, I was flush against the front door and broke character, trembling when he looked at me, sliding the key in the lock so slowly it made me breathless.

The room was dark. The tiny desk lamp he turned on made it shimmer in silver. He placed a chair from his dinette across the small room and turned mine to face him. "Can I get you anything?" he said, easily falling into Michael Douglas' detective Nick Curran. "A cup of coffee?"

"No, thank you." I regained my Sharon Stoneness, sat in the chair, and crossed my legs.

An unused chopstick from last night's takeout served as a cigarette. It was more Audrey Hepburn than the gritty, elegant Catherine Tramell, but it worked well enough to make Rhys slack-jawed with lust as he watched me suck on the tip.

"There's no smoking here." His line was barely above a whisper.

"What are you going to do, detective?" I purred. "Arrest me?"

He somehow regained his composure, ignored the tent in his pants, opened a file folder with math tests from my third graders, and shuffled through some papers like they were case files. "Are you sure you don't want an attorney present?"

"No." I took another puff. "Just you."

"Would you tell me the nature of your relationship with Rhys Carver?"

"I have sex with him. I like having sex with him. He gives me pleasure." I took another puff and re-crossed my legs much slower than Sharon had for her famous money shot. "Lots of pleasure." I barely got the last word out before Rhys peeled off my clothes. We stayed in bed all weekend and called in sick Monday morning.

"I'm sorry for your losses." Misty scribbled something on the legal pad and then set it on the side table like she didn't need it anymore. "How are you handling your grief?"

My head was still swimming with memories of Rhys, and I was grateful she didn't mention Julia or expect me to wax on about her.

Dad could recall the make of his first car, hell, his first BB gun, but I could leave the room and come back a few seconds later, and it was like he was seeing me for the first time. I was a stranger, and he was my daddy, the man who loved me first. The man who unknowingly showed me a glimpse into the future of what my life would be like when Alzheimer's tapped me to be his replacement.

The space between my belly and the top of my ribcage throbbed with loss. Dad was alive. He was the one I should be visiting, but it hurt too much. I'd lost the father who knew me, and there was a good possibility I was going to lose myself to Alzheimer's. What good would it do to get better, to figure out who I am and what I want, only to lose it all to a damn disease?

"Not sure what you mean by handling my grief."

"Maisie, your father, your sister, those are some pretty big losses." And Rhys. Maybe if you told me everything I needed to know about my dead husband, I could scratch that one off the list and get on with my life. "What are you doing to cope with your grief?"

I gave her a puzzled look. "See if any of these strike a chord." She shuffled through some pages and handed me a booklet entitled Natural and Normal Grief Responses with 50 bullet points that actually made me feel good about hoarding thousands of unopened cardboard boxes.

Misty waited patiently as I read each bullet point, mentally checking off the ones that applied to me.

Feeling emotionally numb. I was more like one of those fire batons, cold and unfeeling in the middle, hot and painful on the ends. Why had I felt so triumphant when I hit the Buy button but too guilty to open the boxes when they arrived?

Knowing death has occurred but having difficulty believing the death actually happened. Sometimes, when I wake up facing Rhys's side of the bed, my brain says he's in the bathroom, or he's gone to the gym, and it seems so real I start dreading picking up his soppy workout clothes.

Having the desire to eat more than usual or not eat at all. In two weeks, I'd crossed every Lowcountry restaurant off my bucket list and had found some amazing new places, yet I had lost weight.

The list was long, and I only had about a dozen or so of the abnormalities, or normalities, depending on how you looked at reactions to grief.

Feeling intense anger at your loved one for leaving you. Rhys had abandoned me. I had to work hard not to full-on hate Julia and work even harder at not expecting her to show up with that little shrug that said she knows she'll always be forgiven because she's my sister.

"That's quite a reaction." I looked down to see the half-crumpled pamphlet, my fists shaking so hard, I didn't recognize them. "Do you want to talk about it?"

My hand brushed across my forehead like I could brush away the anger that had it throbbing in time with my runaway heartbeat.

Misty's head was cocked to the side, and she'd added a pair of thick black-rimmed glasses to her ensemble so she could double as a hot librarian. "I had a falling out with my sister, my oldest sister, Julia." She nodded with a thin smile that said she'd pull the words out of me one by one if she had to. I smoothed the wrinkles out of the paper, folded it up, and put it in my purse.

"A week or so before the funeral, I started planning this trip to California for Mom. God, she was so excited about seeing the redwoods with her girls, me, my sisters, Willa and Julia. My Mom always wanted the trip, and I'd wanted to go until the falling out. Julia didn't even know about the trip until I mentioned it at the viewing."

"The viewing for your dad?"

My face flashed red at the slip-up. If I explained it was my husband's funeral, she would definitely put two and two together. She would know I was the only Maisie she'd ever heard of, the session would be over, and I needed help.

" Yes," I lied. "Julia didn't bother to attend the funeral. Never heard a peep out of her as to why she bailed. I was so mad at her that I forgot about the trip, but Mom didn't. Instead, she called all excited, saying it would be good for all of us to get away together. I know she was trying to make us kiss and make up like she used to when we were little, but this is bigger.

"I'm angry at her. But I'm angrier at myself for being such a child, for needing her so much, it felt impossible to breathe without---." Black mascara-laced tears stung my eyes. "Her." I barely got the last word out before my lips slammed into a tight thin line.

"And now? "Misty coaxed.

"Now." I let out a bitter laugh. "Now, I don't want to be anywhere near my sister, much less fly halfway across the country for some slumber party where we all pretend she didn't desert us. I don't know if I can tool around the redwoods like I'm okay with what she did, but Mom wants this trip. I'm doing it for her."

"I understand the loss of your dad has been tough on your family and that you want to do something nice for your mother, but you are grieving the loss of your dad too. You're grieving the loss of your sister. This trip might come at a good time for your mom, but maybe, where you are in your healing, it's not the right time for you."

"The right time for me?" I felt the shakiness of my new reality. Only there was no thrill, just a potent cocktail of guilt and anger I'd fueled with online shopping.

"I'd like for you to go back through the last few days, months, maybe even years and examine the times your sister didn't show up for you or your family. Take yourself out of the equation and look at the possibility that Julia was doing what was right for her at the time." Misty glanced at the clock and then picked up her notebook and scribbled something in the margin. "Whether you decide to continue your work with me or someone else, I hope you'll examine your relationship with your sister and define what you feel. Is it anger? Is it envy or something else entirely?" Her smile was thin but genuine, and those eyes I didn't want to admit were wise beyond their years shone with kindness.

I was shocked and a little sad; I didn't want the session to end. I apologized for paying in cash, but I couldn't very well whip out my credit card that said Maisie Carver, or worse, the checkbook that said Maisie and Rhys Carver.

For a minute, she looked like she wasn't quite sure what to do with the money; then she filled out a receipt. "Bottom line, Maisie," she said as she printed my name in big curly letters, "It's okay to do what's right for you."

# Chapter Sixteen

Aunt Delia was such a good widow. That's what everyone always said about her like it was her job. I was five when her husband died of a heart attack. She was only thirty-seven, but she spent the rest of her life keeping their house exactly as it was the day Uncle Jack died.

For some unexplained reason, Mom thought it would be a good idea for me to stay with Aunt Delia whenever she and Dad went out of town, or my sisters were away at camp or slumber parties, or my parents just wanted some alone time. But it was terrifying.

Every single day, Aunt Delia put Uncle Jack's slippers beside his recliner at 4:30 on the dot. She lay the newspaper folded on the seat before excusing herself to freshen up. She always came out of her room in a little nicer dress or blouse. She cooked the best Lowcountry food, which was my only perk for visiting, and watched the front door like she truly believed any minute Uncle Jack was going to come home and ask what was for supper on his way to his sacred chair.

She claimed to be a teetotaler but made him an old fashion every night. The following day, the glass was always empty. Being five, I was sure Uncle Jack had indeed come back from the dead, eaten a fabulous dinner, thrown back his drink, and left before the Grim Reaper came looking for him again. When I told my mom about Aunt Delia's morbid behavior and that I was too creeped out to spend the night with her, Mom said Aunt Delia loved Uncle Jack so much she just couldn't let him go.

She had been two weeks shy of her eighteenth birthday and fresh out of high school when she married him and had been part of a couple for more than half her life by the time he died. At 37, she had her whole life ahead of her and, coming from a family of long-livers, that meant at the very least another 50 years. But she didn't know how to exist without her husband, so she didn't.

Five years to the day Uncle Jack died, she stepped off the curb on King Street and was killed instantly by some poor tourist from New Jersey. The police report said the light had just turned yellow when the driver hit the gas to beat the light. Stupid, to say the least, in a tourist mecca like Charleston. Mom said her sister was just anxious to make it to the semi-annual shoe sale at Bob Ellis. But I will always believe Aunt Delia just got sick of living with Uncle Jack's ghost.

I'd like to think that heaven is such a perfect place that Aunt Delia did untangle her life and discover her truest self. I can't imagine that would include fetching drinks and slippers for Jesus or Uncle Jack. Seeing how Aunt Delia did her time on earth, I think Jesus would be cool with that, but I wondered what Uncle Jack would think about her true self. And isn't that what widowhood is all about? Finding your truest self, who you are without your spouse, who you want to become?

Unless you decide to chuck it and step off the curb, which is what I wanted to do when I came home from the grocery store the day after my appointment with Misty and found Willa lounging in front of my open garage in one of the comfy chaise lounges I hadn't sent back to Amazon yet because I couldn't get it to fit in the box, it came in. The card table I'd used for my little Return Department was beside the chaise, and Willa was reading one of the many legal pads I'd used as a ledger to keep track of what I'd bought and what was returned. The other legal pads she'd already gone through were in her lap.

"You've been busy." She toasted me with her venti Starbucks iced coffee.

"I've sent back everything that was inside the house and was going to finish the rest today." I motioned to the thirty or so smiling brown Amazon boxes.

She threw the pads down on the table, opened the door to the mudroom, and made her way through the house, which I pointed out was clutter-free. She walked through every room downstairs and then headed up to check out Emma and Jordan's rooms, along with my room and the guest room. She didn't say anything about the gouges in my bedroom floor from the dresser I'd moved across the room. Instead, she stooped down beside Rhys' chair, put her hand under the coffee table, and pulled out his coffee mug from who knows when.

She inspected the mold curled around the bottom half of the cup like a long hairy caterpillar. "So just the boxes in the garage, that's it?" she asked. "There's no series of storage lockers around the Holy City stuffed with—stuff?"

"There's a few here." I opened my closet door. "But they're going back," I added hastily. "All of them." She nodded and stepped into the closet that, a few days ago, had been full of enough merchandise to stock a small boutique. "I don't know how it happened. A lot of it, I don't even remember buying, and that scares me, Will."

"I know," she said because the older we got, the more impossible it was not to worry every little stinking thing we forgot was the beginning of Alzheimer's. ""It's going to get better. You might not see it now, but it will," she said softly. "So, this is all of it?"

"As far as I know, these and the few boxes in the garage are everything," I promised, relieved and grateful she hadn't shown up this morning when the boat I'd canceled was delivered by mistake. "I just got back from seeing a therapist, and I start a grief group on Monday."

"And you promise you'll go to the group and continue therapy?"

"I promise."

She didn't preach or point out the obvious, that I was sick, that I'd be penniless if I'd kept up the spending. She just said, "I'll help you finish," and we got to it.

A few hours later, we were a well-oiled machine and could have easily run Amazon's worldwide return department. Willa never commented on the items I purchased in my grief-ridden state. She simply dug around in the box for the invoice, processed the return, and taped it back up for shipping.

She opened one of the many boxes I'd ordered from White House Black Market. Inside was one of those holiday things they mark down for next to nothing in March, a red satin dress with a horrible cropped jacket, one of the first pieces I'd bought when I started my spree. They didn't have it in my size, so I'd bought the eight to put in the wishful section of my closet that was anywhere from one to three sizes smaller than my normal size ten.

"Oooh." Willa tossed the jacket on the floor and held the dress up by the slender satin straps. "This stays."

"It's pretty, but--."

"Definitely stays. Try it on." She wiggled the dress that was too red, too sexy, too much for a fifty-something-year-old like me, but it felt like a whisper and was so pretty.

"No." If I started keeping things, I'd want to keep everything, or worse, I'd start replacing the things I'd already returned. "Everything goes back," I repeated my mantra from the past five days.

"Just try it on," she said, ordering Alexa to play Gloria Gaynor.

The wishful dress actually fit. Willa clapped her hands and motioned for me to twirl, even though it wasn't that kind of dress. I did and thanked her for the billionth time for everything she'd done for me. She grabbed my hand, and we danced barefoot while Gloria dug into the chorus the way Diana Ross wished she could have and belted, "I will survive."

"You're not just going to survive, sister," Willa shouted over the music. "You're going to thrive."

We hooted and hollered until my cellphone rang with a Facetime call from Mom. I jerked the red dress off like it was scalding hot, pulled on my yoga pants and T-shirt, and looked at Willa to see if she knew what this was about. She shrugged and motioned for me to answer the damn thing because the special FaceTime ringtone was so annoying.

I ran my hands through my hair and tried to look normal. "Hi, Mom!"

"Hello, darling. I called Willa but didn't get her."

For some reason, Mom tried to FaceTime Willa on her landline at least three days a week, which always set off a shit storm of SOS calls from Mom to me about her broken phone or the possibility her new iPhone wasn't all it was cracked up to be.

"Willa's here with me."

"Oh, I'm so glad I have you both. Julia called this morning. She's planned the most delightful outings for all of us to see the Redwoods in Big Basin and Felton and drive up the Pacific Coast Highway. It's really quite the itinerary, a dream come true."

I should not have felt like I'd been shot through the heart, but I did. How could Julia, who couldn't hang around for Rhys' funeral, couldn't bother to call or text or send up smoke signals, hijack my trip? But Mom was glowing, and I hadn't seen her this excited since she'd learned she'd have weekly maid service in assisted living and would never have to cook another day.

"It was so kind of Julia, Maisie. I really do think she's trying to say she's sorry about the funeral. And all you have to do is show up two weeks from today. Isn't it marvelous? Simply marvelous, me and my three girls, in California. Why I've never even been west of the Mississippi. This is going to be such a treat. So, you and Willa get with Julia when you have time and get the details, you hear?"

"Yes, ma'am." I ended the call and gritted my teeth for three full seconds before exploding. "That bitch."

"Calm down." Willa attempted to take the box cutter away from me but thought the better of it.

"I haven't heard a damn word from her since the viewing, Will, not one. And now she expects me to make nice and go along with her and her marvelous itinerary? That's bullshit."

"She called me last night--," Willa began.

"You knew about this?" And suddenly, Willa and Julia were twelve and thirteen with their own secret club and a sign on their door that read KEEP OUT MAISIE. At the time, I was just learning how to read, but Julia had been all too happy to jab her long slender finger at each word for me like I didn't already know I wasn't welcome.

"I was going to tell you, Masie, really I was." Her voice was pleading, and I reminded myself she was the good sister. My only real sister. "But we got busy with the boxes, and then we came upstairs, and there were more boxes. So, I forgot to tell you, and I'm so sorry."

160

On the surface, the trip sounded as perfect as Julia herself. No fuss, no muss, but how, after all these years, was it possible that she could still make me feel like a child? Like it was report card day after she'd already been praised for perpetual straight A's? The same for Willa, except for that nagging B in Math, and Mom was sitting me down on my twin bed to ask me why I couldn't be like my sisters?

I grabbed the last item to be returned and slit the top of the box like it was Julia's long wrinkle-free neck.

# Chapter Seventeen

I was born on Friday, March 18, the year the Mamas and the Pappas set the world on fire with their easy groovy tune "Monday Monday." While Dad was always partial to Elvis and Jerry Lee Lewis, Mom loved the sounds of the sixties and that song so much that she almost named me Monday. I suppose if I was destined to be named after a song, that was certainly better than paying homage to Elvis and Jerry Lee by naming me Corina or Hound Dog.

The story goes that Mom and Dad were at an impasse over my name, and the hospital wouldn't let me leave without one. So, they went old school and named me Margaret, after my mother's grandmother, and Ruth, after my father's grandmother, but nobody ever called me Margaret. Even when I got in trouble, Mom would grit out Masie Ruth. And the times when the world was rough, and I needed soothing, I would lay my head in her lap, and she would stroke my hair and hum the beginning of Monday Monday, just the Bah-da Bah-da-da-da part.

But the Mamas and the Pappas knew what they were talking about when they sang, "Monday, Monday, can't trust that day".

Almost everything bad that has ever happened to me has happened on a Monday. Three of my four grandparents died on Mondays. When I was in the 7th grade, I flunked my first test and was expelled a week later for socking a bully in the stomach, both on Mondays. I wrecked my first car, and both of the kids wrecked their first cars on the first day of the week. Before Emma was born, I had a Monday miscarriage. That, along with my ancient history, made me want to renege on my promise to Willa. But true to my word, I was at the Lutheran church two blocks from my house, sitting on a very uncomfortable folding chair, part of a large circle in the middle of a gym. And since Willa insisted on driving me, I was fifteen minutes early and the only one there.

The doors opened, a long slender leg emerged, then a shoulder and the rest of Misty's stripper body. She struggled with a broad cake box that was big enough for a full sheet cake, her purse on one shoulder, and a reusable Publix bag dangling from one hand. "Maisie! You're here early," she laughed nervously, my cue to get up and help her with her load, but all I could think about was Rhys, sitting on a couch for fifty minutes, staring at those legs.

But Misty knew how to ask for what she wanted. "Can you please get the grocery bag before I drop the cake?"

"Sorry." I took the cake, and she pointed me to a card table where I set the box down.

"I'm so glad you're here. This is a lovely group; you'll see. There was something I wanted to ask you." She cocked her head to the side like she'd had an epiphany. "I remembered where I'd heard your name. You're not by any chance Rhys Carver's wife, are you?"

"No." I was a terrible liar but somehow sold it.

"I'm sorry. I shouldn't have even mentioned it; it's just your name is so unusual." She shook her head. "And I worried that if you were, it would have been

totally inappropriate for me to have seen you as a client."

The door opened again, and a dozen people filed into the room. A few as young as their mid-thirties, the majority older than me. "Welcome," Misty said, "Come on in and take your seats. I want to stay on schedule tonight. We have a lot of work to do." The crowd moaned good-naturedly. "We have birthday cake for James." A little cheer went up, and a stout man, who I assumed was James, waved at the crowd.

Many of the group members were portly from grief or Misty feeding them too much sugar and carbs. But the odd thing, the thing I least expected about the group, was they all seemed so happy. Some of them seemed downright jolly. Twin sisters plopped down on either side of me like Tweedle Dee and Tweedle Dum. "Newbie," one of them sang while the other one giggled, making me wonder if I was in the right place? Maybe this was the I'm So Happy I Can't Stand Myself Group.

"Let's hurry up and start," James said with the exuberance of the birthday boy, clamoring for cake.

"We'll get to the cake," Misty assured. "I want to give Hayden a few more minutes."

"Why? He never comes," Tweedle Dee pointed out.

"That's not true. He always comes on James' birthday," Tweedle Dum reminded.

"It's possible Hayden may feel like he doesn't need the group anymore," Misty said, "and that's okay. Someday, all of you may feel that way as you grow and work through your grief." She glanced at the clock. "We'll give him five more minutes, so catch up with your friends; we have a written activity."

The rest of the group groaned again, like my third graders used to do when they were forced to take out their composition notebooks. After being a little intimidated by Misty and her long legs and feeling like the outsider in the group, I wanted to pump my fist in the air because I was good at writing.

"I'll bet you my cut of the birthday cake Hayden doesn't show," Tweedle Dee whispered. The chair groaned when her sister leaned forward to look at her. "You're on," she said before turning her attention to me. "I'm Dottie, and this is my sister Diane."

"I'm Maisie." We shook hands.

Dottie said, "We're here because our mother--."

"Passed six years ago," Diane said. "Wanna tell us--"

"What you're in for," Dottie laughed. "We work--"

"At the Liberman Correctional institution in Ridgeville," Diane said.

"But we live in Summerville. Group is a long haul—." Dottie said.

"But Misty's so worth it," Diane added.

"I'm Maisie," I said, grateful Misty had given up on the Hayden guy and called the meeting to order. "Do you always finish each other's sentences?"

"Yes." They responded in unison, giggling like tweenagers at a sixth-grade dance.

Misty went down the list of rules like they probably do in AA or Hoarders Anonymous meetings. Everything said here stays here. Share your feelings but refrain from giving advice. Accept everyone as they are without judgment. Dottie and Diane squirmed in unison, making me believe that the telepathic thing between twins is true.

"Everyone who wants to share will have an opportunity," Misty continued. "You may share as much or as little as you want, but you also have a right to remain silent." The twins smirked at Misty's unintentional justice system humor. "Be supportive with your attention but avoid side conversations and interrupting. Try to be aware of your own feelings and talk about what is present for you now rather than dwelling on the past. And please, do not discuss group members who are not here." She gave the twins a sweet but stern look that made them squirm again. "Since we have a new member tonight, let's begin with introductions, and if you'd like to, share what brought you to the group. Maisie, would you like to start?"

"My name is Masie," I caught myself before I said Carver. "Jenkins."

"First names only," Misty chided softly.

"Sorry. I'm here because I've lost --." A sister, a husband to heart disease and God knows what, a father to Alzheimer's, and there's a good possibility I may lose my mind too. Lots of raised eyebrows from inquiring minds asked for more. "my dad."

Everyone nodded and said, "Hi, Masie," like we were at an AA meeting. I hung my head, and Dottie and Diane took turns rubbing my back.

Everyone in the circle introduced themselves and received the same greeting. And maybe the grief group was like prison because they all told what they were in for. James's thirty-four-year-old wife died of cancer eight years ago; "I like the group and want to get better, just not so much better that I don't need to come anymore."

Rutledge lost his long-time partner and husband of one year, Gary, in a car crash five years ago and still can't say his name without tearing up. Seven pretty widows of various ages congregated from me on the opposite side of the room. A lone black man sat beside Misty with his legs kicked out in front of him and crossed at the ankles, his big arms folded across his chest like he didn't want to be there. He nodded at me. "I'm Big G. I'm here 'cause my grandmama got shot dead."

"At the Emanuel church," Dottie whispered. "She raised him," Diane added, drawing a sharp look from Misty.

"All right, that's everyone," Misty said while Diane smugly reminded Dottie she lost their bet because Hayden never showed. "I'm going to switch things up a bit tonight and do our exercise first, and then we'll have time to share what's on your minds before we celebrate James' birthday."

The metal doors clicked open; the sound echoed off the huge room. Everyone looked to see a man every bit as handsome and well-preserved as Rhys striding toward the circle. From a distance, he was Robert Redford if Redford was completely gray and believed in Botox. He took the seat next to Big G, raised a hand to the group, and nodded at Misty. But, on closer inspection, his eyes were much bluer than Redford's, his face more chiseled. He was Paul Newman risen from the dead, shattering the ten-point scale amidst a sea of fours and sevens, except for Misty.

"Hey. Sorry, I'm late," he said to the group. "Traffic."

"That's okay. We were just getting started," Misty said. "We have a few new faces since you were last here. Care to introduce yourself?"

"He never shares, but he's been coming twice a year," Dottie whispered.

"At least for as long as we have," Diane added. "But nobody knows why."

"Hi. I'm Hayden," he said with no story, and the spell he cast was gone from everyone except the group of widows across the room, who were still slack-jawed in his presence.

Misty handed out pens and legal pads with instructions to think about where we were in our recovery and write a letter to the deceased, telling them how we were doing without them. "Be honest. If you're a mess, tell them. If you feel unaffected, tell them. Whatever you feel, wherever you are on your journey, tell them how far you've come since that initial loss, what your life looks like without them, if you know what the future you're working toward looks like."

About half the group just stared at blank pages while Paul Newman got right to it, and so did I. Soon, everyone was letting their feelings ooze onto the page in sticky black ink. When the written exercise was over, Misty gave group members time to share what they'd written. No one broke down sobbing or seemed particularly grief-stricken, except for James, who wiped his eyes when he read a love letter to his wife declaring his life will never be better, just different.

When it was Hayden's turn, he folded the letter up and slipped it into his jacket pocket before resting his hand on James' shoulder and saying something only James could hear. Two of the widows, who looked like they were picturing Hayden naked just minutes ago, swiped away tears when they read letters to their dead husbands about coping with loneliness and the challenges of raising little kids alone. Then twenty pairs of eyes were set on me.

I glanced down at my paper. "I'm--." My voice broke.

*Dear Rhys,*

*I'm good, for the most part, although it still bugs the shit out of me that you wanted a divorce. Maybe that makes us even since I wanted the same but couldn't tell you. When you died, I made myself crazy because I didn't know how to be the widow of a man who didn't want me anymore. I still don't, but I'm learning. I'm not going to lie; there are days you still make me crazy. If you were alive, I don't think you would like the new me, much less love me. But that doesn't matter because I love me and...*

"I'm learning to live without you."

# Chapter Eighteen

The night before the trip, I washed my face, layered on my skincare regime, and pulled on my nightgown before giving the empty suitcases in the corner of my bedroom a triumphant look. It was settled. Sort of. I'd called Mom and Willa early in the morning and told them I didn't want to go to California tomorrow as long as Julia was going. Mom railed about forgiveness but, in the end, said she understood.

"We're going to miss you," Mom said.

"I'll miss you too. Have fun, and don't worry about Dad; I'll check on him every day."

"I know it's hard for you to go to the Memory Care Unit. It's depressing, sometimes even for me," Mom said. "You've had such a rough go of it after Rhys' death. Just take care of yourself. Your father will be fine. I've written a letter for him to read each day, and Willa left her iPad on his bedside table with instructions for the staff to help him FaceTime with me. Willa's taken the travel itinerary you put together married it with Julia's, and the result is a jam-packed itinerary. I declare Willa will go to her grave on schedule." We laughed at the truth, but the grave talk was unsettling because we were all so sick of losing. "You be good to yourself; you hear?"

I promised I would before I called Willa, who was a little pissed at my last-minute decision, but said she understood too. I did not text Julia. Not because I wanted her to see how it felt for someone you love not to show up for something important. I didn't text her because it wouldn't have mattered.

And everything was fine until I'd been asleep for a couple of hours, and Rhys wrapped his arm around my waist, or I dreamed he did. His imaginary arm had the same effect as when the real one was wrapped around me, his huge hand resting on my bladder. I awoke with urgency, a little woozy from the glass of wine I'd had before I went to sleep and went in the bathroom, did my thing, before returning to bed.

The obnoxious lime green light from the digital clock on Rhys's nightstand blinked 2:15. The house was quiet, too quiet. I tossed and turned, which only made me more restless. Finally, I changed sides of the bed, but that had me facing the empty suitcases that had never been to California before, and neither had I. The handle on the large one was extended like an antenna, sending guilt waves my way. *Your mother's 85. This could be her last trip ever.*

*I don't want to go,* I telepathed back.

My words broke the stillness, "Selfish bitch."

Was that what I was? My laptop on the chaise was open but asleep like the rest of the world at such an ungodly hour. I felt a powerful urge to shop, but I'd promised Willa I wouldn't. Even though she didn't make me promise, the oath had kept me away from online bargains that promised to have the lowest prices ever, which was always a lie. And Mom had lied to me, not when she said she wanted what was best for me, but when she said it was okay that all of her daughters would not be together on her bucket list trip. I threw back the covers, got out of bed, and started packing.

Mom and Willa were giddy when the Uber driver let me off in front of the airport. "You came," Mom sang. "My sweet girl, you came." Willa gave me her know-it-all look that said she wasn't a bit surprised, and we headed into the terminal. Flying out of Charleston meant that we would have to connect in Atlanta. Since Julia couldn't get a direct flight to California, she was meeting us there too.

"My husband and I flew that one time, connected in Atlanta, and then all the way to Miami when my brother had open heart surgery," Mom said to the nice man behind the Delta counter who checked her bag. "Such a busy airport. Why I'd never seen such a thing," Mom gushed. "My husband used to say when you die, God routes you through the Atlanta airport." The man laughed and finished checking our bags before directing us to security.

The plane was full, a commuter with only two seats on each side of the aisle. Cheeks flushed with excitement, Mom turned and waved to me. She and Willa were in seats next to each other in the first few rows. Since I'd waited until the last minute to check in for the flight, my seat was in the next-to-the-last row, across from the bathroom.

The knot in my stomach tightened from a lack of food and too much coffee. The fact that I'd still tossed and turned after I decided to go on the trip did not help matters. A young flight attendant at the front of the plane recited the safety litany. At the same time, a simmering anger rolled off of her much older coworker.

The angry one looked battle-worn, like she didn't want to be here either. Her dead eyes caught me staring before she offered a creepy fake smile to her coworker that was hard enough to burn a hole through the woman. Her shoes, almost flats compared to her young coworker's spiked heels, said she'd been at this for a while and was too close to retirement with free worldwide travel and a permanent Buddy Pass to find her inner Norma Rae and stalk off the job.

The pilot announced we were next in line for takeoff, which didn't seem necessary for such a tiny airport. The bitchy flight attendant in flats strapped herself into the jump seat across the aisle and directed her rote smile at me. It was both annoying and so sad. I wanted to share the gospel of Misty and tell her it was okay to do what was right for her too.

The plane barreled down the runway before the wheels left the ground, climbing up and heading to Atlanta. "That's your Mom up there?" the flight attendant across from me asked. "The gentleman in the window seat across from her wanted to sit on the aisle. When the pilot turns off the seatbelt sign, I can see if he'd like to switch."

Mom was three rows from the front, her hands talking as excitedly as she was. Beside her, in the window seat, Willa's head was tipped back in laughter, the two of them in full-blown Julia mode, anticipating a child, a sister rarely seen, at least for the last couple of years. And I was the youngest by ten years, my father's last hope at having a son, at the back of the plane, envious of their little fan club but too sleep deprived to move.

Julia would be waiting at the gate when we landed in Atlanta, and the love fest would continue. "No thanks." I needed to get over Julia, I needed to get over myself, but most of all, I needed to sleep.

I slept hard and would still have been asleep if we hadn't touched down in Atlanta. Before the plane eased up to the terminal, seat belts were unclicked, and cell phones fired up. The plane stopped in front of the gate, and Willa and Mom stood to stretch their legs. Willa's phone rang the minute she switched it on, and Mom was trying to open her phone to check a text when my phone pinged with a message, most likely from Emma with the wedding dilemma du jour.

Willa answered her phone, and her face fell. Mom glanced at a text and then gave me a worried look. I looked at my phone to read Emma's message, Urgent. Call me.

I stabbed at the screen; the call took forever to connect. Mom and Willa were about a dozen passengers ahead of me when Emma answered. I could barely breathe. "Emma, what's wrong?"

"Uncle Tank is in the hospital. He called me not long after your plane took off. He's having an appendectomy in a couple of hours, three tops. He said he knows it's not a life or death kind of thing, but he put me in charge of hunting the twins down and Aunt Willa before she got on the plane to California."

"Appendectomy," I breathed. Not stroke or aneurysm or a near-fatal car accident.

"It's supposed to be an easy surgery," she said. "But after Dad."

"Are you okay?"

"I'm fine, Mom. I just want everyone I love to stay alive and stay out of the hospital."

"I know, honey. Me too." I told her I loved her and ended the call.

Mom and Willa huddled around Julia at the gate when I finally got off the plane. Translator of all things medical, Julia was on her cellphone, talking to a doctor friend of hers at the hospital in Charleston. Willa suddenly looked worn and pale, and Mom looked like this trip was too much for her, too much for all of us.

I cut across the sea of people just as Julia ended her call. "Tank's fine. He called me when they admitted him. I've spoken with the attending physician before you landed and again just now. They're taking good care of him." Julia put her hand on Willa's shoulder the way she might have if she were delivering bad news to one of her patients. "It's a simple appendectomy. Nothing to worry about."

"Just this morning, he said he didn't feel well. I thought he was just putting on because he didn't want me to go on this trip," Willa said

"Didn't want you to go?" Mom huffed. "Well, why not?"

Tank had probably groused at the same things Rhys would have if he'd lived and we were still married. He would have to forage for food or eat one of the many meals Willa put in the refrigerator, plates marked with menus and instructions on how long to heat them in the microwave. If Tank changed clothes as often as Rhys, he'd have to take his laundry to the cleaners because God knows, if a terrorist broke into the house and demanded he separate and wash a load of laundry to avoid getting blown to bits, that would be the end of him.

"The attending said the procedure would be done laparoscopically. As surgeries go, it's not life-threatening and is about as easy as it gets. Tank's a big guy, which might make his recovery a little more difficult, but he should be fine," Julia assured.

Fine. Until now, I didn't remember the cardiologist coming into my room not long after my surgery to tell me he'd completed Rhys' bypass and he was going to be fine. Willa had heard the same spiel; now she looked like she was going to throw up.

"I want to be there." She nodded. "I need to be there."

"Of course, you do, darling." Mom wrapped her arms around Willa. "We should all go home."

"No." Willa swiped at tears, sucked in a deep breath, and then let it out slowly. "Julia's right. It's not major surgery or life-threatening, but I need to be there for him and the girls."

"I thought you might," Julia said and handed Willa a yellow Post-It note. "The next flight to Charleston is just a few gates over and boards in thirty minutes. I spoke to the customer care attendant at the end of the terminal. They know the situation and will get you back to Charleston, but you need to go now."

Willa broke down when she looked at the bright yellow sticky note that was stamped with the logo and the name of some medication that was impossible to pronounce. She wiped at her tears and threw her shoulders back. "All of you are under strict orders to go to California and have the time of your lives. I'll be with you, just not there. I love you all to bits." She took off and didn't look back.

As we walked toward the gate for our next flight, Mom called Dad to ensure he was okay while Julia and I walked in silence. I was wearing a dress that had been in the Extremely Wishful section of my closet for the last six years, an almost sexy olive-green T-shirt dress rucked up one side that looked shabby next to Julia. Dressed in loose-fitting, white linen pants and a crisp long-sleeved linen shirt buttoned up to the hollow of her throat, she looked like she'd just raided Nichole Kidman's closet.

"You look really good, Maise. How are you?" Julia dodged some guy on his cell phone who nearly body-checked her. "How are the kids doing?"

I stumbled over her words before righting myself and giving her the death stare. Mom ended her call and turned her attention to me. "What is this?" she demanded.

"Oh look, the food court," said no self-respecting Charlestonian foodie ever. "And a Chili's that serves breakfast."

"Maisie Ruth Jenkins," Mom growled, "are you still not speaking to your sister? What in the world is going on?"

"It's fine, Mom. I just asked how she and the kids are," Julia said. "Chili's works for me."

How was I? How were the kids? It had been two months since I'd heard one word from her. "I don't give a rat's ass what works for you, Julia."

"Maisie. You girls are sisters,"

"Lots of choices," I ignore both of them. "Five Guys, Atlanta Bread Company." More bad food ideas, but I honestly did not know what to say to Julia after she deserted me when I needed her the most. Sure, I'd sent her a nasty text after the fact, but we were not even, not by a long shot.

"No, Mom said flatly and stopped in her tracks. "We're not taking another step. We're not eating a single morsel, and we're certainly not going to get on some airplane until--," she stammered. "The two of you hug each other's necks this instant and say you're sorry."

I wasn't the least bit sorry, but when I opened my mouth to say so, Julia beat me to the punch. "It's nothing worth ruining our trip over, Mom. Right Maise?"

# Chapter Nineteen

There is an unwritten law that no matter how mediocre or bad a restaurant chain's food is, it's always ten times worse at their airport location. That rule was alive and well at Baja Fresh, which was neither Baja nor fresh, but repressed anger always made me ravenous. So I perused the menu that doubled as a placemat and chose number ten, which consisted of coffee, a breakfast wrap, and long crinkle-cut French fries dubbed home fries because they were served before 10:00 a.m.

Mom and Julia opted for coffee and fruit cups. I didn't notice the calories in small print italics next to each menu item on the placemat until my plate was clean. That couldn't be right; it hadn't tasted like fifteen hundred calories. Julia asked Mom if she was sure she didn't want anything to eat. Mom looked at the diners around us, their plates newly delivered and half empty, and shook her head. "I believe I'll just get a little something on the plane."

"It's a long flight, Mom. You should eat something," I said as Julia's phone pinged with a text. As a daughter and a doctor, I expected her to chime in with some medical research on the negative effects of those glorified graham crackers and minuscule pretzels the airlines pass off as snacks.

"It's fine, Mom," Julia said, in her, I've got everything handled voice. She checked the message and then shoved her phone back into her bag. "I had your tickets bumped up to first class, so we'll have a nice breakfast on the plane and bottomless mimosas."

"Wonderful," Mom gushed, and I don't think I'd ever heard her so excited. "I've never flown first class before. I do hope we're all sitting together."

"We'll know when we get to the gate," Julia said and asked for the check. The server returned in record time. But, when Julia and I reached for it at the same time, a bitter memory flooded my senses.

I was in first grade; Julia and Willa wanted to go to the beach with the rest of their high school friends. Mom was hosting bridge club and had me tag along, a kind of mutual babysitting to ensure nobody got in too much trouble. Willa and Julia took turns watching me play most of the day with a little tourist girl about my age from Canada. When it was time to go, Julia and I had a tug-of-war over my beach towel that looked the same as hers. She'd called me a little shit in front of her friends, so I'd dug in my heels and pulled harder than any six-year-old in the history of Tug of War. And then Julia let go, and I went flying while she and her friends held their tanned flat stomachs and laughed at me.

"I've got it." I yanked at the check holder, but she didn't let go. Her smile was genuine but shaky like she'd almost forgotten how.

"Please." The word hung between us like one of those rickety old bridges made out of worn ropes and decaying wood, and maybe this was a bridge.

Mom watched us intently, not physically pushing us together like she used to when we were little and were forced to apologize. But then she didn't have to. She'd perfected her powers of détente so that invisible hands pushed my heart toward Julia's in what our mother hoped would be a lasting peace. As much as I didn't want to make up with my sister, I wasn't going to be the one to disappoint Mom. That was Julia's forte.

"Thank you," I let go of the check as Mom beamed.

The one and only time I'd flown before, I'd traipsed through first class to my coach seat, thinking those passengers were fools for paying triple for a seat that came with a few more inches of legroom and free drinks. Come to find out, most of the passengers in first class didn't pay actual money for the privilege; they just have a gazillion frequent flyer miles like Julia used to upgrade our tickets.

Mom and I were in the first row of a dozen seats, and Julia was in the last. Shortly after the pilot took off, breakfast was served, a choice between a biscuit with chorizo gravy and scrambled eggs or a sausage or vegetable frittata. I was a little baffled as to why I was still hungry. Maybe it was because the food was free or because I wouldn't eat for another five hours, but I ordered the chorizo thing along with another round of mimosas for Mom and me and made her promise to eat her breakfast before she tackled her second drink.

After a fair amount of orange juice diluted champagne and consuming two full breakfasts in as many hours, I should have been exhausted. Mom was already asleep, occasionally snorting herself awake to look out the window and offer the clouds a kid-in-the-candy-store smile that said she couldn't believe she was really doing this.

As much as I missed Willa, as awkward as it was to have Julia along, my body was electric. The girl who'd idolized her big sister wanted to turn and look at Julia, but the girl on fire, said, Does she really get off so easily? A simple, Please, and all is forgiven?

Our pilot liked to play tour guide, pointing out microscopic specks of interest no one but him could see from thirty-six-thousand feet. Mom was too sacked when he announced we were west of the Mississippi to have marked this first for herself. So, I drained the last of my mimosa and gave the glass to the flight attendant, who seemed to anticipate our needs before we knew them.

The biscuit sat heavy in my stomach, and I was in mid yawn when she presented a navy blanket and a pillow with a knowing smile. Paper crinkled as she opened a package with a sleep mask, another first-class perk. Before I could ask, she'd grabbed another blanket out of a gunmetal gray bin and spread it over mom. When I pulled the blanket up to my chin, I was too amped up to sleep. I liked the cozy blanket but was less comfortable with the feeling that Julia was watching over me.

But something was off. That was never how forced apologies went; they were always followed by go-to-hell looks or tongues sticking out when Mom wasn't looking. I craned my neck around in hopes that feeling my sister's eyes on me was my imagination, that her long pink tongue would dart out of her mouth, or she would flip me off. Instead, she smiled and flashed a peace sign like she used to do when she was my cool sister. I wheeled around in my seat and pretended to sleep until I did.

The landing barely jostled me awake. When I nudged Mom, she threw off her blanket, nose pressed to the window. "Good golly! We're here?" Everything was a wonder to her, including the

185

concrete tarmac that looked like all concrete tarmacs everywhere. We deplaned and made our way to Baggage Claim while Julia went to get the rental car, which for a mortal person normally takes forever. But Julia was waiting at the curb in a shiny black Cadillac Escalade when Mom and I pushed the luggage cart out to the car.

Mom settled into the front passenger seat while Julia and I loaded the luggage. I took the seat behind Julia in hopes of getting a glimpse of Mom's face when she first saw the redwoods.

"I checked in with Willa," Julia said and eased into the traffic to exit the airport. "She says Tank is out of surgery. He's still in and out but complaining about having to stay in the hospital overnight."

"He's complaining. That's a good sign," Mom said.

Julia nodded in agreement. "He made them wait until she got there to take him down to the OR. Willa said he's acting like he's the first man in the history of men to ever have an appendectomy, but she'll straighten him out."

"And baby him. I do wish Willa were here, but we are going to do her proud and have a fabulous time." Mom said. "Let the adventure begin!"

Her enthusiasm was contagious; I couldn't remember the last time something felt so exciting and new. Julia, who'd always seemed to know everything about everything, didn't ask Waze or Siri how to get to the Chaminade Resort, which was a little less and an hour away from the airport. Soon we were breezing down the freeway, taking hairpin turns like a slalom gold medalist and making my full stomach queasy. I rolled the window down to keep from getting sick. Even though San Jose and Charleston were on their respective oceans, the Pacific air smelled different and cleaner.

"There they are," Mom gasped and pointed to a stand of Redwoods by the roadside. The trees were everywhere but didn't look anything like the gargantuan ones I'd seen on the internet.

"Just wait till you see the ones in Big Basin or Henry Cowell State Park," Julia said. "But first, we're going to take a little detour before we head to the hotel. It won't take long."

A half-hour later, the Pacific Ocean came into view, and it was my turn to gasp. I put my hand on Mom's shoulder as Julia pulled onto a lookout so we could have a better view. Mom and I couldn't get out of the car fast enough to gawk at the Atlantic's showier sister, who seemed bigger and more beautiful. The plain dirt parking lot doubled as a majestic cliff line that went on as far as the eye could see over the ocean, putting her east coast sister to shame.

Clouds moved quickly across dark indigo waters that turned a deep azure in full sun. Torrents churned hard and then crashed onto the beach, making the air salty and sweet. To complete the postcard picture, gulls circled above us.

Julia swiped at tears and pointed across the broad expanse of wonder. "Two o'clock. Just watch the water." The wind picked up as if on Julia's cue, blowing mom's well-coiffed bob about. The three of us squealed like kids on Christmas morning as a lone whale breached to gawk back at the three sobbing Southerners standing on the edge of beauty.

"It looks like a dream," Mom wrapped one arm around my waist and the other around Julia's. "It is a dream."

That was when it hit me, and I think Julia, too, that time and circumstance had worn Mom down. She was always a few inches taller than me and nearly eye-to-eye with Julia for as long as I could remember. Now Julia towered over her, and I could see over the top of Mom's head. She squeezed both of us hard, making us squeal like little girls and making me grateful that her strength and wisdom were simply concentrated into a smaller form now. She blessed the hearts of some tourists who'd joined us and didn't have better sense than to feed bread crumbs to seagulls over their car.

We mooned over the ocean for a few more minutes before piling back in the car to head to the hotel. The road meandered up the mountain until we reached the three-hundred-acre resort at the top. The mission-style hotel sprawled across the landscape and looked nice but less fancy than I'd expected a AAA 4 Diamond resort to be. But the property itself was breathtaking. Three hundred acres of primarily redwood and eucalyptus trees framed a sliver of Monterey Bay in the distance.

"Oh, my," Mom said. "Isn't it amazing?" She gushed as Julia pulled up to the valet stand.

"Well done, Maise," Julia said as the valet opened our doors and started loading our bags onto the cart.

"Thanks, Julia," I said, grateful the bargain hotel package hadn't turned out to be a dump. "We have a king suite, so I thought you and mom could take the bed, and I'll take the couch."

"I don't mind the couch," Mom piped up.

"No, you two take the bed. I'm used to sleeping on the couch," Julia said, and I wondered what that meant. She had a huge house, big enough to sleep in a different bed every night for a week, or she had last I heard.

The lobby was bustling with guests and so many canines. Most of them were on leashes, most with those clips that attached their leashes to their owner's waists. Of course, there were the off-leash showoffs, the random German shepherds or Labs who were quivering for their master's next command. An unruly sheepdog puppy walked the little boy attached to his leash.

Rhys was never a fan of pets in general and was certainly not a dog person. I thought I wasn't either until Jordan came home with a stray chow retriever mix he found in the neighborhood when he was six. He dubbed him Shadow, and he lived to the ripe old age of ten when he passed away and broke our hearts, even Rhys'.

A tall, tanned thirtyish looking couple set off the welcoming committee when they entered the lobby with their feisty terrier. Even with the barking and controlled chaos, it made me want a dog again.

A stunning Asian woman checked us in, handed us our hotel keycards, and instructed a bellman to show us to our room. The bellman was equally gorgeous, one of those shiny blond California boys who looked like he lived to surf. He led us to the elevator and then to our room which had spectacular in-your-face views of the redwoods. He unloaded our bags but didn't stand around making friendly conversation like his counterpart down South most definitely would have to cajole a nice tip.

Mom started unpacking. I followed her lead while Julia toed off her shoes and shook off the traveling dust with a slow sun salutation. The sun answered back, dipping curiously low for not quite 7:00 Pacific Standard Time.

As I'd packed, The Weather Channel had warned me to be prepared for warm days and cold nights, especially by Charleston standards. I had a giant suitcase full of clothes and a little carry-on for shoes, makeup, and assorted grooming products, although the carry-on wasn't little enough to fly for free. Mom's suitcase was large enough to hide a young Big Foot should we find one wandering around amongst the redwoods, while Julia had a small duffle.

Mom put her things in the dresser and hung her outfits in the closet, at least two for every day, while Julia sat cross-legged on the floor meditating. Still dressed in her loose linen outfit, her face was the essence of peace, while I was the woman in the Harry Met Sally diner scene who wanted "what she's having."

Some children ran down the hallway like earsplitting sopranos in a high-powered shriek fest. The shrill pitch made my ears kiss my shoulders. At the same time, Mom blanched and flashed a disapproving look and a fake smile at the door. Still, Julia didn't move until she'd had her daily recommended allowance of vitamin Zen. Finally, she opened her eyes and smiled. "I hope you don't mind, Maise, but I made dinner reservations for 8:00 if that suits you; or we could order in if you're too tired to go down to the dining room."

Mom lived to go anywhere, especially out to dinner. She insisted she wasn't the least bit tired, pulled a dress with the tags on it out of the closet, and headed into the bathroom. Julia grabbed something black out of her bag and went into the bedroom, leaving me to stare into the living room closet to figure out what to wear.

The thermostat in the room swore it was a comfortable seventy degrees, but my own personal summer said otherwise. I chose a white tank I knew would draw a disapproving look from mom for my bare shoulders on such a cool night, but I had to honor my summer that had been curiously absent since the funeral. Even when I was part of the ovulation nation, my body was never reliable. But the last five years of the change had been ambivalent as change itself, lurking, flickering on hard. Stress and cortisol partied hard with my raging hormones, and then suddenly were gone like they were never there, to begin with.

I grabbed a pair of turquoise skinny jeans I probably should have left in the wishful side of my closet. They were stretchy and not so tight I had to lay down on the couch to zip them, but they did require an elaborate interpretive dance to put them on. Julia emerged from the bedroom in the black version of what she'd worn today, pants and a thin linen long-sleeved shirt buttoned at the cuffs and up to the hollow of her throat. She ran a brush through her blond hair that fell just past her shoulders and caught me staring like I used to when I was little, and she was getting ready for a date. I pretended to look past her to admire the bed that had a giant abacus for a headboard.

"You look great, Maise," she said, like things between us weren't complicated. She went to her handbag, pulled out a little pouch, and rummaged through it until she found a necklace to put on me. It was heavy and silver with lots of turquoises and was absolutely stunning. "I had this made the first time I went to Sedona." I ran my fingers over the smooth stones. This was the first time in years that Julia had mentioned one of her gazillion trips, and I hadn't rolled my eyes. Or secretly hated her a little bit for being so well traveled and for being so—Julia. "It looks perfect on you."

And this was what I'd missed from my sister, what I'd always wanted even when I swore I didn't, this closeness. For years there had been something between us, something visible and invisible. Had she always been an enigma? With all the mystery that surrounds a big sister, yes. But there was something else now, something bigger between us. I just didn't know what it was. A week ago, even twenty-four hours ago, I wouldn't have given two shits about Julia, but, looking at her smile, I longed to know what happened to this sister I didn't know and when the Julia I loved was coming back.

I accepted her peace offering and put some silver hoops on that looked good with my new haircut since it had grown out a bit, the perfect complement to the fancy necklace. Mom came out of the bathroom in the standard garb typically worn by someone twenty years younger than her. Julia and I told her how gorgeous she looked so she didn't have to fish for the compliments she relished. She put on a sage green wool duster and then rubbed my dewy arms, not noticing or not mentioning that they were sweaty and muscular or more muscular.

"She's fine, Mom, we're all fine," Julia assured, pulling on a black jacket. And God, I hoped she was right.

The evening temperature coaxed goose flesh on my arms as the waiter led us to the outdoor terrace. The full moon danced with the evening fog, making the distant redwoods look soft and dreamy. Our table had a fire pit in the center, the dark shadows and amber light softened the lines on my mother's face, and she looked closer to my age than her own. The firelight caressed Julia's face as well. With her blond hair down, she could have passed for a California cover girl for Vogue or maybe that AARP magazine I get that I never signed up for.

We ordered from the menu, then ate like grateful food snobs, savoring every morsel, including the thick, rich cabernet Julia discussed at length with our waiter. Another impossibly good-looking California boy, he was home for a break after finishing his sommelier training. He was thrilled to talk wine with Julia, and by the time he brought the check, he was a little smitten by her.

"That was lovely," Mom said as we entered the elevator.

"It was," Julia said, almost dreamily and maybe a little tipsy since the cute waiter talked her into ordering another bottle of wine. We'd drunk a little more than half of the second bottle tucked safely under Julia's arm and would make a delicious nightcap for a very long day.

In the room, I put on my pajamas and slathered on my nighttime face regime. By the time I emerged from the bathroom, Mom and Julia were in their PJs too. A half dozen tea lights that, as far as I knew, were illegal in a hotel room glowed. And Mom glowed too, from the wine, from the decadence of finally doing something just for herself. Music played on a small Bluetooth box, a Billie Holiday tune I couldn't name. But it was the perfect complement to this new world that was so different from Charleston.

Julia smiled, meticulously dividing the last of the wine between three glasses. She handed me mine, and I gave her necklace back, my head swimmy from the wine, from my love for my mother and sister. I took a sip and watched Julia run her fingers over the intricate silverwork and the smooth turquoise stones like she was seeing them for the first time.

"Thanks," I whispered, tipsy enough to let everything between us go. She looked up at me quizzically, like I'd just given her the most wonderful gift.

"Wow," she said, and I wondered if she slipped out onto the balcony for one of her funny cigarettes when Mom and I were getting ready for bed. Spreading the necklace out on the small round wooden coffee table, she was teary. "Thanks, Maise, It's so—wow."

Her face flushed from high dollar cabernet while I played along like I really had given her the most beautiful gift. But it wasn't the necklace. The poison I'd held onto for so long had evaporated, and all I felt for my sister was love and forgiveness.

# Chapter Twenty

Around seven the following day, Mom and I emerged from our room bedheaded and a little hungover. Julia's sheets and blanket were neatly folded and stacked on the back of the couch, and she was already dressed in black compression capris and a soft-looking red long-sleeve T-shirt. The necklace she'd loaned me wasn't on the coffee table anymore and was probably stowed away in her duffel. She sat facing the window in a deep meditative state with her legs crisscrossed, her hands resting on her knees, palms facing upward.

"I wish she wouldn't do that," Mom whispered loud enough to hear herself, which was hardly whispering. "It's unchristian."

"Mom," I chided. "There's nothing wrong with meditating."

"I never believed one bit in all that cross-legged hullabaloo. One of the CNA's who works with your daddy tried to get him to do it, said it slows the progression of Alzheimer's. But I told that woman I'll not have your father worshiping Buddha."

"She's not worshiping Buddha; nobody does. It's a philosophy. Besides, we were raised within walking distance of a dozen churches, and somehow none of us are particularly religious."

"That's my downfall," Mom sighed. "We went from time to time, usually when I had a new dress to show off but nowhere to wear it. Church was always good for that. Back then, I never gave heaven or hell that much thought, but when you get old, you think about those kinds of things." She'd missed the tag under the arm of her sporty new outfit. "It's never too late, you know." She fluffed her hair and then licked her index finger to tame her silver brows, which were bushy compared to my barely-there ones, another lovely gift of menopause.

Julia opened her eyes and smiled her Cover Girl smile. So Zen, so blonde, I hoped she didn't hear Mom. "Ready for breakfast?" she chirped, with no pesky hangover residue.

We headed down to the Sunset Restaurant and were seated at a table overlooking the forest. Mom was almost star-struck, glancing back and forth from her menu to the view like she was worried the redwoods were going somewhere before she could see them up close.

"We should head over to Henry Cowell State Park today," Julia said. "It's just a few minutes from here near Felton. We can come back to the hotel after lunch and rest and then go into Santa Cruz for dinner on the wharf."

"I didn't come here to rest," Mom declared. "I want to see everything."

"Relax, Mom, we have plenty of time," I promised. "Henry Cowell sounds like a great place to start, and we can bounce back and forth between the coast and the state parks, eventually work our way up to Big Basin."

"There are so many beautiful places to see along the way." Julia stirred her coffee thoughtfully. "We should definitely take a day to head up the Pacific Coast Highway, take a peek at San Francisco, or just hang out in some of the cool little towns along the way."

Three teenagers at the table next to us whined to their parents about being forced to hike a stupid mountain today when they could be home surfing. They took turns complaining like Willa and Julia, and I used to, a tag team method of protest that provided endless torture for our parents.

"I want to see it all," Mom said. "Pack as much as we can into seven days and then some."

"Let's see how things go this morning," Julia said. "If you're still feeling ambitious, we can do dinner on the wharf tomorrow and take a picnic dinner up to Wilder Ranch and watch the sunset."

"Don't worry about me. I feel terrific," Mom bragged. "By the end of the week, I might get out there with one of those surfboards and hang— whatever it is they hang."

The dark-haired teen who was the most vocal smirked to himself in the way teens do when they believe they are superior. And I wanted to laugh at him for underestimating my mother and her capabilities. In less than three minutes, she could talk him into offering her his beloved board and have him begging her to keep it.

Mom's cell boomed with a Bugle Call ringtone. Most of the diners, even the teens, turned to glare at the noise. Mom made a show out of fumbling in her purse for her phone. Then, she looked apologetically at the diners who'd already forgiven her because she was a cute little old lady. "It's your sister," she announced, "maybe she has Daddy on the line."

"Hello." Her voice was as breathy as a twenty-year-old anxious to talk with her fella. "Why, Willa. How are you?" She mouthed to Julia and me that it was Willa. "And Tank's recovering well?" Her voice was more tinny than usual from holding back the question she really wanted to ask. "And your father? He's well?" The words spilled out like one sentence. She didn't breathe until she heard Willa's answer. I couldn't hear what Willa was saying, but I knew from the way Mom slumped in relief that Dad was fine. Then her body snapped to attention. "He is? Are you sure?" Mom nodded as Willa talked for some time, but she seemed more annoyed than worried.

She put her hand over the lower half of the phone like she was talking on the old phone in the kitchen where we grew up that had a cord so long, I could wrap it around myself four times. "Willa says Katherine's got your father believing he's on the cruise boat with her," she whispered. "Yes. I'm still here, Willa, but I'm not entirely sure how I feel about that."

Funny how Mom never minded Dad believing with all his heart that he was young and in between jobs. Maybe in her mind, she pretended that she was too, and that was why she never redirected him when he daydreamed about getting a job at the strip center across the street. On those days, he was always hellbent on making enough money to move them to a little bungalow on Folly Beach so they could go dancing on Saturday nights. But let one of the other residents try to sell Dad on their delusions, and Mom shut them down in a heartbeat.

"Because anybody can see the Memory Care Unit is not a cruise boat, dear. Why I've taken Katherine to that window five hundred times and shown her, there is no boat, no captain with her children. For mercy's sake, Katherine doesn't even have children."

Mom listened intently and nodded until it was her turn to speak. "Well, as long as your father is okay, I suppose it will have to be fine until I get back. Yes, I'll tell your sisters you said hello. Goodbye, dear." She looked deflated as she put her phone in her purse, and maybe even a little helpless that she couldn't control Dad's day-to-day world from her California command post.

"Mom." She looked up suddenly like I'd startled her, like she'd forgotten Julia and I were even there. "Going along with Katherine's reality is part of the validation therapy; you know that. And Dad loves to feel like he's helping out. He'll help Katherine look for her children all day, and he'll be calm because he'll want Katherine to be calm. It'll be okay. They'll help each other out and stick together while you're gone."

"That's exactly what I'm worried about," she huffed.

From the time Dad was diagnosed, we'd prepared her that he may not know her someday. Or worse, she might walk into Memory Care and find him in bed with another woman he believed was his wife. All of us knew the ABCs of the horrible disease, but Mom And Dad had been lucky. Every time without fail, he knew her name, knew her face, and had always had such a peace about him when she was near. Something I never had with Rhys.

"Maybe I shouldn't have come," Mom said. "Maybe we should just go on home now."

"Not until you've hugged at least one redwood," Julia said. "And once you get started, you won't be able to stop."

I know being away from Dad must have felt odd. I was just grateful Willa hadn't called to say, Annette, the Memory Care unit harlot, as Mom called her, hadn't slept with Dad. Of course, Mom made up for the slur by always pointing out that Alzheimer's had made Annette powerless over her urges. Still, the woman had bedded half the unit, both male and female.

"Everything's okay. Willa can handle Dad, and Tank, and Donald Trump if she had to." I gave Mom my most reassuring smile. "Dad will be fine. You'll see."

A little girl who was maybe five distracted Mom when she sauntered by our table with two adoring dads in tow. Well aware she had an audience, she settled into the booth and proceeded to hold court while the men exchanged looks that are universal to all parents when their child does something cute. It made me think of Jordan and hope someday he'd change his mind about not wanting kids.

The little girl gloated over the tiny pinecone-looking thing in her hand. She proclaimed it her treasure and looked around to see who was basking in her cuteness. Of course, everyone except the griping teens was. She grinned at Mom, who, to this day, even though her daughters are in their fifties and sixties, still looked at little girls with such a longing for that time in her life when we were little.

"You are such a lovely young lady," Mom said. "And what is it you have there?"

"It's a wedwood." The little girl crawled out of her seat to give Mom a closer look. "And one day, it's gonna be a giant wedwood twee. My daddies say it will take a vewy vewy wong time."

"Thank you for showing me. You know, you're such a lucky girl to see the redwoods at your age. I'm very old and have never seen one up close, and certainly not close enough to get this tiny seed," Mom said in the voice she reserved for small children. "But I'm going to see them today."

After breakfast, we headed down the mountain. The car strained under the weight of our anticipation. When we reached the end of the road, Julia put her blinker on to turn north. As a southerner who didn't live by north, south, east, and west directions, everything was either left or right. But even I knew Henry Cowell State park was south and to the right.

"Where are we going?" I asked as Julia waited for her turn to pull onto the highway.

"To Big Basin." Julia gave me that same pitiful look Rhys used to when I made him turn around to go back to the house because I was sure I'd left the iron on, only to find the iron and ironing board unused in the laundry room closet.

Mourning inner twined with self-renaissance had given me a little vacation from Alzheimer's that felt like thin, sticky strands of cobwebs I could never get off of me. But, God, I hoped there would be at least one person I knew every time I saw their face, the way Dad knows Mom or Julia. One person I called by name, the right name. One person I felt at home with, who was my home.

"No worries," Julia said softly, "We can start at the park in Felton if you want, Maise." I nodded as Julia pulled onto the highway headed toward Felton and wished I could forget about this damn disease.

# Chapter Twenty-One

**W**e missed the park near Felton thanks to spotty GPS reception and turned around at the Big Foot Museum, which was doing a lively business for a weekday. At the park entrance, Julia bought an annual family pass she'd probably never use again, but it was her way of contributing to the California park system.

The place was not what I'd expected; there was no fanfare, no gaudy flashing neon sign announcing to hikers they'd entered the Greatest Show on Earth. Instead, a more touristy train station was on the left side of the parking lot behind a stand of small trees. I couldn't see it or the train, but I could hear it grunt and whistle while it waited to take passengers around the park or over the mountain to Santa Cruz beach. Finally, to the right was where the greatest show of nature awaited, where Mom's bucket list would be complete.

"I'll meet you at the trailhead," Julia said, gathering her camera and small backpack. "I'm going to grab us tickets for the train ride after we're done with a short loop that should be doable for you, Mom. We can take our time and then take the train for a different perspective of the park."

"This is so exciting," Mom grabbed her cane. She trembled hard when I cupped her elbow and giggled at my concerned face. "It's just the excitement, dear.

"Everything is just so different. Different shades of green than back home. And the trees, Lord, the trees, they're so magnificent, part of me wonders if they're real. But they are, and we're here. It's momentous." She laughed and wrapped her arm around my middle. "Why, I don't think I've ever used that word a day in my life, but that's exactly what these trees are to me, to us. They're the dream from my past, a symbol of my girl's future."

As spectacular as the forest looked, that was a pretty tall order, but Mom was right. Everything was different from the Lowcountry, more than just the topography. The air was thin, California clean, and lighter than the thick salty air back home. The greens of the forest were different, more muted, without the high gloss of leaves from gnarled live oaks, but still beautiful. And the trees were so tall they made a whopper hundred-foot Loblolly pine back home seem puny and small.

"I'm so glad we came," she said. "I miss Willa and wish she were here, but I'm so glad we came."

Julia joined us at the trailhead. The three of us posed next to a crosscut of a redwood tree while another tourist snapped our picture. I never thought I was a stereotypical tree hugger, but I trembled with excitement. Being there for Mom's dream, for a dream I didn't even know I had, was the most important thing I'd done in a long time. And there was also a peace about it, a promise that the world would keep spinning because I was right where I was supposed to be.

Mom ran her hand over the crosscut's rings with little historical markers that showed it had been growing tall for thousands of years and shook her head, her breath short and quick.

"Mom, are you okay?" I asked as Julia thanked the man who took our picture.

"I never should have waited this long," Mom's voice was thick with emotion. "I've wanted to see these trees since I learned about them in grade school. I don't even remember how old I was. Young, very young. I should never have risked missing this."

"But you're here now," I said.

"I know, and I'm grateful, so grateful." Mom grabbed my hand as we started for the trail. "It's just all that time; I missed this because your father didn't want to travel because it was too far or it just seemed like too much. I spent my whole life convincing myself something I wanted so much was something I could do without, and look what I almost missed.

"Promise me you won't do that, Masie. Promise me you'll be more like Julia; see everything you want to see. Do everything you want to do before you're old like me."

For the first time in all my born days, I smiled at the notion that Mom was asking me to be more like my sister.

With her fancy camera, Julia snapped a few pictures of a tiny purple flower in a stand of ferns that was somehow thriving in the shadow of a giant redwood tree. Mom pulled away from me to press her cheek against what looked like a relatively young tree, maybe a thousand years old. She closed her eyes and smiled. I did the same on the other side of the tree and felt a flash of warmth that didn't feel like my inner summer.

The train whistle blew. Mom unwrapped herself from the tree and stooped to pick up a tiny cone like the little girl at the restaurant had. The redwoods were everywhere, yet this patch that began along the Northern California coast and ended in Oregon was the only place on earth you could find them. Mom put one of the tiny seeds in her pocket and then handed one to me without saying anything corny about putting a miracle in my pocket, but she didn't have to. I felt the same connection with this place that she did.

The loop was flat and easy for her. We took our time and arrived at tree number eight on the map. It stood over two-hundred feet high, was estimated to be over two thousand years old, and had a hobbit hole at the base. To our amazement, a group of schoolchildren began to spill out from inside the tree like a clown car.

"Oh, my," Mom laughed as a teacher wiggled out of the opening. "Look. Grownups can go inside too."

"Yeah." A sweaty little boy who looked to be maybe ten said. "It's big in there, real big, but we didn't break the record."

"And what is the record?" Mom asked as the kids continued to pile out of the tree.

"Two teachers and seventy-five third graders," he said while watching the last of the kids stream out of the tree. "We had a chance to break the record, but a bunch of kids in the other two classes are out with a bug. That means they're sick. Not that they have some giant bug inside them, but that would be cool."

"It would indeed," Mom said.

We sat at the picnic bench and watched two more adults duck walk out of the opening in the tree. It took a little doing for one of them, but not enough to make the entrance to the tree off-putting. The grownups did a headcount; satisfied they'd collected all their charges, they headed down the path to the next wonder. Both Mom and I leaned back on our elbows on the picnic table and gazed up in amazement at the sky-high tree while Julia, who had probably seen them a thousand times, looked at the pictures she'd taken.

The clamor of excited children became fainter and fainter until we were left with the quiet of the forest and a sort of reverence. Like the woods were church, a church I wanted to be a part of, and God was under every rock and inside every tree.

A young couple with matching Michigan T-shirts walked up with more serious-looking hiking gear than our sneakers and Mom's cane. Their lean bodies and fresh-faced good looks could have landed them in the Patagonia ad with Jordan or maybe a Patagonia ad for lovers. And they were lovers, bodies leaning in, looking at each other like there was no one on earth they'd rather be with.

During our Basic Instinct days, Rhys used to look at me that way. Compared to our marriage, that time of adoration lasted a minute. But that's what I wanted the next time around, if there was a next time.

The girl on fire said, you're damn straight there will be a next time, and you will know to hold on to the sweet spot that comes in the beginning so that it never ends.

The guy ran his knuckles across the woman's cheek and then led her to the tree's entrance. They were young and agile enough to stoop and go in rather than duck waddle like the teachers. My chest felt tight as they disappeared into the hobbit hole. A few minutes later, the couple emerged from the tree so starry-eyed, you'd have to have been dead to look at them and not want what they had. The woman caught me gawking and blushed, "So amazing in there."

He looked at her like she was the only wonder in a forest of wonders, nuzzled her ear, and whispered something that made her blush again before he took her hand and led her down the trail.

Julia was still going through her photos and showed me the one she took of Mom with her face against the tree, eyes closed, grinning like a fool. She swiped the screen for the next pic of both Mom and I hugging the tree. "My favorite so far," Julia said. "I texted this one to Willa."

"Send it to me; I'd love to frame it," I said. "How'd the one the guy took of us at the entrance turn out?"

"With this camera, they're all perfect." She showed me the proof and scrolled through tons of pictures she'd taken in just the few minutes we'd been there.

"Girls," Mom said in her moderately firm mom voice. "I want to go inside."

Suddenly, the hole in the tree looked tiny and way more ominous than it did when the kids and the lovers were piling in. "Mom—," I began.

She knew I was shutting her down and put her hands on her hips. "Hush now. I've already figured out how I'm going to do it. I'll use my nylon jacket, tie it around my waist and then scoot in on my bottom." Her chin wobbled in defiance. "If it's the last thing I do on God's green earth, I am going inside that tree." She trembled with resolve to crawl into the blackest hole, and it was clear there was no stopping her.

I looked at Julia for a bit of support, but she just shrugged. "She wants what she wants, and she's come this far, so why not?"

"I don't know because she's eighty-five? Because she's our mother," I snapped. This was so like my if-it-feels good, even if it kills you, do-it, Julia. "The only mother we have. Besides, we don't know what's in there." I glared, daring Julia to shrug one more time at the idea of feeding our mother to a black hole so that I could come across the picnic table and snatch her blond head bald.

"I'm doing it."

I whipped around to see Mom with her Columbia windbreaker tied around her waist as she slipped into the opening. "She'll be fine," Julia assured, taking the lens cap off her Nikon and disappearing through the entrance. "Come on," she called. "You don't want to miss this."

If the redwood forest was back in the Lowcountry, there would be snakes inside, glorified roaches called palmetto bugs as big as your hand, and spiders with thick webs that were impossible to unstick from anything, especially your hair. But this was the part of California where everything was pristine and strangely debugged. I followed Julia inside the tree; she pulled a small flashlight out of her bag and shone it straight up.

The ceiling jutted at least twenty feet into the darkness. Rays of light cast a faint glow around the surprisingly large space that could have very well held seventy-five smallish school children, as well as the brown pasteboard boxes that overtook my home for a brief period.

The wonder of the hobbit mansion, the claustrophobia from total darkness, and, well, being inside of a massive redwood was literally breathtaking. My chest heaved. I glanced at Mom to make sure she was still alive and found her still sitting on the ground with her neck craned up at God's cathedral ceiling and grinning like a fool.

I tapped the flashlight on my phone and shone the light on the smooth, polished walls that whispered secrets and wisdom. A lone heart carved into the wall flooded my own with promises to do what I could before Alzheimer's washed me clean of resolve and regrets. I leaned my forehead against the wall of the tree and surrendered like a child. The hum of life and energy passed around me, through me connecting to every living thing.

Julia said something, but I ignored her. Her voice was more urgent like maybe it was time to go. I turned away from her and pressed my face into the smooth surface. Tears flowed for the new life I promised myself and the one I wish I'd done differently. From here on out, I would be the me I was meant to be before I learned to live life on the back burner.

"Maisie," Julia's scream ripped through the bowels of the tree. My sister, who had never been hapless or helpless a day in her life, stared down at our lifeless mother like they were separated by an impenetrable wall.

"Help her, Julia." My words bounced off the walls of the tree that had swallowed us whole. I shoved Julia forward through the barrier. Her look was blank and confused.

"Mom. Mom," I shrieked. It was too dark to see the rise and fall of her chest. I pressed my fingers into the side of her neck for a pulse. Nothing. I yanked my phone out of my pocket, but there was no signal. "I have to go outside and call 911, but you have to help her, Julia. You have to help Mom now." Julia didn't move. "Damnit, help her."

The invisible thread holding Mom's head up snapped. It lolled to one side before landing inhumanly low on her chest.

"Now," the scream ripped through me.

Julia nodded and dropped to her knees. She found the right spot on our mother's chest and pumped like I had for Rhys. But, this time, it would work. Julia wasn't just a doctor. She was a goddamn deity.

"She's not responding." My sister's voice said she was back from whatever haze she was in. She barked out a command at Mom and pumped with wild perfection. Everything was going to be okay. This was Julia. A hotshot cardiovascular surgeon with better rhythm than the BeeGees.

The hole in the tree seemed to close up, but not enough to stop me. I dropped to my belly and elbowed my way outside. Sunlight blazed through a gap in the thick limbs like a spotlight. My eyes fought to adjust to the blinding light.

The signal on my phone registered half a bar. I shook it and pointed it at the sky, but the bar disappeared. I stood on the picnic table and scanned the heavens until a speck indicating the tiniest signal appeared. The Gibb brothers screamed, Whether you're a brother or whether you're a mother, you're stayin' alive, stayin' alive.

But they couldn't scream because they were all dead.

No, my diseased brain said. One BeeGee was alive. I couldn't remember which one, but that didn't matter because Mom was staying alive. The Gibb brother's double-edged falsetto pierced my chest. Somebody help me. Somebody help me. I punched 911 into my phone and stood stock still for the call to go through.

An unholy scream ripped through the giant redwood.

# Chapter Twenty-Two

Julia clung to me, and I to her as the paramedics eased our mother out of the tree. Lying on the stretcher, Mom looked peaceful, her body still warm when I kissed her forehead. I had a million things I wanted to say to her, to thank her for, but the words were lost in a deluge of tears.

I wrapped my arms around my sister and held on for dear life, for our dear mother's life. Bound together, every shaky breath paid homage to the woman who bore us, raised us, loved us and taught us how to love, and we ached in the way only motherless children do.

Too many EMTs scurried about the area around the tree that had swallowed our vibrant mother whole and spit her out lifeless. Three men talked quietly as they wrapped the area with yellow tape like the place was a crime scene. The overkill made me wonder if this had ever happened before.

A blond buff Cali guy with huge biceps made notes while speaking quietly to his walkie. "Eighty-five-year-old female, deceased. Possible heart attack or stroke." The person on the other end of the walkie answered back, something intelligible only to him. "Copy that," He said and nodded at a female EMT, and the two of them started toward Julia and me.

The two of us sat on the picnic table like we used to in our backyard, but this was not a sweltering Lowcountry day. Wrapped in thin fleece blankets, we shivered like we did when we were kids, and Mom would take us to Folly Beach on a sunny February day and watch us pretend to be Yankee polar bears. The icy waters had thrilled, racking our pasty white thin bodies with pain before we ran out of the sweet Atlantic to be soothed by the sun. But there was no sun under the giant redwood, and the sheer magnitude of our loss made everything hurt.

Every beat of my heart said it couldn't be possible she was gone, but my brain knew better, and the shaking would not stop.

"I'm Angel Hernandez, and this is my partner, Chrissy Chapman."

Angel's eyes were the truest shade of blue, and I wondered if that was his real name? Was he really an angel? If he was, I wanted him to ring a bell or clap his hands and call Mom out of the body bag like Lazarus. Instead, he talked, but I didn't want him to tell me what I already knew, so my mind wandered as far as it could go from the body bag on the gurney that was close enough to touch.

Desperate for a distraction, I almost asked him about his name, about his Hispanicness or lack thereof. But that would have been racist, something I would have fussed at my father for doing before Alzheimer's turned him into Captain Tolerance.

"We're sorry for your loss," he said, and Chrissy bowed her head in agreement. Angel looked at Julia. "I understand you're a doctor. Cardio, right?"

Julia sat up so straight it should have hurt. "I am." Her Dr. Julia Watson voice was strong; I reached for her hand and held on tight.

"Can you tell me what happened?"

"Mom wanted to go inside the tree. She never stood up. At least, I don't think she did. We were all sort of caught up in the experience. One minute she was sitting on the ground, leaning against the tree, smiling." Chrissy offered her a bottle of water and then handed one to me. Julia cracked open the bottle and took a long draw before wiping her mouth with the back of her hand. "I decided to take some pictures and glanced at her every so often in the dim light of her cellphone flashlight.

"She was so happy to be inside that damn tree. I remember thinking, 'Good for her.' I was playing around with my camera, trying to get some good shots because the bark is——. It's just so amazing, you know to be inside there. When I looked back at Mom, even in the dim light, she didn't look right. Her eyes were hollow, but she was smiling like she had been just moments ago, so I knew it wasn't a stroke."

He scribbled something on his pad. "And that was when you started CPR?"

"Yes. No. I—I don't know," Julia's face crumpled. She looked confused and desolate. "I don't know."

"Yes. She started CPR." I squeezed Julia's hand hard until she winced and continued. Her voice was different now, more like her doctor's voice when she says, It's okay. Everything's going to be okay.

She broke into medical speak with the EMTs. She could have had the same conversation in Italian, Spanish, German, or Russian if she'd had to. But she could have been speaking Mandarin Chinese because I didn't understand a word she said. She had both EMTs nodding in agreement until her voice tailed off at the end of the story, the end of our mother. Impossible.

"I couldn't save her." But Julia couldn't blame her failure on skipping the last half of CPR class. She'd held beating hearts in her hands and massaged ones that didn't beat to life. She'd cut and stitched and forced life into organs clogged full of calamity and cholesterol, but her sorrowful look dissolved into tears. "I tried, Maise."

"I know you did," I said, and I meant it.

"Don't blame yourself," Crissy said. "Short of having a defibrillator in the tree, there's nothing anyone could have done." Julia nodded at the words but didn't believe them for a second.

"At her age and under the circumstances, I'd be surprised if the coroner does an autopsy." Angel handed me a pink business card that said, GLOW in big script letters. "We'll take her to the morgue until you decide which funeral home you want to use here. We're not allowed to make recommendations, but my step-sister, Lisa Joyner, works at Santa Cruz Memorial. Even if you don't use them, she'll be glad to answer any questions you have about getting your Mom home. And she makes really nice candles; it's a side business."

He gave the guys by the gurney a nod, and they wheeled it in the direction of the parking lot. The path was bumpier than I remembered, but their pace was slow and reverent. Julia wailed when the gurney slipped out of site. Grief pulsed like a living thing between us, inside us, as we shared the same broken heart and cried hand-me-down tears for our beloved mother.

Julia and I didn't utter a word after the paramedics left. Hours passed; a ranger took away the yellow crime scene tape and told us to stay as long as we wanted. We huddled together on the picnic table, the aftershocks from crying so long and so hard rippling through us, but we were all cried out.

Two rangers posted about a hundred feet in either direction from the tree, stopped hikers, spoke in hushed tones about Mom's death, and encouraged them to take a detour around what the map had gushingly described as a must-see. Most of them did, but a fair number of lookie-loos came to see the grieving Jenkins sisters and the tree that swallowed our mother, but not a single soul went inside.

Hikers who chose to ignore the detour didn't talk to us or each other. They filed past quietly, without stopping to say how sorry they were or how this was all part of God's plan. Some looked wary, as if grief and death were contagious. They gave the tree a quick once-over before heading to the next point on their map. A few of them looked sad, like they remembered their own irreparable loss. One woman's face was soaked with tears well before she reached the tree; she disappeared down the trail before we heard her break down.

The train whistle shrieked every fifteen minutes, a reminder of one more thing Mom would never get to do, but I was grateful for the noise. Julia could be silent for hours, for years, and I just couldn't take it anymore.

"My butt hurts," I said. Julia smiled for a beat and shoved my good shoulder hard before pulling the blanket tighter around us. "It does, Jules." God, I hadn't called her that since before she deserted me before she deserted us.

"I know," she whispered.

"We have to pick a funeral home like the guy said. We have to call Willa and tell Dad or let her tell him. I think that's best. He shouldn't hear it over the phone. We can split the rest of the family between you and me. I don't want to put it all on Willa. And the kids, God, I hate doing this to them again." The to-do list in my head multiplied exponentially with things Willa and I would have already handled by now. I waited for Julia to say something, but she didn't. "We have a lot to do. We have to go."

"I don't want to go back to that hotel," she blurted and slammed her teeth over her lips.

I rubbed her arms. They were cold, and I felt like a space heater on full blast. "We have to."

"Mom's not there. She's not anywhere." She raked her hand over her face. "God, I'm so sick of death. It just won't stop, and now Mom? I can't go back to that hotel. I just can't."

We stood like we were connected by marionette strings. Julia shivered so hard she could barely walk. I peeled off my blanket and wrapped it around her. The relief from the cool breeze was so heavenly; I was sure Mom must already be up there running the show. Julia muttered her thanks and pulled it tight around her as we headed for the parking lot. There was no discussion when I took the driver's seat, no reminder Hertz said only Julia was allowed to drive the car. I started it up, cranked up the heater for Julia, and rolled down my window while pulling up a last-minute hotel site on my phone.

It seemed impossible there were no vacancies within a twenty-five-mile radius, so I started making calls. Everyone I talked to seemed surprised I didn't know the World CrossFit competition was in town. Rhys had mentioned he was toying with the idea of joining some travel team at the gym. He never said a hot blonde nurse was toying with him to get him to go, but maybe this convention was what he meant. Finally, my last-ditch call yielded a cancelation at the Carousel Beach Inn.

The chatty reservationist said two rooms had opened up when one of the guests competing in the 60+ division dropped dead of a heart attack in the shower this morning. Lucky for us, they had already booked the dead guy's room, and there was just one left, a king bed. I scrolled through photos of the hotel that looked like a cross between the old Myrtle Beach Pavilion and the State Fair back home, complete with a Ferris wheel and plenty of rides to make you scream.

"Let me ask my sister." I left out the part about the dead guy. "Everything in Santa Cruz is booked except for this one room; it's across the street from a boardwalk on the beach and will be noisy. Maybe we should look at another town further up the coast or inland."

"I want to stay in Santa Cruz until we can take Mom home," her voice was flat. She pulled her shades out of her backpack and put them on.

"Okay. It'll just be for tonight," I said more to myself than to her before I went back to the call.

She put her hand on my arm. "No, it won't. That guy was right. There's red tape shipping a— body. We'll be here two days, maybe three, more if they decide to autopsy her, but I don't think they will."

I booked the room through Tuesday to be on the safe side. The woman apologized for the sky-high weekend rates but promised they'd be cheaper after Saturday night. I ended the call and headed the car down the mountain toward Santa Cruz.

The road was a ribbon of twisting asphalt, the trees slightly less remarkable when you're driving. Julia found a Classic Rock station on the radio and cranked it up. The lead singer of Nazareth affirmed what we already knew. Love hurts. Love scars. Love wounds and marks. I'd always hated that song, the weird rhythm, the way the music never fit the rocker's voice, but God, he was right. The words were like the plip plop of rain after the worst of a heavy storm had passed, and that was where we were in all this.

The road straightened enough for me to glance at Julia. She was a blonde ghost with dead eyes that, just hours ago, could have lit up the entire boardwalk when she gave me that shrug and followed Mom into the tree. I couldn't blame her for what happened to Mom any more than I could promise her I wouldn't blame her when grief pecked at my bones. But in that moment, I would have given anything to see that light in my sister's eyes again.

Please, God. Let me see the light.

# Chapter Twenty-Three

The role reversal was something I'd fantasized about when I was younger with lots of big talk. "If I were the big sister, I'd boss everyone around and be better at it than Julia." But it felt heavy and odd to give Julia commands.

"Stay here," I said firmly as we pulled up to the hotel entrance. She didn't argue or get out of the car to go inside and get her things.

Instead, she closed her eyes and leaned her head against the window to wait for the world to return to the way it was, the way it should be, with Mom anxious about which outfit she should wear to dinner.

The valet was annoyed he had to ask for the keys a second time. "We've had a death in our family and have to check out. I won't be long."

No one argues when somebody dies.

I waved off the bellman and took a luggage cart up to our room. Julia's things were already packed up, but her duffle was unzipped. I looked around the small living area to make sure she hadn't dropped anything. Years of family vacations with two kids and a husband who never picked up after himself had me on my hands and knees with the flashlight on my phone to check under the couch.

Near the back crease, something dangly shone back at me. Unable to reach it, I stood up, jammed my hand between the cushions and the sofa back, and fished out the necklace Julia loaned me. I shoved it into her bag and loaded it onto the cart.

The bedroom door was standing open, the bed freshly made, and my heart twisted for last night's sheets with Mom's signature fragrance, a blend of Chanel No. 5 and Final Net hairspray. I pressed her pillow to my face to breathe her in, but it didn't smell like anything, not even detergent. I wasn't prepared for the loss of her, for the loss of her scent. My chest heaved. The room blurred with tears. But I couldn't afford to cry, not with Julia alone in the car, hurting, blaming herself.

My suitcases were a jumbled mess of clothes exploding over the sides, miscellaneous mismatched shoes scattered about. It took a few seconds to stuff everything back in. I put them on the cart mechanically. That was what I needed to be to get our things and get the hell out of there, a machine.

When I opened the closet, I crumpled to the floor. The crying jag lasted a little longer than the few minutes I allotted myself before getting to my feet and back to the task at hand. Never one to live out of a suitcase or a dresser drawer, Mom's new clothes that didn't smell like her were all on colorful travel hangers she had me order for her a few weeks ago. She'd loved the hangers though she wasn't crazy about the screaming primary colors and had wanted all white, which even Amazon didn't have.

My bones ached under the weight of things my mother would never wear. I couldn't look at them without remembering the fashion show she'd put on for me at her apartment, how she'd looked at herself in the mirror like she was young enough to be my sister. The way she'd blushed at the pricy jacket she adored and whispered, "Don't tell your father."

How could I tell my father? My sister? Jordan and Emma?

"God," I said to no one, not even the deity, "It hurts. It hurts." I could barely breathe. All I wanted to do was surrender like a child to grief, to loss, until my butt buzzed. I took my cell phone out of my back pocket to see a one-word text, misspelled, imperfect, and so not Julia. Hury.

I shoved the rest of Mom's things into her bags and headed for the door. The woman at the front desk was kind and efficient as she checked us out of our room. "I'm so sorry for your loss, Ms. Carver." I thanked her, and before I could muscle the overloaded baggage cart out to the car, the bellman was there, and all I could think was I had no money to tip him. I rarely carried cash because my mother never carried cash.

"Those little cards are just so much easier," she'd say, "and if you lose them, they just give you another. But if you lose cash, it's gone for good."

Gone for good. My fingers dug around in my purse for loose change, for anything to give George for putting our bags in the car. His name tag said he was from Idaho. He had a nice smile that paled in comparison to the California-beautiful waiter Mom and Julia had flirted with last night. I dug and dug, like that would make a ten or a twenty magically appear. I yanked out a tissue and stared at it. He waved me off, but I wanted to give him something.

"That's okay, ma'am," he said softly and turned to go.

He was as caught off guard as I was when I grabbed his arm and spun him around to face me. The words wanted to die in my throat, but I wouldn't let them. "Call your mother." I looked into his somber brown eyes so that he knew this was the most important tip he would ever get. "Call her and tell her you love her."

Julia and I headed down the mountain toward the Carousel Hotel; neither of us spoke. A part of me kept waiting for her to take her place as the doctor, the big sister, but she just leaned her head against the window.

"I'm glad she died here." Her words startled me as much as they angered me. My knuckles went white on the steering wheel. Mom shouldn't have gone into that tree or died three thousand miles away from everything she loved. "I think Dad would remember if she'd died with him. Even with Alzheimer's, I think he would remember every day, and it would kill him."

On that much, we agreed. My brain ordered my hands and the rest of me to relax. "I feel for Willa having to tell him," I said. "But she'll haul Tank out of bed to help her. He's good with Dad. He always thinks Tank is a guy he worked with just after he and Mom married."

We pulled into the Carousel Beach Inn parking lot. A far cry from the Chaminade, it looked more like the no-frills motels that used to dot the Grand Strand in Myrtle Beach before the megaresorts took over. There was no bellman, but we didn't need one with the luggage carts lined up at the entrance. We loaded up a cart and headed for the front desk.

I took my ID and credit card out of my wallet and put them in front of the attendant. "Maisie Carver. I reserved a room a couple of hours ago."

She looked young enough to be a college intern, but her demeanor was still more like a high school cheerleader's. "I remember you. You're the lucky one who got the last room," she gushed. "Bet you're glad it's not the one that guy died in this morning."

Julia's head jerked up hard enough to get whiplash. "You wanted to stay in Santa Cruz, Jules. This is the best I could do. Do you want it or not?" That shrug again. God.

I gave the cheerleader my credit card while she yammered on about all of the really cool things to do within walking distance. And they must have been really cool because she said that about ninety-five times before she handed me our room keys.

The elevator was small and smelled like coconut oil and chili dogs.

"We didn't have to stay in Santa Cruz, Jules. We could have gone to Monterey, even San Francisco." Or other places I'd never been. And I had a fierce craving to see them all, to fill Mom's bucket list and mine with the rest of California, the west coast, destinations I didn't even know I wanted to go to until now. But Julia said nothing.

I'm sure the reds and blues of the carnival decor were meant to complement the beach boardwalk theme. The walls were a blinding white with an inordinate number of startling fire engine red accents and framed pictures of the boardwalk rides at sunset. A picture of an arched rock like the one I saw on someone's Pinterest page made me want to park Julia in the room, take off, and see everything like Mom said.

Damnit, Mom. You tricked me into believing you would live forever.

My nose stung hard, a prelude to an ugly cry, but nothing came not one single tear. I swiped the plastic key, and the lock clicked open. I pushed the door open and was assaulted by another red-rimmed mirror that magnified the tracks of tears from my face and down my neck like a funhouse mirror. The little bit of mascara I'd put on this morning said I was ready to suit up for "Monday Night Football." At the same time, Julia was a beautiful blonde zombie, the special guest star on "The Living Dead."

"You need to eat something," I said, unpacking my suitcase so I wouldn't walk right back out the door. "We need to call Willa."

She nodded, laid across the king-size bed, and curled up fetal, eyes closed while my brain buzzed with the to-do list of everything Julia would have already done by now. After everything, including Julia's things, was put away, there was nothing else to do but call Willa. When I sat down on the edge of the bed, Julia scooched over and laid her head on my lap.

"You rest." I swallowed hard. "I've got this."

Did I? Really? The call connected before I could chicken out. "Hey, you." The noise in the background said Willa and Tank were still at dinner. "I dragged Tank out tonight. He said he'd only go if we could go to the Charleston Grill. Lo and behold, they had a 9:30

seating. So, how goes it? And spare me the truth because I know those Cali chefs can give ours a run for their money."

"Will." Her name came out shaky. Julia gripped me tighter, but I couldn't say the words. I just couldn't. There was a clatter, like a fork dropping onto a china plate, but the words still wouldn't come, and Julia was sobbing again.

"No," Willa said, "Maisie, no."

"It's Mom." I stroked Julia's hair like Mom used to do for the three of us when the world was hard. "She died this morning."

"This morning?" Willa barked, like calling her sooner would have changed the outcome. "And you're just now telling me?"

"I'm—." What was I? Stunned? Aching from loss? Writhing in pain from the unimaginable? Sure Rhys had lost his mother, and Tank too; I had other friends who had suffered the same loss, and I'd wept with them, pitied them because their mother wasn't immortal like mine. "Sorry, Will, I'm so sorry. We're just now getting back to the hotel, and Julia—. She's—both of us are barely holding up."

Willa sobbed. I could hear Tank comforting her. "Maise?" His voice was concerned but had an edge because my words had crushed his beloved. "Tell me what happened."

"We don't know—."

"Hold up, here's our waiter." The dining room clatter disappeared, and I imagined respectful diners trying not to gawk at my sister. "Would you get our check? We have to step outside. I'll be back in a moment to settle up."

The clatter resumed; Willa was crying, but I could hear the sound of water in the background, which meant Tank had taken her out by the fountain at the hotel's main entrance. "She wants to talk to you, Maisie." He must have handed her the phone, but all she could do was whimper.

"It happened around 10:00 a.m., maybe 11. There was nothing anybody could do. One minute she was smiling, so happy to be here." This was not the time to tell her our mother died inside a tree. "And the next, she was gone. Julia worked on her, but she was gone before the paramedics arrived."

Willa cried ugly. I squeezed my eyes shut and wished our tears were part of some joint account that was all paid up so she wouldn't have to feel the loss. "It was peaceful." Such a stupid thing to say. If her passing had been so peaceful, why was it ripping us apart? Tank said something and must have tried to take the phone away from her. "No," she whimpered, and Julia started up again, matching Willa's mewling cry like the twin crinoline dresses they used to wear with matching patent Mary Jane shoes.

Eleven months apart, they were Irish twins, and I was the baby, always the baby, but not today. I listened to Willa cry, to Tank's attempts to comfort her. After a while, she pulled herself together enough to say, "I'll tell Dad." Before I could open my mouth to thank her, she broke down again. "What do I say to him that won't make her die every day for the rest of his life? It's gonna gut him. Oh, God, she's gone. I can't believe she's gone."

"Baby. Baby, give me the phone." Tank soothed "Masie? I'm so sorry." His voice broke like his heart was breaking for his wife. "Don't worry about your dad. He'll be asleep now. Tomorrow, we'll talk to the folks at Sunny Side, find out the best way to tell him, and then we'll stay with him. When will y'all be back?"

"Thanks, Tank, but we don't know, probably a few days. We have to talk to a funeral home here to make the arrangements. I know Mom had a plan; maybe Willa knows where it is. If she can't find it, we'll use the same funeral home we did for Rhys. If that's okay with her."

"You know we don't get caught up in worrying about stuff like that. We'll look for the plan when we go over to talk to your dad tomorrow. Is Julia all right?"

I stroked her hair, wishing she still had all the answers "No. Both of us are wrecked. If you and Willa take care of notifying Sunny Side and telling Dad, we'll call all the relatives and make the arrangements on this end."

"We can do more, Maisie."

"I know, but I really want you to concentrate on Willa and the kids, and on Dad. This is going to be horrible for him."

"Done," he said and ended the call.

Funny how death was so final, yet there was always the next thing for the living to do. I took the business card the paramedic gave me out of my pocket and waited for the call to connect. "Santa Cruz Memorial, Lisa Joyner speaking."

"Hi. Your stepbrother gave me your card. My mom died today, and I have to get her home to South Carolina."

The woman's voice was what Jordan would call very chill, which I'm sure came in handy in the funeral business. "Of course, I'm so sorry for your loss. How can I help?"

"I'm going to call the morgue and tell them to take Mom to your place. I don't know what getting her back home will entail, and right now, I don't want to know."

"I understand. Would you like for me to make the call to the morgue?"

I was so happy to have someone else be the grownup. "Yes. Thanks. My sister and I will come by tomorrow to make arrangements."

"If I can help with anything or if you have any questions, please don't hesitate to call. And again, I'm so sorry for your loss, Ms. Carver."

"Masie. Please call me Masie, and thank you," I said and ended the call. "Jules, it's late back East. We'll let the rest of the family know tomorrow." I flopped back on the bed, grateful for the three-hour time difference.

Even with Julia spooned up next to me, I was so lonely all I could do was cry. That was what losing Mom felt like, so goddamn alone. And just when I was sure neither Julia nor I would sleep, I closed my eyes and saw Mom smiling at me.

# Chapter Twenty-Four

**E**ven the California sunrise was chill, making the glorious ones back home borderline obnoxious. Julia was face down on her pillow, sleeping hard. The paranoid part of me, waiting for the third death that would have made the superstition real, checked to make sure she was still breathing. The steady rise and fall of her chest tamped down my paranoia; when she snorted, it was all I could do not to laugh.

It was almost 6:00 a.m., late enough to start calling everyone back East. I slipped into a pair of jeans and grabbed the pink Henry Cowell State Park T-shirt Mom bought for us yesterday before we hit the trail. My mind replayed her buying the matching shirts, hot pink ones, how proud she'd been when she'd pulled hers on over her Ralph Lauren turtleneck. I gave myself a once over in the mirror and fully expected the tears to start, but they didn't, just a warm pressure pulsing tight behind my eyes. My key card was on the dresser beside Julia's. I scribbled a note and headed downstairs.

The continental breakfast was the same as at every hotel, which always made me wonder why they bothered. But the coffee was decent enough. I was the only guest in the dining room and imagined all the CrossFitters who'd booked up the hotel were in their rooms drinking something vile and green or microwaving egg whites and broccoli. I could almost see Rhys, with his cheaters on just after he joined the gym, grunting at the proposed diet to make him bigger and stronger. By sixty-plus male standards, he ate extremely well, except he hated CrossFit staples like fatty fish, broccoli, cabbage, asparagus, celery, and carrots and barely tolerated sugar snap peas. Likewise, he despised kale and did his own Lowcountry version of the diet that would have had the folks here tsking him.

I threw back half of my drink and got a refill before sitting down at a two-top in a corner of the room. Emma would be at work now. I swiped her number and waited for the call to go through.

"Hey, Mom. I'm getting ready to go into a meeting, but it's good to hear from you. Are y'all having fun?"

"Emma——." That's as far as I got.

"Something's wrong. Oh my God. Grandma?" She sucked in a breath. "No, Mom. No." Ever the professional, she didn't bawl; she sniffled and listened while I went over everything that happened yesterday. "When will you be home?" Her tone was even, but the last word was a whisper. Someone in the background asked if she was okay, and she snapped, "Yes," before her voice gentled. "Sorry."

"I don't know when we'll be back. Julia and I are going to the funeral home this morning to find out. I know there are procedures for transporting a body from one state to another. From what I understand, it will take a few days."

"Cam's college roommate's dad used to be a California senator. I can ask Cam to see if he has some contacts who can speed things up."

"That would be appreciated, but my gut tells me we're going to be here until they say we can take her home."

"Can't hurt to try," she said. "How are you and Aunt Julia and Willa holding up? And, oh my God, Grandpa?"

"We're all shaken, and I don't know about Dad. Willa's going to tell him today. It will wreck him, and then he'll forget and start asking for her, and then it will gut him all over again. I know Willa won't leave his side, but that'll wear on her and make it as fresh for her as it does for him every time. If you and Cam could relieve her when you get off work, that would be great."

"Of course. Have you called Jordan yet?"

"At 9:00 your time? No. But I texted him and told him to call me when he got up. Are you okay?" I asked hesitantly.

"As good as I'm going to be," she said. "Want me to see if I can get the morning off and help you make calls?"

"That's okay, honey. Mom outlived so many of her friends there won't be as many people to call as the last time I did this." The words were almost careless until their full weight settled over me. I didn't make the calls when Rhys died. Willa and Mom did.

My heart galloped, and my head swam at the thought of telling the same sad truth over and over again. But I could not go back to being the nutcase I was when Rhys died, not with Julia falling apart. The very idea of her breaking down was foreign, impossible. Yet, I couldn't get the image out of my head of her standing in that hollowed-out tree, watching our mother die, too freaked out to save her.

"Julia's going to take half of the list, so it shouldn't take us long. Don't be insulted if you get a group text with our travel arrangements. It's just easier that way, but I'll call you as soon as I can. Are you okay?" She swore she was, but she was lying, and I let her because I needed her to be okay.

"I love you, Mom." Her words sounded breathy and frightened, like she was worried I would be next. "I love you."

The other forty-six calls weren't as easy as I thought. The rest of the world wasn't as shocked as Julia and I that Mom was gone. There was more resignation in their voices than sorrow. It seemed wrong, but it helped me stay on message like a gubernatorial candidate on a whistle-stop tour the day of the election. Tears stayed in check until I talked with friends of Mom's that were her age or older who had sadly grown accustomed to such phone calls.

"Hey." Julia slid into the seat across from me with a Styrofoam cup of coffee, her phone, and a hotel notepad with names scribbled on it. "Why didn't you wake me?"

"You were sleeping like the dead." I looked up, horrified, before taking a look at her notepad. "You were asleep." I flipped through the pages. "Guess there were less people to contact than I thought. I've called all but four of these."

"Thanks." She winced at the coffee, as much of a coffee snob as she was a wine snob. She glanced at what the hotel claimed were fresh bagels and pastries but looked like the shiny plastic ones I used to play with in my pretend kitchen when I was little. "I'll call the others, and we'll get out of here to find some decent coffee."

"Okay." I switched to orange juice that was not fresh squeezed like the dispenser swore and listened to Julia and her doctor's voice as she made the remaining calls, which was good because I couldn't believe I'd forgotten to call Jim and Sal, Mom and Dad's oldest and dearest friends.

Dad had just turned barely twenty-two when he took Sal to a square dance at the beach pavilion on the Isle of Palms. Mom was eighteen, trying to decide whether Jim was good husband material when she saw Dad attempting to square dance. By the end of the night, Dad talked the country western band into playing a Rogers and Hart tune and then swept Mom off her feet.

Julia's voice was steady, and I couldn't judge her for sounding scripted. I was no better; the words were always the same. "I just wanted to call to say Mom passed away yesterday." The people on the other end must have had a script too. All of them were sorry. The older folks wanted to know all the details to ensure the same thing didn't happen to them. Everyone asked about the arrangements, making me think we should have waited until we knew what they were.

Julia ended the last call and put her phone away. "Let's get out of here, eat some breakfast, and maybe have a bloody Mary or two before we head to the funeral home."

"I could use a drink." I tapped the restaurant app on my phone. "There's a place .2 miles away. The Beach Street Cafe."

"I've been there." Of course, she had. "They only serve beer and wine. I'm going to need something stiffer than a mimosa to get me through the funeral home. Johnny's Harborside is about a mile from here. We can have a nice walk, and they serve liquor."

I started to ask my perfect sister if she needed alcohol or pot to deal with every crisis. But after making the bulk of the phone calls, I saw the wisdom in her thinking. The numbness had begun to set in. I'm not sure I was Novocain numb or eighteen shots of tequila numb, but I must have been to call all the people who loved Mom and tell them she was dead.

We walked at a good clip down Murray Street. It was mostly flat and gorgeous in places. We didn't talk, didn't try to keep up with the flock of super fit elderly who breezed by us, most sporting road warrior braces on their ankles and knees, and were fast enough to make Dave Wottle proud if he was still alive. With the restaurant in sight, Julia picked up the pace. Moments later, we were pushing through the doors.

Julia made a peace sign for a table for two and told the hostess to have our server bring bloody marys when he came to the table. I gave the menu a quick study and opted for the Morning Mule, a drink that promised a refreshing pick-me-up with a kick.

The obedient server was as handsome as the tanned garden variety ones we'd had so far. I was certain that somewhere among the vineyards and organic farms in California was a farm where they cloned beautiful people. His smile was brilliant when Julia nodded thanks for her drink and told him to 'keep 'em coming.' He went through the morning specials that were a lot of the same things you'd find on any harborside menu, but I would have killed for a plate of shrimp and grits from the Hominy Grill back home.

I ordered crab cakes benedict, "And coffee. Lots of coffee." Julia ordered the same, then drained her drink. "So, are we gonna do this drunk?" I asked.

"This is going to blow. You know it, and so do I; we've both done it sober, at least I did when John died, so why not?" The reference surprised me; Julia never talked about her husband's death. She polished off her drink and rattled the ice. The server appeared like magic with drinks for both of us.

Julia made a show of looking into my copper cup to see it was almost full. "This is Mom we're talking about, Masie. Better get at least two of these in you before we hit the funeral home."

Our food came, and we ate in silence. I didn't like the way Julia was pounding the bloody marys and was about as keen about propping her up at the funeral home as I was about leaving her at the hotel to sleep it off. At least she was eating or inhaling her food, and she'd ordered a third drink.

"It's not your fault, Jules."

She was putting the last morsel of food in her mouth but stopped. "Excuse me?"

"It's not your fault," I said. "What happened to Mom wasn't your fault."

"I know that." Her tone was dismissive. She pointed at her empty drink, and the server scurried away to do her bidding.

"I'm sorry. I was just saying what I thought you needed to hear, what I'd want to hear if I were in your shoes."

"My shoes?" She plucked the orange slice off my plate, removed the peeling, and ate it before forking the parsley garnish on hers and eating that too. "There's nothing to be sorry about, Maise. Mom was gone fast. Maybe faster than Rhys." She eyed the key lime pie the lady next to us was having for breakfast and ordered one too.

I sipped my coffee while the ice melted in my second mule and watched Julia eat the pie like she could fill something bottomless inside her. "It's just that you hesitated to help her, that's all. I get it. It was a shock."

"Jesus, Masie. You don't know what I did or didn't do. You were off in your own little world, but it doesn't matter. Mom's dead, and we have to deal with it." The last thing Mom would have wanted was for Julia and me to have a good old sisterly knock-down drag out. But then she'd also be mortified that Julia was plastered well before noon.

Julia motioned to the server for the check. "Look. There are much shittier places in the world to do what we have to do." And she should know. Her husband died on their thirtieth wedding anniversary trip on a near-deserted island in Singapore. Her voice gentled, "So, let's just get through today. Okay?"

Back at the hotel, Julia claimed first dibs on the shower. I sat on the tiny balcony with a view of the parking lot and an ocean mural. The mural reminded me how jazzed Mom had been to see the real thing when Jordan called.

"Morning. Saw your text just now. I got invited to a premier party last night for a new Broadway play and didn't get in until really late. I was so close to getting a part in it, it was hard to go. But I saw the director. He said he loved me in that thing I did in Brooklyn a couple of months ago." His voice was sleepy but sweet. "God, making it as an actor in New York is hard. Sometimes I think I should just pull up stakes and move to LA. How's California treating you?"

"Good," which was true, "And bad. Grandma passed away yesterday. I would have called, but with the time difference Julia and I thought it would be better to wait until today."

"You're kidding," he said. I swallowed the lump in my throat. "You're not kidding. Wow. It's just so hard to believe."

"I know." And told the story again for the fifty-seventh time.

"How'd Emma take it?"

"About like everyone else, sad but not surprised. Willa was inconsolable, but she's got Tank and the girls. She'll pull herself together to tell Dad."

"Grandpa's really gonna have a hard time with this."

"I know. That's the part I dread the most. Anyway, I just wanted to let you know. As soon as we know the arrangements, we'll text everyone. It looks like we're going to be here for a few days until we can bring her home."

"I'm sorry, Mom. Do you need me to come out there and be with you?"

"No, honey. I'm okay. Really sad, but I have Julia. If you want to go to Charleston to be with Emma and the rest of the family, let me know, and I'll book you a flight."

"I don't know." There's enough silence to worry me. "Emma's still pretty torn up over Dad. I get it; I miss him too. I'm sorry he's gone. It's just that she was so close to Grandma that I don't think I can deal with another display. Not that I doubt hers was authentic," he added hastily. "It's going to be hard enough watching you and the aunts bury Grandma so soon after Dad. It's all just—. The only way I can describe it is weird."

"I know, honey. Let me know if you change your mind about going home. I'll get you on the next plane out. I love you, Jordan."

"Love you back," he said as Julia came out of the bathroom, dressed but with a towel wrapped around her head. "And Mom?'

"Yeah, honey?"

"I'm so glad you're alive."

"Me too, baby. Me too."

I took my turn in the bathroom while Julia called the funeral home to let them know we'd be there within the hour. I stripped and glanced up at my reflection in the full-length mirror on the back of the door, surprised and maybe even a little shocked to see the dirt caked into the skin on my forearms from where I belly-crawled out of the tree yesterday.

The shower felt good, and I was grateful I'd swiped some of the fancy shampoo and body wash from the Chaminade. Squeaky clean, I turned the hot water off and left the cold on. The jolt made my heart race well enough that I was sure I wouldn't be the third shoe to drop. When I came out of the bathroom, Julia was dressed in a long-sleeved gray maxi T-shirt dress mom bought in the youngish department of the Finicky Filly back home. Her hair was damp but pulled back in some kind of twist, something Mom used to do. Something Julia never did. She looked so much like Mom did twenty years ago that my knees wobbled.

Julia smoothed the dress over her waist and looked almost embarrassed. "Mom would be mad if she knew I didn't bring a dress."

"God. The lecture. 'Be prepared for anything and everything.'" We laughed, and she blushed, something Julia was always too confident to do. "You look great, Jules. Really great."

"I didn't know if you'd be okay with me wearing it. If you're not, I can put on something else."

The resemblance still had me reeling. I barely managed to shake my head before blurting. "I'm fine with it."

She didn't seem to notice the price tag peeking out from under her arm. I thought of Mom, how much she lived for the excitement of wearing a new outfit, and how she adored pretty clothes. How in the last couple of decades, more often than not, she always forgot to take off the price tags.

When I was a kid, and my heart got broken, Mom's remedy was a full day of shopping and a good meal. Always with the disclaimer: "Shopping and good food won't solve all your problems, darling, but they sure as hell don't hurt." I swallowed hard and could almost hear her sweet laugh as I snipped a tag off her dress for the last time.

# Chapter Twenty-Five

"Three days? From today?" Julia snapped, making the young woman behind the desk at the funeral home flinch. But hadn't Julia agreed with the EMT after he'd said the same thing?

Lisa Joyner was close to Jordan's age, a sun-drenched Cali girl who looked more like a model than a funeral director. She was dressed in a smart black skirt with a silky turquoise top. Her bracelet and necklace were funky, a mix of copper intertwined with chunks of turquoise and cobalt. Her wild blond hair was tamed into a loose ponytail clasped at the base of her neck, a standard issue black blazer slung over the back of her chair, only hers was made of a thick nubby weave and cropped.

"Please understand, it's the paperwork between our states that takes so long, not our process. I faxed all the forms first thing this morning, but these things take time." Her thin smile was genuine and not at all creepy for a millennial undertaker.

"That's bullshit." I squeezed Julia's hand hard to calm her down and shut her up.

"Your brother mentioned it would take some time," I said. "My daughter's fiancé has a contact here in your state government; he's trying to expedite the process, but we don't even know if that's possible."

"This has only happened a couple of times since I started working here. In all of the instances, the deceased were military." She opened an antique-looking brown binder with Mom's name on the spine. "On the phone, you said you were using the Stuhr Funeral Home in Charleston. I have their contact information and have already spoken with the director there before you came in. He sends his condolences."

Julia smiled and squeezed my hand again.

Years ago, when our Grammy died, her cousin, a chocolatier in the Adirondacks, couldn't come to the funeral but sent a huge box of artsy chocolates and a beautiful greeting card with condolences stamped in thick gold script letters. I was only six and thought condolence was a fancy name for chocolates, and Julia and Willa did too for about a minute. So for years, whenever I had a chocolate craving, I would beg for condolences.

Mom let it go because she thought it was cute; my sisters did the same because it affirmed I was mentally inferior to them and most likely adopted. Not that one has anything to do with the other; it was just that big sister kind of love that always came with a generous dose of humiliation.

"I'm pretty sure the funeral home in Charleston sold Mom and Dad some kind of program, like college savings plans where you pay a little for the funerals over several years," I said.

"They did," Julia said. "Willa should be able to find it in Mom's files."

"I'll circle back to Schur. They should have a copy in their files if they sold her the policy. Depending on the type of plan your parents purchased, there's a possibility it may cover transportation," Lisa said. "We need to discuss container options and clothing. If your mother had a favorite outfit back home that you'd like her to wear, you can have your family overnight it to our address."

While I didn't know much about funeral layaway plans, I knew Mom picked out what she wanted to wear to her funeral a few years ago. The outfit was in the back of her closet, a cream-colored silk blouse with an expensive azure blue suit that was two sizes too small. Mom knew that when she bought it but reasoned she'd probably have shed a few stubborn pounds before her death, and it would fit fine.

The jacket had pulled hard across her shoulders, but the sleeves, which she always had to have let out for her long arms, had fit just right. Though she wasn't particularly religious, she took it as a sign from God as she stood on the pedestal in front of the three-sided mirror, holding the skirt that wasn't even close to zipping with one hand while fluffing up her hair with the other. Even though I was completely creeped out by the idea of mom buying a funeral trousseau, I could see she was hopelessly in love with the outfit and was practically forced to buy it since it was half-price.

"Or we can shop for something here," Julia said.

I wasn't sure how Mom would feel about being buried in something that wasn't Charleston chic, but there had to be a store here that catered to the eighty-plus crowd. And she would have adored the idea of Julia and I shopping together.

"If you're not overnighting something from home, I'd like the outfit today. If this is too difficult, let me know what you have in mind, and one of our staff can purchase something for you."

"We'll do it," my sister and I said.

"Jinx," Julia whispered.

"Good. Now, on to containers." Lisa scribbled some notes before looking at us with practiced, gentled eyes. "I understand your mom has probably purchased a casket back home, but we have to get her there. You could buy one here and ask the funeral home for a refund on the one she purchased. Since she paid for everything some time ago, it's doubtful you'll get it. The industry discourages prepaid funerals for a lot of reasons, primarily because funeral homes can and do go under, and most of the ones that don't rarely offer cash-back options. Still, it never hurts to ask. If they say no, and you don't want to purchase a casket here, there are two options."

I tried not to look horrified, but the options were terrible. Mom would be dressed to the nines, put in a plastic bag, and placed in a corrugated container, which was just a glorified term for a cardboard box. Even more horrifying, option two offered the same clear plastic zippered bag, minus the box.

"Like a Ziplock bag?" I asked, and Julia burst out laughing. "What is wrong with you? One minute you're drowning your sorrows in bloody marys and breakfast food, and the next, you're cackling like a hyena in a funeral parlor."

"It's okay," Linda said. "Laughing is as much a part of the grieving process as crying."

Julia swiped at her eyes and sighed, but there were still little hiccups of laughter. "What?" I snapped.

"Don't you remember?" She snorted. "How we used to tease mom about Ziplock bags?"

Mom always put everything in zippered plastic bags, not just things in the cupboard or the refrigerator. Even more so after she and Dad moved to Sunny Side and she was forced to consolidate their belongings. She was such a Ziplock fanatic Julia used to tease, "Thousands of years from now when archeologists unearth your domicile, they'll find everything perfectly preserved in plastic." At the time, Mom had played along with the joke, but it wouldn't have surprised me one bit if she'd risen from the grave and put her foot down on wearing a body-sized Ziplock bag.

"So our only options are just a plastic bag or one that comes with a box?" I asked.

Lisa steepled her hands on the desk. "Look, I'm definitely not trying to push another casket on you, but your only other option is to buy an inexpensive one to get your mother home. Lots of companies sell discounted ones online, even Costco and Walmart." Mom loved price rollbacks as much as anyone, but she wouldn't go for a Walmart coffin, not even temporarily.

Lisa tapped on her iPad and then put the screen in front of Julia and me. "This company can provide one for less than two thousand dollars. They're the only ones I trust to get it here today, which you will need should your contact with the government come through for you."

A good idea, but it was hard to get past the name of the company, Coffins To Go.

"What do they have in blue?" Julia asked.

"The color of the ocean," I added.

Lisa took the iPad back to search before placing it in front of us again. "Nothing from their regular stock." She pointed to the lone blue one on the clearance page that was not a pretty Pacific blue like I'd hoped and looked like it had been dyed to match Papa Smurf. "This is the only blue one, but I know for sure they will get it here fast."

Julia and I scrolled through the other pages. Even with all the crazy shit I bought after Rhys died, it was hard to believe we couldn't order a decent-colored blue casket online. But it was seventy-five percent off, and Mom always did love a good sale.

The banner at the top of the page screamed, "Prices slashed to the bone." We scrolled through page after page of heavy ornate wooden models and showy metal ones. Another banner claimed none of the caskets had "protective rubber gaskets that can cause gasses to build up, and in some cases make the casket explode." So that was a plus. With no more blue models to choose from, we scrolled back to the Smurf one. The website confirmed they had fifteen in stock.

"Maybe we should just get her a good one," I said to Julia.

"You can do that," Linda said. "We have a good selection, but they start at just under ten thousand dollars."

"The one she chose at home is blue." Julia ran her finger over the picture of the smurfy one. "This is a hideous color, but it's just to get her home."

"Alright." Lisa took Julia's credit card and finished up her notes. "You have my card, and I have your contact information. You can drop the clothes off at the front desk. Someone will be here until 9:00 tonight, and again, if shopping is too much, we're here to help."

"Shopping is never too much," Mom's words came out of my mouth. But after six hours of trying to find elderly Charleston chic in northern California, we gave up and went back to the hotel to look through Mom's things. Julia changed out of the gray dress that was the favorite for now. I went through Mom's seventeen outfits for a third time, but none were right.

"She always loved the way a nice gray dress set off her silver hair, but I don't think she'd go for that look now," I said. "Not with the startling blue casket anyway."

Julia pulled a pair of yoga pants out of her bag and fished around in my suitcase until she found my dirty Henry Cowell State Park T-shirt. "She should wear this. We can wash the T-shirt in the laundry room down the hall. It's perfect."

"You've lost your mind," I folded the gray dress into the plastic hotel bag, along with Mom's powder pink bra and panties, her favorite black Stuart Weitzman sling-backs. "This is what she would pick out. If she were—." The tears started to build again, and how could they after yesterday's marathon crying jag?

"But this is what she was wearing when she died," Julia said. "And she was happy, Maise. So happy."

The vote was tied, so I called Willa. She said Dad was a mess but that his Memory Care unit friend Katherine was sure Mom was somewhere on the cruise boat with her children and the captain. "They've been walking around the facility and the courtyard looking for them for hours," Willa said. "Honest to God, I just don't have it in me to tell him again that Mom's gone. Not today, and if I have to choose between deluding myself and the truth, I'm right there on that boat with them.

"How are y'all holding up?"

"We're okay," I said. "Did our thing at the funeral home. They're saying we might be able to take her home Wednesday."

"Emma told me she's got Cam on trying to get y'all home sooner."

"I know. I'm not counting on it, but we have another problem. Julia and I are at odds on what to dress mom in."

"Didn't you get my text?"

I clicked on my messages, but the last text I'd gotten from Willa was when Tank was still in the hospital. "No."

"I'm sure I sent it this morning." She growled and swore to herself. "No wonder I forgot to press the Send button. The gist is

I overnighted Mom's funeral suit to your hotel. You should have it by 10:00 tomorrow morning. I didn't send underwear because she packed plenty, and she's got those black sling-backs she loved so much she bought two pairs."

I blew out a breath. "That's a relief; I'll let the funeral home know. Julia wanted to dress her in a T-shirt and yoga pants."

"Tell Julia we'll dress her in a T-shirt and yoga pants when she dies, but not Mom."

Julia smirked and threw an arm around my shoulder. "We're shopping anyway, Will. Mom always believed in having at least one backup outfit. Sure, she has seventeen, but it's a good excuse to shop.

"I just texted you the tracking number, but you all go ahead and drown your sorrows in retail therapy. I won't judge."

No, she wouldn't, but the joke she didn't intend to be a jab hit home. It had been weeks since I returned the last box from drowning my own sorrows. I wanted to promise Willa I'd be good, but that might mean explaining to my perfect older sister just how far off the rails I'd gone after Rhys died. "Thanks, Will. How are you doing?"

A tired sigh followed a poor attempt at a laugh. "Does it count that I tell everyone I'm fine? Probably not. It's so hard to believe Mom's gone, but it shouldn't be. She was eighty-five. I'm the only one of my friends whose mom is still living, so in my head, I get it. It just doesn't feel real. I'm not sure it ever will."

# Chapter Twenty-Six

It was our mission to find Mom's backup outfit that made me give in to the magnetic pull that drew me into every single shop and boutique. The same for Julia, only she favored any place that hawked jewelry over clothes and shoes. But the problem with shopping for someone else is you can never find anything for them, but you find everything you don't need but adore for yourself.

I repeated the mantra that never worked on impressionable school children or myself. Just say no. Just say no.

Julia's penchant for pretty accessories landed us in the Artisan Gallery, where she found a necklace similar to the one our server at breakfast wore. I doubted she bought hers here because the piece Julia asked to see and a collection of similar pieces were expensive and showier in an understated kind of way. The chunks of cobalt and turquoise bound together were bigger. The chunky copper wire reminded me of the Pacific at sunset. Julia announced she'd take the necklace and bracelet and surprised me by buying what even I would call ear bobs. Though she always dressed in longsleeved tops, she added the matching wide cuff bracelet to her haul, but we still had nothing for Mom.

"That clutch." Julia pointed to a gorgeous piece in the if-you-have-to-ask-how-much-it-costs-you-can't-afford-it section of the store.

The saleslady's face flushed. Her voice raised an octave, and I was pretty sure she was close to orgasming over the possibility of such a big sale. Handing the purse to Julia pushed her and her breathy voice right over the edge. "It's made by a local artisan who only does commission work. I saw some of his at a show in Seattle and begged him to do a few for us. The purse is veneered with redwood. Young redwood, of course, which is easier to work with."

Julia examined the gold trim and opened the clasp that the woman pointed out was genuine onyx. The lining was midnight blue, an odd choice of color, but it would look nice with Julia's other purchases. "I'll take it." The woman quivered as Julia handed over her black Amex card, but we still didn't have a backup outfit.

Two stores later, we gave up and went to a Mexican restaurant that didn't look like much, but ninety-seven percent of the reviews on Yelp claimed the food was fantastic. Our hostess was pretty and petite, with long dark hair and dark eyes. She was dressed in a short baby doll tank dress and bearing enough skin that I was sure she was inked from the base of her long slender neck to her ring-covered toes. I'd never thought of tattoos as art, but hers were beautiful.

"You want?" Julia's words made me realize I was gawking, but it was hard not to try to read the fancy script words wrapped around the woman's wrists like bangles. Was there an overall meaning to all that ink? Did it hurt like hell? She offered us menus and announced the drink of the day, a cocktail called a detox. It sounded yummy, vodka, fresh grapefruit juice, fresh lemon, and basil-coriander served up in a dainty little martini glass, but I passed when our server came and just ordered water. Julia, who was never a cheap date, ordered two detox drinks and a gordita, which was apparently not a Taco Bell creation like I'd thought.

Of course, everything on the menu was organic and local and sounded delicious. I was not very hungry until another server strutted by with a mouthwatering plate of goodness. Our server saw the lust in my eyes and said the dish was something made with roasted corn, squash, onions, cheese, and sour cream called a calabacitas.

"Okay. That." I pointed to the calabacitas instead of slaughtering the Spanish language with my Charleston drawl. Julia rattled off something in Spanish. I wondered if she ever wakes up on some days and feels the burden of being perfect and knowing everything.

Until now, I'd never really thought about her superpowers being more of a curse than a blessing. Especially when it came to working on Mom, trying to revive her while the practical part of her brain screamed Mom was already gone. Or Dad laid up in the ICU with tubes protruding from him. Rather than standing there, nodding at the doctor and not understanding a word he said like Willa and me, Julia would have known exactly what he meant, every possible thing that could go wrong, along with the mix-and-match horror stories that went with them. Then she would have had to dumb it down for Mom, me, and Willa.

Who wouldn't hide out from that if they could? Who wouldn't choose Fiji, or any place for that matter, over having to translate medical speak while her heart was breaking? God, I'd been so stupid, so selfish, holding on to my anger. I snagged one of Julia's drinks when the waiter put them on the table and downed the liquid courage.

I wiped my mouth with the back of my hand. "I have something to tell you."

"You want to wait for another?" Julia asked.

A tiny basil leaf floated in the dregs that were so good I wanted to lick the glass. "That was really good, but no. I have something I need to say to you."

The server returned in record time with two more drinks. "I do, too, Maise. I've been working up the courage all day, and if I don't tell you now, I'm going to be really, really drunk."

First born, first in everything. "Okay, you go."

"This is hard to say." Her voice was tentative, without a trace of the good Doctor Watson. "I know you were upset with me for not going to Rhys's funeral, and you have every right to be. The truth is I just—forgot. I—."

I didn't recognize the low growl of my voice until the screaming ensued. "You forgot my husband's funeral?" This was so like Julia and her whims to come and go, to extend her Fiji vacation just because. What about her family who needed her? What about me? "My husband of thirty-two years? God, Julia, you were always selfish in that I'm-a-professional-and-I'm-entitled-sort of way, but this is a new low, even for you. Hell, forget about Rhys' funeral and how much I needed you; you deserted us when Dad fell. Me, Willa, Mom, we all needed you. God, we needed you, but you've given yourself a pass to opt out of all the messy things that come with family. What the hell is wrong with you?"

The words continued to spew out, rancid bitter words I'd never be able to take back, and I didn't want to. The freedom of letting them fly was more potent than any cocktail. But people were staring, and the manager was talking to our server. Julia put her hand on mine to stop my screaming.

"I have Alzheimer's, Maise."

The room spun like a roulette wheel, pockets marked with names instead of red and black, Willa, Masie, Julia. Spinning, spinning. A sing-songy voice from my childhood hollered, "Someone's gonna get it. Someone's gonna get it." I'd been sure that someone was me.

"I have the genes," Julia said. I grabbed her hand and held on for our dear lives. "They tell you not to get tested; they say if you have the genes, it doesn't mean you'll get it, and it will mess with your mind."

"But you got tested?" The clatter returned to the dining room; ice melted in glasses while my heart broke.

She nodded. "I got the results when I was on vacation in Fiji, and Dad was in the hospital. I have all four genes, Maise. It was a lot to wrap my head around.

"After that, I started second-guessing myself, trying to appear competent on the outside but making myself crazy inside. I told myself I was just being paranoid, but my work began to suffer. Then, last month, I stood over a patient to do a simple coronary artery bypass graph. I've done hundreds of them since I've been practicing, but I didn't know what to do. I couldn't remember, Maise.

I told one of the nurses I was sick, and I left the OR. I saw a doctor a few days later. She confirmed the diagnosis."

"We'll get a second opinion," I blurted.

"I did," she said softly. "Four of them."

"Then get five. Damn it, Julia, get as many as it takes to tell us you don't have--." I couldn't say the word. My body vibrated with anger at the Alzheimer's roulette wheel for having the audacity to land on Julia. Part of me was thrilled it hadn't been me, but a voice in the slippery recesses of my mind hissed maybe the disease would claim a twofer.

"I do, Maise. The scans don't lie. After the incident in the OR, I took an immediate leave of absence. It was self-imposed, but there was nothing else to do but retire. A few days later, Rhys died, and I had to come for you, for Mom and Dad. Seeing Dad like he is always does me in. All I can think about when I visit the Memory Care unit is this will be me one day. It's going to be me." Her voice tailed off until it was so small, I could barely hear her over the restaurant noise. "I don't know what happened the day of Rhys's funeral—."

"That doesn't matter now, Jules." It had been such a big fucking deal then. Now her absence was an explanation, a confirmation of the impossible. "It doesn't."

"I wanted to be there for you. It's just that my mind got messed up, and my body went right along with it. I woke up sometime during the night, dressed for work, got in my car, and drove to the hospital. I knew something was wrong when I pulled into the hospital parking lot. Aside from being exhausted, I knew I didn't belong there anymore. I fell asleep in the car and saw your messages when I woke up. I wanted to tell you what happened, to explain, but this disease is so tricky. I feel fine physically, hell, I even feel okay mentally most of the time, and then something will happen to remind me I've got this disease, that it's going to win. It's going to take my mind. That's why Mom is dead. She's dead because of me."

"That's not true, Julia. You said so yourself, and so did the paramedics."

"I'm a cardiac surgeon, and I couldn't even remember how to perform CPR on my own mother." Even when she cried, she was beautiful. "I'm so sorry."

The food came. I picked at my meal while Julia dug in like her life depended on it, and maybe it did. She ordered another cocktail, and I finally got it now. She wanted to feel full; she wanted to feel that swimmy feeling from too much vodka. She wanted to grab onto life and hold on tight until she didn't recognize it anymore, and I couldn't fault her for that. After hiding an entire house full of brown cardboard boxes, I couldn't fault her for hiding the horrible truth that was bound to get one of us. "I'm sorry for being mad at you."

"You didn't know." She dismissed my guilt with a wave of her fork. "Believe me, if you'd done the things I have, if you hadn't showed for John's funeral, I would have been livid."

"Dad takes medication—," I blurted.

"Some drugs claim they can slow the progression, but they can't stop it. Plus, they make me sick, so sick I decided to just do without. The pot helps. Sometimes I think I'm better." Hope radiated from my entire being until she qualified her diagnosis. "At least I feel better without the prescription drugs. I still have the hiccups that draw me back to my old life. They seem so real. It terrifies me, Maise.

"But it's a fact, one day, I'm going to be like Dad or Katherine, and I'll wander some memory care unit looking for the OR or for John." Her deep blue eyes were lonely and scared and brimming with remorse. "I know where this train is going. I'm not happy about it. It took me a long time to get to where I am now, but I accept I have this disease. There's peace in that. What's not okay is that I hurt you. I'm so sorry."

# Chapter Twenty-Seven

Truth is as exhausting as death, but not for Julia. She tried to talk me into lounging on the beach, but I needed a nap. And to be honest, after watching her consume two heavy meals and a half dozen drinks, her boundless energy made me feel old.

I opened the sliders to hear the ocean. Even though we were across the street from the mighty Pacific, the only noise that filtered into the room was from cars gunning up the hill on Riverside Avenue. I drew the curtains before pushing Julia out the door to stroll the beach or swim a couple miles to wear herself out while I napped. But I couldn't sleep, couldn't stop thinking about what she must have gone through since her diagnosis, worrying if and when the symptoms would show up, doubting herself every time she forgot or mislaid something.

It made sense she couldn't tell the family. She was Julia, after all, and would have probably broken her neck trying to climb off the perilously high pedestal she'd been on since birth. At the restaurant, she told me she'd told Dad about her diagnosis on one of her visits to the memory care unit. His response was the same as it would have been for a skinned knee or a broken heart. It's gonna be all right. And God, I hoped he was right. Still, there was a fluttering of sick pleasure in my chest from finally knowing something about my big sister that nobody else knew. Still, I didn't want this secret for her.

The wind picked up and bowed the bottoms of the curtains like starched, red hoop skirts while the Pacific did her best impression of puny Atlantic waves. The noise lulled me into a hard sleep, and I was at home, on the phone with Mom. She is telling me how wonderful she heard the new iPhone 30 was. "Is that what you want?" I teased.

"What do you want, Masie?" she asked in her best heart-to-heart tone.

I wanted Dad's mind to be right, and I never wanted Julia to lose hers. I wanted to know what to do about her secret. And what about Rhys' secrets? Did he know he was sick before he died?

He used to tell me everything. When did he stop, and why did he stop loving me? Was there a moment, like some doctor saying, "Yes, Mr. Carver, you're missing the half of your heart your wife occupied?"

"What do you want, Masie?" Mom's voice was so faint I could hardly hear her.

I opened my mouth to answer her, but the hotel room door clicked open. I was barely awake when I whispered, "Jules?" The bathroom door closed. The shower started, and I drifted back to sleep, back to my mother and Rhys.

They were Dick Clark people, beautiful, godlike beings who never aged. Men like Rhys choose women like Julia. Why did he choose me? How could he feel like he belonged to me when I never felt like I belonged to him? It took a while to get past his looks enough to know and love him until I didn't anymore. What made me stop? A moan yanked me out of my dream.

Oh, my God. Julia must have fallen in the shower. I sprinted to the bathroom door and turned the knob until I heard a different, throatier moan and a voice that was not my sister's. Julia said something back, but not loud enough to make out what she said. A man laughed. She shushed him. Both of them laughed. Julia's sharp gasp sent me scurrying back to bed.

What was she doing? God, I knew what she was doing, but this guy was a total stranger. He had to be. What was she thinking? Was this part of her eat, drink, and be merry philosophy? But grief and shower sex and Alzheimer's just didn't jibe, or maybe they did.

I feigned sleep until the hotel room door opened and closed, and Julia came into the bedroom. "How was your nap," she asked.

She was dressed in her black linen outfit that was somehow never wrinkled. Her hair was still damp from the shower, and her face was flush from sunshine and sex. I didn't have to look in the mirror to know I looked like hell, and my stomach felt like it was somewhere down around my ankles.

Julia couldn't have Alzheimer's. She just couldn't. I wanted her to burst out laughing and tell me that whole bit was just a cruel joke. I wanted her to tell me about the guy, but she didn't.

"Get up and get dressed. I want to go down to the boardwalk." She put on a pair of gold hoop earrings that Mom would have said were too big for her to wear at her age. But then what would Mom have said about the mystery man in the shower? If Mom were here, that wouldn't have happened. If she were here, Julia probably wouldn't have told me about her diagnosis. She would have gone on pretending for all of us until when? Until she got in the car for a loaf of bread and ended up in Florida like Dad did?

"You know I hate puke rides, and you'll want to ride all of them," I said. "Let's just go to dinner and call it a night."

She tossed a pair of her yoga pants at me, along with my Henry Cowell State Park T-shirt that was somehow freshly laundered. "But you love funnel cakes and saltwater taffy and caramel apples and fried Twinkies."

She had a point, several points. The breeze off of the ocean was too cold for the T-shirt. I put on the pants, plucked Julia's red longsleeved T-shirt out of her bag, and pulled it on. I loved this double-role reversal. I loved being the little sister with Julia in charge. "I've never had fried Twinkies."

"Well, we're having all that and chocolate-covered jerky too." Her poor imitation of Sam Elliott made me laugh. "Beef. It's what's for dinner."

Although I can't speak for chocolate jerky everywhere, carnival food generally has a universal standard of being too sweet or greasy. Still, everything we'd had so far, especially the jerky, was delicious. I ate my way through half the boardwalk while trying to ignore Julia's attempts to get me onto thrill rides with names like Cliff Hanger, Typhoon, and Shockwave. There was also one called a Fireball that looked like a giant eggbeater and promised to provide "disorientation at its finest. "No, thank you," I said for the thousandth time.

We ended up standing in another food line while I answered texts from Emma and Jordan. I felt a little guilty about forgetting them all day, but it had been a really weird day. When I glanced up from my phone, we were not in line with the thick rope of people waiting for fried Twinkies. We were in line for the Ferris wheel, which was admittedly tame in comparison to the puke rides. But I got dizzy just standing on a chair to reach the top shelf of my pantry.

I turned to bolt, but Julia grabbed my arm. "I am not doing this, Jules." My head shook so hard it rattled. The ride behind me started. I felt the swish of the cars as they twirled into the air. Up. Up. Up. Obnoxious calliope disco music blared out of speakers to camouflage the old ride's creaks and groans that screamed, Look at me. I'm a death trap.

"I'm going to be sick." A lie guaranteed to part a crowd.

"No, you're not." Julia laughed and held on tighter. "Come on, you're doing this for Mom."

"I'm not doing this. Period." I tried to pull away, but she was surprisingly strong. "You know I'm afraid of heights. Besides, Mom hated carnivals."

"She did. She thought they were tacky and dirty, but she adored the Ferris wheel. And she wouldn't want you to be afraid, Maise. I don't want you to be afraid."

The brawny operator brought the ride to the traditional stop at the top. People in the upper cars screamed because they were dying,

275

while others laughed and waited for their turn at the top of the world.

"Maise, I'm not afraid," and I knew she was not talking about Ferris wheels.

Operators of puke rides always have a sick sense of who to terrorize. "Good luck," he smirked and winked as he slammed the bar down, locking us in the flimsy metal death trap. My knuckles were white against the skinny sliver of metal that was supposed to keep us from plummeting to our deaths. The ride jerked to a start. My eyes slammed shut as it stopped to fill the next car and the next until we were going up, too far up. "I want out. Oh, God, I want out."

The sadistic operator made the ride spin faster. My heart hammered hard enough to break. Julia laughed and pried one of my hands off of the bar. The constant sense of rising and falling confused my brain, but when she threaded her fingers in mine, I was untethered yet grounded. Bound to my sister and floating.

"We're flying, Maise. And the view is so big, and the sunset, it's so damn beautiful."

How could the insane rise and fall be good? God. Oh, God, the ride stopped, but we weren't on the ground. Julia squeezed my hand. "I've got you, Maise. Open your eyes."

I did, just enough to see the world the way she did, and the sunset stole my breath right along with my fear. Even when the car rocked, my eyes were wide open. The wind blowing off of the ocean

276

stung my cheeks. "It's gorgeous up here and quiet," I marveled, and so close to heaven, so close to Mom.

Julia stared out at the fading sunset. "I fucked a boy. At least he was a boy to me," she said matter-of-factly, and I prayed Mom couldn't keep up with her hearing aids in heaven any better than she could on earth. "He said he was mid-forties, but I think he was younger."

"What makes you think that?" She looked at me and laughed? "What?"

"His ass was truly spectacular. Men in their mid-forties don't have asses like that. Unless you're Hugh Jackman, or Derek Jeeter. The guy had a really nice one at the age when muscle mass usually starts to go." Not Rhys. Maybe it was genetics or all the workout stuff he did even before CrossFit, but he had a terrific ass.

"Oh." I tried to sound nonchalant, "Was it good?"

"That is so not what I expected you to say." I squeezed Julia's hand as the ride jolted and then made a quarter turn before stopping like it was presenting us to the Pacific ocean.

"What question would that be?"

"My guess would have been, 'What were you thinking, Julia?'" She'd gotten that right. "Why did you do it?"

"Why did you do it?"

"I just wanted to feel what it was like, to be naked, to feel that close to someone again. To just feel." Her last words were almost wistful. "Maise, I don't know what this disease is going to do to me. And I'm so tired of ticking off the stages of progression in my head on the days I remember them. I just want to feel alive." The ride jolted again, and we floated back to where we'd started. The operator's smirk was gone, and he even looked a little disappointed I hadn't fallen apart.

"Rhys asked for a divorce before he died." I almost hoped she didn't hear me above the boardwalk noise, but her incredulous look said she did. "Not like weeks or even days before. It was like he lived just long enough to say the words. Then he died."

The ride jolted to a stop again. Julia put her arm around me. "Why didn't you tell me?"

"Because I was mad at you. Because you're perfect."

"I'm not perfect," she said. "Are you okay?"

"I thought I was, but I don't know. Most of the time, everything's fine, but it's hard to get that out of my head. I wish I could forgive him. I wish it was like the honey-dos he gave me that I always forgot." I cut myself off. "I'm sorry. That was thoughtless."

"Stop. It wasn't thoughtless," she said. "There are things I'd like to forget but haven't. Yet. You're okay, Maise. You may not know it, but you are okay."

There was no need for a tattooed lady attraction; almost everyone wandering the boardwalk was inked. A hoot considering back when I was a kid, people used to pay good money to see the tattooed lady who would blend right into the masses here. The man in front of us in the frozen cocktail line had the most beautiful eagle spanning the entire width of his massive shoulders. It peeked out from under his CrossFit tank top that matched his date's. Only hers was tied up to show off her belly. Intricate bangles inked her impressive biceps, and the head of a lioness just above fancy script letters disappeared into her jeans.

"Stop staring." Julia nudged me. "It's rude."

"I'm not staring," I whispered. She gave me a look. "Okay, they're just really tacky. Besides, it's not like I've never seen a tattoo before."

"You want one," Julia she teased and ordered two frosty red drinks in elaborate plastic cups that screamed Apocalypse Now.

"No." My face flushed harder than when I was six, and Julia caught me trying on her bra. "God. No."

"You do want one." She laughed as I attempted to steer her away from all the beautiful, tatted people. "There's nothing wrong with them. If you want one, why not?"

"Because I'm terrified of needles. Because I'm not twenty, and there's such a thing as gravity." I took a long draw of the twisty turny straw and tried to blink away the alcohol-fueled brain freeze.

"Because of that commercial where the guy gets No Regerts burned into his arm."

"You're an ex-teacher. There's no way you'll let anyone get away with a misspelled word. Besides, they're not the kind of needles you're thinking."

Sure, I knew that. I'd seen movies and that commercial where you don't see actual needles, but you know that's how the ink gets under the skin. "Tattoos just seem prettier here. If it didn't hurt, and I know it does. I might get one. Something small, someplace that will never sag and look like melted crayons." Was there such a place on a fifty-something-year-old body?

"Come on," Julia said and downed the rest of her cocktail. I made a lousy attempt to finish mine because I really needed it if I was actually considering this. "I know a place."

Of course, she did, this Julia who remembered I loved trashy carnival food but conveniently forgot how much I hate needles. Before I could back out, we were sitting in the waiting area, having a ball, flipping through notebooks of tattoos, the tame, the racy, the beautiful, and the hideous. Some were just—I don't even know. But there was not a misspelled word in the bunch.

"How about this one." Julia pointed to a simple design that said Sisters in pretty script letters and had little pink roses at the beginning and the end of the word. "He could put the roses together there." She pointed under the center of the word. "Make three of them for you, Willa, and me."

"Okay." This actually seemed doable, and we were already here. "There's a cute tattoo place on Johns Island. We'll have to drug Willa to get her through the door, but she'll thank us later."

The problem with getting a tattoo is that you can't just walk in and get one. There was a lot of consulting and waiting while other, more serious human canvases got inked up. But my Slurpee cocktail was wearing off, or maybe the constant buzzing of the machines was sobering up this virgin. That was what they called me even before I told them I was a first-timer, and God, it was as scary as the first time I had sex, only there was no foreplay to distract me from the fact that this was really happening.

A happy customer left while the artist got ready for us. He discussed the design with Julia and excused himself to make what Julia explained was something like the fake tattoos my kids used to wear when they were in middle school. He returned with the template, which I would have been perfectly happy with, and grinned. "Which one of you is first?"

His name was Shaun; he was dreamy and, from the look of it, was inked everywhere. He had that easy California way about him that would make anyone jump at the chance for him to jab needles into their skin.

"You go," I said at the same time Julia said, "Maisie's first."

Shaun gave me a conciliatory smile and then looked at Julia. "Okay, if you go first?"

281

"Sure," she said and sat in a chair beside his table. They chatted for a few moments, discussing colors and where Julia wanted the design. She said the forearm. Shaun nodded and readied to ink my sister. Julia unbuttoned the cuff of her prim linen shirt that always came off as sexy.

"Fuck." A beefy guy on the table across from Julia made me jump.

God, was it hot. Or was it me?

The burly guy winced hard as the other artist on duty jabbed him with needles. Hundreds of tiny needles. The giant eagle's claw on the beefy guy's jugular was red and puffy, and why would anyone even think about doing anything that hurt so much?

"Fuck," his bark was sharp. The artist backed off and asked him if he was good to go. He was being tenderized with ink. Of course, he wasn't good. But the burly guy was no virgin. An elaborate dragon head snaked out of the waistline of his pants, mating underneath his tank with a smaller snake, the two of them in a love dance that looked like it covered his entire chest, their heads meeting in an Eskimo kiss at the base of his throat.

But the neck couldn't have hurt any worse than having his chest or below tattooed. And what did the artist do when he got to the nipple? Did he leave it plain, like a third eye? Or did he jab the needles into—?

"Jesus, fuck. That hurts," the brawny dude looked at me with tears in his eyes.

My heart jackhammered. The room spun like a puke ride, and I barely made it to the unisex bathroom. I hugged the toilet and tried not to think about how men are pigs, which was why I avoided unisex bathrooms at all costs, much less hugging a toilet in one. Everything I'd eaten for at least the last week came up, but the room wasn't spinning anymore. And, from what I could tell, the room really was surprisingly clean. I rinsed out my mouth, wet some paper towels, and sat on the toilet lid. God, I was such a chicken.

The burly guy had stopped swearing. At least I couldn't hear him with the vent over the toilet blowing cold air on the back of my neck, but my heart rate was nowhere near normal.

This was silly. Sister bonding ink wasn't worth dying for. I should just march myself out there, like a grown-ass woman, and say, "Thanks, but I'll just take the press-on tattoo."

I turned on the faucet and washed my hands three or four more times because I really had been on my hands and knees in a public restroom. I rinsed my mouth out again. The mirror was filmy and old, so I looked filmy and old. But I embraced my age. I embraced myself.

"I can't do this because I'm not brave enough," I said to the girl on fire, who was a little green around the gills too. "I'm not Julia," who was probably smiling and chatting with Shaun while he worked. Who knows? Maybe he was hitting on her, and she'd bed a twenty-something for a nightcap.

I was not, nor will I ever be my sister, and that was okay. I threw open the door to tell her so and froze.

Other artists were busy working. The burly guy was gone, and a skinny blonde was in his place. But my sister—. God, my sister. She was wearing a black spaghetti strap camisole; her trademark linen shirt was folded beside her on the table. The realization that I hadn't seen her in anything other than something high-necked and longsleeved since—. I couldn't remember the last time I'd seen her in anything but.

My mouth gaped open at the good doctor, the perfect child whose back and arms were covered in ink. Needles buzzed like killer bees. Incredulity and curiosity to see her story, to know her story propelled me forward until I was touching her. She looked back at me to assess my reaction to her torso which was completely inked. John's name was a cliche within a heart over her beating one, the rest—. There was just so much ink I couldn't make sense of it all.

"Maise?" she said. "Are you okay?"

Shaun glanced up at me, his eyes jacked the way a kid's are on Christmas morning. "Your sister has some exceptional work. The tat she got in Vancouver should be in an art museum." I nodded blankly and touched her skin that still looked young, so much younger than her sixty-five years. There were random words and phrases that held no meaning for me. A storybook mermaid with long, flowing red hair and tiny intricate scales was perched on a rock between her shoulder blades. A tribute to her daughter, who always swore she was going to be a mermaid when she grew up.

Intricate angel wings spanned delicate shoulder blades with writing too fancy to make out. Mother was written just below the base of her neck and sat alongside Father. Underneath were Dad's words, his beautiful truth. It'll be all right.

I traced my fingers over the script letters on the wing to try to figure out what it said, what it meant. Up and down, up, down and again. My God, it was my name. I did the same with the other wing. Willa. Julia covered my hand on her shoulder with her own while Shaun raved about the artistry of Julia's body. He put the finishing touch on the last of the tiny rosettes below the word Sisters, then covered the fresh ink with sticky plastic. "They're just for me," Julia said softly, touching one of the angel wings. "I'm afraid I'll forget you and Willa have always had my back, will always have my back. I don't want to forget, Maise. I don't ever want to forget."

I swiped at my tears and rolled up my sleeve.

# Chapter Twenty-Eight

In the end, it took four full days to get Mom home to Charleston, and during that time, she died a thousand times for Dad.

It would have been cruel to give her the kind of funeral she wanted with an open casket and have him there, and we just couldn't do that to him. Mom had always put in the effort to look beautiful, no matter what the cost, but in her azure suit that the funeral home in Santa Cruz slit up the back to make it fit, she was stunning.

Before her body was prepared, I'd hit up Google for information on smiling corpses, something she'd asked for when she made her funeral plan. Could it be done? Was it an actual thing or something that might terrify mourners? Not that that was her goal. Mom loved her body, especially her face, and was always so happy. And as creepy as the idea of a smiling corpse was, I wanted to see her smile again, the crinkled lines around her eyes that would, of course, be closed. Granted, the idea would probably seem morbid to the average funeralgoer, but that was what she'd wanted. And part of me believed her death would be easier to take if we could all see her smile one last time.

My Google search on smiling corpses produced thousands of Instagram images of men posing with lifeless wild animals and murder selfies—I didn't click on those to find out what those were. Then there was the occasional grinning soldier posed with his lifeless enemy. With no clear etiquette or precedence, I told the funeral home to do their best with the smile and just make her up like they normally would. Either way, she looked beautiful.

Not long after we told Dad, we stopped reminding him she was dead. It was the humane thing to do. So, on the day of Mom's funeral, he was still as happy and laid back as he'd been his whole life, though he spent most of the day looking for her. Thankfully, he'd gotten it in his head that she was shopping, something she adored, perpetually shopping, something we'd all remember her for.

Tank picked him up to go to Dairy Queen before we headed to the service. After lunch, they went over to the Isle of Palms to see the annual sand castle competition. Truth be told, if the pastor asked for a show of hands, we'd probably all rather have had an Oreo cookie Blizzard and a trip to the beach than attend another funeral.

I sat between Julia and Willa, our arms linked in love and grief, inked with a single word no one knew about but us. Willa's tattoo was from the temporary ones Shaun made for us. Willa would probably never set foot in a parlor, but in that moment, we were the Jenkins girls, bound by ink and blood, there to say goodbye to our beloved mother.

Jordan sat in the pew behind us with Julia's daughter on one side of him and Emma and Cam on the other, and then Tank and Willa's girls. Most of Mom and Dad's friends were long gone, so it was just a few friends and us. Apparently, there was a sliding scale for relatives who turned out in droves when people like Rhys died young. Not so much for Mom, who should have, at the very least, gotten a gold star for making it to eighty-five. She just didn't rate a personal appearance.

From top to bottom, the service was all Mom's show, but nothing like her. We weren't sure how or why she chose the two hymns that played on a continuous loop, thanks to the diligent organist who looked like she didn't have a pulse. I guess those were the only ones Mom knew, and she was worried about the last impression she'd leave.

She booked the gig like it was a seven-day cruise where everything was different. Not bad different, just not her. If she had been true to herself, she would have picked tunes from Eddie Fisher, Perry Como, names that still made her swoon until the day she died. And Frankie Lane, God, how she loved him, and Elvis. But she opted for "How Great Thou Art" instead of "Jezebel" or "Hound Dog." That hymn bled into "Morning Has Broken." Cat Stevens joined in my head in that squeaky, small voice that made me wish we'd hired a soloist to break up the drone of the organ.

Jordan put his hand on my shoulder, which was finally healed, and gave it a squeeze. I turned to smile at him and Emma. He was dressed in what he called his funeral suit since it was the same one he wore to Rhys's service, the only one he had. He owned a very nice tux he bought to wear to some fancy New York thing. He thought Mom would like it if he wore that to her sendoff, and she probably would have, but the matching shoes pinched his feet, so I told him the funeral suit would do just fine.

Emma was dressed in her King Street finery but looked like hell. Her stress-induced eczema, which had almost always been kept to discrete but annoying places, had crept up the back of her neck, headed for her beautiful face, and made huge patches on her hands and feet. I kept asking her if she was okay. She swore she was, but her body said otherwise.

Was it work? Was it Mom's or Rhys' death? Was it me? I tried to talk to her, but she begged off and said not to worry. The eczema was better, and she was getting better. But she wasn't. It was clear from the way she looked at me that she bought into that death comes in threes thing. If I told her about Julia's Alzheimer's, that would really send her over the edge. Cam nodded at me with his serious lawyer smile, but I could tell he was worried about her too.

The pastor took the podium and talked a lot about heaven, how pretty it was, and the fine gowns all the angels wore. Mom would like that, but she'd want to make her own adjustments to the outfit, lobby for more than one style, just to change things up a bit, or maybe a gown for each season if there are seasons in heaven. And shoes. I can honestly say I've never seen a painting of an angel with shoes. Mom would put a stop to that with really cute comfortable shoes, or maybe the high heels she adored and wore for a decade or two longer than she should have.

The sadness was different, more like a dull buzz than the gushing barely contained vat I carried when Rhys died. Part of it was a fairytale that said Mom could not possibly be gone because she has always been. Maybe that was where this bittersweet resignation came from. That and my gratitude she didn't go from cancer or dementia, from anything that disfigured her or affected the little sashay she always had even when she wasn't in too-high heels.

The pastor finished his bit, and Emma's daughter Vanessa, the firstborn grandchild, rose to give a eulogy all five grandkids helped write. Julia's already regal posture stiffened with pride at her only child, the good and brilliant doctor who would one day outshine her mother. But Vanessa didn't know about the Alzheimer's, something Julia wanted to fix before Vanessa left.

She was tall and blonde and had a serious boyfriend she showed off in Charleston last summer, also a brilliant doctor from London, and they'd made no secret that their plan was to settle there. Vanessa wouldn't drop what she was doing across the pond to come home and tend to her mother. Not that she needed to now, but who would take care of Julia when those hiccups she talked about turned into everyday life? She couldn't stay in Richmond alone, with just a few friends who were busy doctors.

"Our grandmother taught us a lot," Vanessa began. "She taught Emma how to rock high heels when she was six, and she's an absolute master." The small crowd laughed. "She taught the twins how to dance the shag when Jordan and Emma and I proved to have two left feet. She taught Jordan the true meaning of love and acceptance when he came out to her when she hugged him and told him the only difference between her love for him when he told her five minutes ago, was five minutes. She loved him more, would love him more with every breath she took. And me—." Vanessa's voice cracked and stopped. Her head dipped with the weight of grief, but only for a second before her tear-stained face rose with the strength of a warrior.

"For me, it was the way she cared for Grandpa when he had his bypass surgery. I was only 7, but I was hyperaware of the way she tended to him. By the time he was released, she knew almost every patient on the floor and not just what they were in for. She knew their stories.

"My mother is the finest doctor I've ever known, but I remember thinking then that I wanted to be a doctor like my mother but practice medicine the way my grandmother lived."

The pastor nobody knew closed the service. We filed out of the funeral home and piled into the stretch limo.

I was different now. The flip-flop sisterhood that took me back to the time when I was the little sister was gone for good. But my question was answered. Who will care for Julia?

I will.

A sort of good game mentality comes when a body makes it to eighty-five, happy and stupid in love. I couldn't even feel the grief, but I imagine it was still there, smoldering with the convolution of feelings I had and probably would always have for Rhys. I'd just been too busy dealing with Mom's death to feel them.

We waited our turn to put a dainty shovelful of Lowcountry dirt into the grave. Jordan, who was sitting beside me, said, "Break a heel," and everyone laughed.

I looked down at the Jimmy Choo pumps on my feet that Mom had hidden in the back of her closet. Sleek black five-inch spiked heels that had me teetering when I stood. As best we could figure, Mom bought them on a rogue shopping trip just this year, which was good. Just watching her attempt to walk in them would have been terrifying.

While I totally got the azure suit she bought, we were all at a loss over the Choos. I suggested we bury them with her along with the stunning redwood clutch Julia bought for the occasion that was loaded with Mom's compact and favorite tube of Elizabeth Arden lipstick, her wallet, and canceled credit cards. The consensus was that Mom should stick with her comfy Stuart Weizmans, but each of us would wear something of hers to her sendoff.

Mom's long rope of very good fake pearls was still knotted like the picture of Vogue she was trying to copy. They looked beautiful on Willa, who was perpetually slim and didn't have the boobage Julia or I had that made some of those long necklaces look stupid. Julia chose the dangly pair of earrings Mom bought at Forever 21. Emma and I had taken Mom shopping and couldn't find her. When we finally found her in the store, she pretended to be lost and a little addled, but she really wanted those earrings. And, I think in Mom's mind, she really was forever twenty-one.

Since the shoes fit me and they came from a wishful place, the sisters thought it fitting for me to wear them.

Julia tossed a shovel full of dirt into the grave and handed the short spade to Willa, who did the same. When it was my turn, I stood, threw back my shoulders the way Mom taught me.

"Walk heel to toe, sugar. That's right. Visualize walking a straight line and make small steps. And never rush. The world will wait for you, Maisie, darling. Don't you ever doubt that for a second."

# Chapter Twenty-Nine

The gathering at Willa's stately home South of Broad was everything our mother adored, gorgeous table settings with plenty of delicious Lowcountry food and excellent wine from Tank's collection. Petal pink crystal vases with impressive arrangements from Willa's garden were everywhere, along with enlarged photographs on white easels of Mom in various stages of her life. My favorite was one of her and Dad at a shag competition. The photo caught them in mid-twirl, grinning at each other like they'd already won the contest before it started.

Dad had them practicing for weeks to The Platter's "With This Ring." He'd convinced Mom the judges would get a kick if he pulled out a little black box with a Cracker Jack ring, dropped to one knee at the end of the tune, and pretended to propose. Mom thought it would be cute and promised to really ham it up for the judges. But she didn't have to. Dad never bought that Cracker Jack ring. When he dropped to one knee and opened the box, there was a beautiful engagement ring inside, and like the refrain of the song says, a promise to always love her.

An arm slid around my waist. I looked up at Jordan and then laid my head on his shoulder and sighed. "I love this picture."

"I do too. She looks so happy," Jordan said. "That's one thing I'll always remember about her and Grandpa. I know their lives weren't perfect." I gave him a doubtful look. "Okay, maybe they were perfect, but they were just happy people. I don't have a single memory of them being anything but."

"Except when you were four and decided to pretty up Grandma's entire living room with crayons."

He shrugged. "I was artistic and bored. That's a bad combination with sixty-four Crayolas and a built-in sharpener."

The next poster-size photo in our makeshift gallery was of all five grandkids gathered around Mom in their Christmas pajamas, the only present they were allowed to open on Christmas Eve. She was reading The Night Before Christmas, her face warm and animated. The twins were asleep while Vanessa and Emma, and Jordan hung on her every word. My finger trailed over the image until tears threatened. "I miss her." But I was tired of crying, tired of sadness and loss. "I'm always going to miss her."

"Yeah." Jordan hugged me. "She was a great mom and grandma; it's part of the reason you and Aunt Julia and Aunt Willa are going to be okay. But I'm worried about Emma, Mom."

She was across the room talking to my mother's second cousin Bart who could be chatty and even a little flirty after a half glass of wine, but Cam knew this and was there by her side. Bart's face was flushed and grinning as he told some funny tale, completely unaware of how sad Emma and Cam were.

"I am too, honey, and I've told her so." Cam nodded and said something to Bart before taking his bride-to-be out to the garden. "She won't talk about whatever's bothering her. Says it's work, and honestly, maybe it is. But her eczema has never been this bad, not even during her first year of law school."

"If I were to bet, which I suck at, I'd say it's Dad. She can't talk about him, won't talk about him." Jordan's words sat heavy in the pit of my stomach. Other than the day Emma took me to task in the cemetery, neither of the kids had said much to me about their dad. Was that the reason Emma was hurting? Because we didn't talk about Rhys? Was Jordan such a great actor that he covered up his grief?

297

"And how are you doing with that?" I asked, not for the first time.

"I was calling his number at least once a week to tell him about an audition or just to check in. I'm down to once a month now. That's better, but I can't imagine a time when I won't miss him," he said. "Have you tried to talk to Cam about Emma?"

"Other than saying he's got this, Cam's as mum as she is, so I don't know what's going on. I'd say they're having pre-wedding problems, but I don't think that's it. Just look at them out there in the garden, the way he holds her, the way she looks at him, leans on him."

"She used to call and text too much. Was I seeing anyone? Had I seen any good shows? How'd my audition go, and then back to was I seeing anyone? Now, she doesn't call or text, and she doesn't always respond when I call or message her. Maybe I'll get a canned text a week later that says, 'Thanks for reaching out,' or "Love you too.' But that's all, and it's just not like Emma."

I gave him a good poke in the ribs. "So, you do miss your sister calling every five minutes."

"I love her." My boy sounds weary. "Maybe it's because I am so far away, but I worry about her as much as I worry about you."

"I'm okay, Jordan, and even if I wasn't, it's my job to fix that, not yours. I can't make Emma spill her guts, and neither can you. We just have to trust that she's taking care of herself and that she and Cam are handling whatever this is."

Aside from our immediate families, all the friends and relatives who stopped by the wake were gone by four o'clock. Everyone rolled up their sleeves to set Willa's house back to picture-perfect. None of us knew what to do with any of the poster-size pictures of Mom. Last night we'd sat around Willa's kitchen table and dealt a huge deck of old black and white and color photos evenly before trading them like baseball cards. We did this while sharing our best stories about Mom, and we all walked away with at least one favorite picture. I chose the one of Mom and Dad at the shag competition. I wished the newspaper photographer had had the presence of mind to take a picture of Dad's proposal, but I got the picture I wanted most.

At one point, even Emma joined in, flipping through the photos she was dealt and discarding most of them until she found a half dozen or so she wanted to keep. There was so much good-natured teasing around the table and laughter from remembering shared pasts. I saw Emma smile a couple of times. Really smile. It gave me hope and made me wish I'd had the desire or the presence of mind to have done something like that when Rhys died.

These days, they call funerals celebrations of life. That's what last night was, what today was. We called Rhys's service that, but it was hard to celebrate someone's life when it was cut short. Too easy to be caught up in the shock of it all. And if the deceased threw out a zinger like Rhys did and then up and died, it made it even more impossible to celebrate that life. Maybe it would have helped Emma if we had gone through the photos of Rhys, the videos and talked about the really good times. And there were a lot of good times. Maybe it wasn't too late.

Kitchen duty called, and too many of us banged around Willa's kitchen until she threw us out. Emma and Cam said they'd meet us at Sunny Side for dinner with Dad tomorrow. They hugged everyone goodbye. Emma lingered with Vanessa, who'd made her and Cam promise they'd come to the UK in September. Emma took Cam's hand and waved goodbye.

"You still feel up to taking dinner to Dad tomorrow?" Willa asked.

"Yes. I think everyone will be there." And then I remembered what Julia had said about how hard it was for her to visit the memory care unit. "But Julia and Vanessa probably want some alone time before Vanessa heads back to London tomorrow."

"We're going." Julia's look said she was okay with it, for now, at least. She filled a bag with cookies and brownies and those pralines Dad loved so well. Her smile was sad and sweet as she sealed the Ziplock bag, the overall mood a little more somber as we loaded up the food to take to Sunny Side for our first big family dinner without Mom.

When Jordan and I arrived in Memory Care, everyone was in the private family dining room. Dad was in great spirits after his Blizzard and the beach yesterday. He wasn't sure who any of us were or why we were there, but he doled out hugs to everyone and said he was tickled to death to see us. He kept asking if it was Christmas because there were so many of us. He hugged Julia long and hard and then introduced her to the rest of us as his daughter.

"I wish my wife was here so you all could meet her. She'll be around directly. Must be off getting the camera; she's such a fool about taking pictures," he said. "I'm just so happy you all are here."

He didn't recognize me or any of us except Julia, but there was such love in his eyes, so much love. We set the table in the family dining area. Last night, we debated over whether we should make a place for Mom. We'd decided not to in hopes that Dad wouldn't notice, that it would be a small step toward forgetting the one person he'd never forget., although it would be easier for him if he did. It would be easier if I came back tomorrow or for my Sunday visit and found him occupied with helping Katherine find her children on the cruise boat or his next-door neighbor, George, who's about Dad's age but was stuck in his late teens and was always worried about being late for a biology class that doesn't exist.

Dad did a quick headcount. "Julia, dear, set a place for your mother."

Julia did and sat down beside Dad, who took his place at the head of the table. He didn't know her smile was pained as she struggled with the empty place setting on one side of her and a glimpse of what her future will be like on the other. Dad squeezed her hand and introduced her to us again with the same fanfare he used to have for Willa and me. "This is my daughter, Julia. Why, she's the smartest, prettiest girl you'll ever know. Just got out of med school and is a——." It rattled him that he'd forgotten the few lines he always remembered.

"Cardiac surgeon," Vanessa added.

"Yes! You'll have to excuse me. I just don't remember things like I used to. Yes. She's a cardiac surgeon." Dad beamed. "But I'm sure you know since you all are friends. Anyhow, she's Millie's and my only child." He looked at Mom's empty place and asked Julia, "Where's your mama, honey? I hate that she's missing the party."

"She's here, Dad." Julia swiped at tears, "She's somewhere around here," she added when he looked confused at the empty place setting.

Ever the perfect host, Dad raised his glass, and we all did the same. "Millie and I just want you all to know that any friend of Julia's, is——." Without Mom, the fact he didn't know me hurt more than the usual twinge in my chest that reminded me it was just his Alzheimer's.

"Family." He was delighted his struggle to find the right word was over and laughed. It was such a nice sound. It made me grateful he has always taken everything in stride, including his illness. Tank poured the last of the expensive red into Dad's glass. Dad smacked two little pink packets on the table, opened them, and then added enough Sweet N Low to suit his palate before raising his glass. "To family!"

The dining staff wouldn't let us do anything to clean up. In thanks, we left a mountain of food and sweets along with the flower arrangements from the wake and filed out to our respective cars with somber little smiles from Mom's sendoff. Cousins hugged and promised to keep in touch. Everybody congratulated Jordan, who checked his email after dinner and found he'd gotten a *Law and Order* guest role. He'd never been a fan of the TV show, but a gazillion successful actors had turned up on the show at one time or another, so it was a big step in the right direction. I was happy for him but sad he had to catch the first flight back to New York tomorrow. Vanessa was heading home to London, too.

The love fest continued until it was my turn to hug my daughter. "I love you, Em."

Her eczema disappeared in the dim streetlight, and she was stunning with her father's thick dark hair, his angled cheekbones that made her look like a runway model, and his perfect nose before some perp broke it back when he was a beat cop.

"I know you get tired of me asking, but how are you doing?"

"I'm fine, Mom." She shook her head and pulled away.

"Are you?" Everyone else was still laughing, saying their goodbyes.

"Not here," she barely got the words out. She missed my mom; I knew she did. But every second of every day, she missed Rhys, and no wonder. She saw him every time she looked in a mirror. "Please. Not now."

Cam rescued her and said they had to go. It wasn't so long ago that he was begging for my help.

I was grateful Emma had Cam, but it stung that she wouldn't let me help. "Why don't you come over this week?" Whatever was bothering Emma, she and Cam were tackling it together. I knew that was the way it should be. Still, their autonomy left a hollow space inside me that would only get bigger when Jordan headed back to New York tomorrow. So before Cam or Emma had time to make up an excuse, I added, "Or whenever you have time, both of you. Come for dinner, or we can go out if you want."

"Sure," Cam said. "Emma has my schedule; she'll check hers and set it up." Emma slanted a look at him, and I knew not to hold my breath.

"Can't wait," I said, but it was hard to watch her go.

Rapt in conversation about theater and fashion, Jordan and Vanessa were as entertaining as they were when they used to argue Legos versus K'nex and Barbie's unfortunate wardrobe choices. It was a lovely sight after such a long day.

All of us had earned another glass of wine, or twelve, but since the kids had early flights tomorrow, we were drinking coffee, de cafe for me, and munching on benne wafers and Key lime cookies. I'd already tucked a bag of each into their respective carry-ons so they would carry a little bit of Charleston home with them. Knowing Jordan, he had already stashed his cookies in Vanessa's suitcase so he wouldn't have to work them off at the gym, but also because he adored her.

"New York doesn't appreciate you, Jordie," Vanessa cooed, the only person who'd ever been allowed to call him that. "You're a brilliant actor." She swatted at him when he snorted. "Stop it. You are. They're all just too stupid to recognize your talent. Come to London, Jordie. Oh, please. You'd be a superstar." She punctuated the thought with jazz hands.

"I'll get right on that, Molly Shannon." He toasted her with his empty coffee cup, then put it in the sink. "But if I want to make that 6:00 am flight, I have to go to bed." He kissed Julia's cheek and then mine. "Love you." Vanessa squealed when he picked her up and gave her a little spin. "And you rock."

"No, you rock." Vanessa parroted the words they'd said to each other for decades and gave him a long hug.

Julia stood and stretched. "It's almost one in the morning. We should all go to bed."

We headed upstairs to our respective rooms. Julia and Vanessa elected to bunk together in the guest room since Vanessa had been here for less than forty-eight hours. I got ready for bed and then noticed the St. Michael's medal Rhys wore when he was a street cop. I'd meant to put it in Jordan's suitcase along with the cookies, but I forgot.

I threw on a robe, walked down the hall, and knocked softly on his door before opening it. He was sitting in bed with glasses on, something new, the glow from his laptop illuminating his beautiful face. "Sorry to interrupt," I said. "I know this probably offends your fashion sense, and you won't wear it, but I found your dad's medal. Thought you might like it."

"Thanks." He took the necklace, studied the charm, and then looked at me. "You okay?"

"Yeah, I'm just so tired of grief, honey."

He nodded. "Is that what's wrong with Aunt Julia?" This was not my secret to tell, not even to my son. He held up his hand. "You don't have to answer that. I'm just worried about her too." My sweet boy with a biting wit and the biggest heart. "I know you said she's okay, but nobody's okay, and I feel bad about leaving tomorrow." He looked at his watch. "No, in a couple of hours."

"Honey." I sat down on the bed like I used to do when he was little and wrangled me into as many after-bedtime minutes as possible. "Early on, you and your sister sort of chose up sides. I know that's not how it should be, but Emma gravitated to your Dad because they were so much alike. You did the same with me. Your Dad and I tried to fix that over the years, even things out, but after a while, it was apparent to both of us that's just the way you and your sister are wired. That doesn't mean he loved Emma more than you or I love you more than her; it's just how it was. I know Emma is still struggling with your dad's death, and, my guess is, you are too."

He tried to shrug it off, but his sad smile said different. "I just miss him."

"I know you do, but from the moment Emma entered this world, she was a daddy's girl. She's always come to me when she has girl problems, but anything else, she went straight to your dad. He loved that, and I was glad they were so close." There was no jealousy or hurt in his eyes because Rhys had been a good dad to both of our children.

"I know he loved me." The affirmation wasn't some consolation prize. Jordan's eyes and his voice said he knew as sure as he knew his own name.

"He did. With all his heart, he did." I swiped at my tears. "Look, I really didn't know what you or Emma felt until my own mother died. I had her for fifty-three years; I can't imagine losing her when I was in my twenties. I just can't. What I'm trying to say is, it will take time for all of us to deal with your dad and your grandmother's deaths. But my guess is it will take Emma a lot longer."

He looked at his watch again. I took it as my cue to leave and kissed him on the cheek. "Love you. What time do you want me to take you to the airport?"

"Don't worry about it," he said, settling into bed. "I scheduled an Uber. I'll sleep for a couple of hours and then head out around 4:30."

"Not happening. I'm taking you." He rolled his eyes at me, but his smile said he still liked a little mothering. "Cancel the ride and get some rest."

I headed down to my bedroom at the other end of the hallway. The light in Julia and Vanessa's room was still on. There was a soft, steady voice, and someone was crying so softly I wouldn't have heard it if the house hadn't been so quiet. I knocked but didn't wait for permission to open the door. Julia and Vanessa's heads turned toward me. Vanessa's arms were wrapped around Julia's tatted body that told her story. One of the spaghetti straps of Julia's camisole slipped down her arm. She pushed it back on her shoulder and somehow maintained her doctor's face, but she was broken from telling her daughter the truth.

# Chapter Thirty

**E**ven though Vanessa's connecting flight to New York didn't leave until midmorning, she poked her head in the kitchen just after 4:00 am. Fresh-faced and dry-eyed, she surprised me by asking if she could catch a ride to the airport with Jordan. "Sure." I pulled another travel mug out of the cupboard.

"Help yourself to coffee. I made two breakfast sandwiches. You and Jordan can split them."

"Brilliant," Vanessa said, digging into her sandwich while filling her cup with hot black coffee. She took a long draw. "Coffee," she sighed. "Hospitals everywhere would shut down without it."

She looked so different than the crushed, broken young woman I saw in her mother's arms just a few hours ago. Maybe it came from her ER training that demanded she stays calm. But her strength, her determination that everything would be okay, was the Julia in her. I felt for her. She'd lost her father when she was an undergrad. Knowing that at some point in the not-too-distant future, she was going to lose her mother to Alzheimer's was a lot for someone her age.

"Good morning." Julia stood in the doorway of the kitchen, her silk robe tied snugly about her perpetually thin waist but not covering her tattoos completely. Vanessa's cheery demeanor cracked for a second when her mother kissed her on the cheek. She wanted to stay, but if I knew my sister, she wouldn't let Vanessa stay. Not when she was on the career path she'd always wanted, not when she was head over heels in love with a sweet man and his equally lovely country. But was that really fair to Vanessa? Wasn't this the time she should be here? When Julia had far more good days than bad? "Packed and ready?" Vanessa nodded. "Good girl."

Jordan bounded into the kitchen and headed straight for the coffee pot. "Hello, gorgeous." Vanessa gave him a peck on the cheek before he could take the first sip. She giggled when he wrapped his arm around her neck like he was going to give her a noogie, but she knew Jordan had rather muss his own perfectly coiffed hair than spoil hers. Still, she squealed like she did when she was ten.

He let go of her and then kissed Julia and me on the cheek and did a good job of not being stunned by the ink that, until now,

Julia had kept well hidden. "Nice," said the boy who celebrated quitting his real job to become an actor by getting a tattoo of a phoenix on his upper arm. "Are you riding to the airport with us too?"

"I think I'm heading home." Julia cut me off before I could protest with a look that said, Relax. We'll talk.

"You're sure, Mum?" Vanessa's Southern accent morphed into a British one from time to time and was as thick as if she'd already crossed the pond.

"I'm sure. And you should leave now, or Jordan won't make his flight, and he'll miss his possible toehold on stardom." Julia gave Jordan a hug. "It's really hard for a doctor to say this but break a leg." She doled out hugs and kisses to the kids and raised her coffee cup to me in a promise that we'd talk when I got back.

I was not surprised when her car was gone. The cute magnetic pad stamped HONEY DO on the refrigerator had a note from Julia.

*Dearest Maise,*

*I'm headed back to Richmond for now. I need to figure out what I want while I still can and make arrangements for when I can't. Please don't tell Willa about the Alzheimer's, not now. When I get things figured out, I'll do it, and I'll need you with me when I do. But I'm just not ready, and after everything she did for us and for Dad, and for you when Rhys died, I think it's better not to tell her just now. Although, she'll probably be a little pissed at me for keeping this secret.*

*I'm glad you know, and Vanessa. She wanted to stay and take care of me. I'm just not there yet. And I can't let her give up her life and the love of her life to sit around with me and wait for this disease to progress when I have no intention of sitting around and waiting for this thing to overtake me. I'm okay. For now, I'm okay.*

*I miss Mom and imagine I always will, but I'll be okay, because you and I are good again. And that means the world to me, Maise. Call me when you get home from the airport. It's a long drive back to Richmond, and I could use the company.*

*Love, Julia.*

I didn't think I would feel good about Julia going back to Richmond, but after talking her home to Virginia for the better part of six hours, I felt much better. And it was downright inspiring, the way she was getting on with her life, heroically taking control while she could.

"Thanks for talking me home. The GPS says I'm 15 minutes away."

I added the last item to my grocery list for Trader Joe's. "Are you kidding? You did me a favor. I had you on speaker phone the whole time and got the yard weeded, closets cleaned out, and did three loads of laundry."

Julia laughed. "Willa would be proud."

"She'd be shocked about the laundry, although I don't know why I'm actually putting it away. I'm still waiting for the world to be like it was on the Jetsons."

"Ah, the Jetsons. Pretty sexist with George coming home from work and having poor Jane and that robot wait on him hand and foot. They set up a generation of girls for disappointment when we got to adulthood and discovered there were no robots to do everything, including laundry."

"But it would be cool if there were." I shoved the last stack of towels into the linen closet. "Someday."

"I've got to run into the grocery store for a minute, but thanks for talking me home."

"And I'll talk you back. Anytime."

"Love you, Maise." She sounded happy and normal and not at all like a ticking time bomb. I hated that she had Alzheimer's, that Willa or I could have it too, but Julia had the right idea. Live and love as big as you can, for as long as you can.

"Love you back."

Trader Joe's was the great equalizer in the Holy City. Everyone from semi-hippie millennials to Charleston bluebloods, from construction workers to yogafide soccer moms, was there for cheap produce, great food, and a happy vibe.

Although I had come in for just a few things, my basket was almost full, and I was magnetically drawn to the freebie area at the back of the store. The sample table was hopping with a hoard of health-conscious shoppers who shunned the sweet lemon pound caked and lined up for samples of soy ginger kale salad. I was ready to belly up to the bar for cake when I saw the CrossFit nurse from Rhys' viewing.

Munching on free kale, she stood out in the sea of shoppers and was more beautiful than the rest of the health nuts. Her long hair was balled up in a messy bun. Without her scrubs and makeup, her face looked younger, her rock-hard body intimidating in her capris-length workout pants and sports bra. Her midriff was bare with bulges of solid muscle where most women had a healthy layer of fat. A gold belly button ring glistened against her tanned skin. She was deep in conversation with the sample guy as she nibbled on salad from a tiny paper cup with an even tinier wooden fork.

I maneuvered my cart behind her to listen to the sample guy, who was obviously hitting on her, go on about the virtues of kale. The guy said he loved the stuff but teasingly said he was more of an arugula man. He grinned and flirted and tried hard to keep his eyes focused on her face but failed miserably. I had to agree her boobs were kind of fascinating. While my sports bra smushed mine into submission, hers were so perky and firm, I bet you could have bounced a quarter off of them.

She wore the extra muscle she carried well, unlike some CrossFit women who looked like they'd strapped on a Michelin Man suit. Something about love was tattooed on her lower back in curly blue script, which probably didn't qualify as a tramp stamp since she must mean Jesus or her dad. At least, I thought it said love; I couldn't make it out. My eyes bore a hole into her backside when she turned around.

"Mrs. Carver?" She blushed and was a little creeped out that she'd caught me ogling her tattoo. "I'm Cassidy Kramer—from the viewing. Rhys-- Mr. Carver's viewing. How are you?"

"Um. Fine. How are you?" I chirped and met her beautiful, sad eyes. Had she had a bad WOD? Had another patient died on her watch?

"Good. I'm really glad to see you." But her expression wasn't good. She bit her bottom lip and sucked in a breath. Her upper abs did a fascinating dance when she blew it out again. "I know this may sound weird, but I'd like to talk to you. Do you have a minute?" Her tone made my face flush hard. Was she the reason Rhys wanted a divorce?

Cassidy swiped at her eyes, laughed, and apologized for her tears. At least, I hoped that was what she apologized for. "There's a new coffee shop next door. I won't take much of your time."

"Sure. Just let me check out."

She went to her checkout lane, and I went to mine. Her basket was full of superfoods. Mine was full of comfort food and chocolate. When she paid and glanced up to see if I was still there, her smile was off. If she was the answer to why my husband was grieving, I was good with not knowing. I was good with forgetting everything except the six oversized chocolate bars in my cart. I just wanted to leave the store and eat as many of them as possible before I got home. But her eyes were sad, so sad.

The Now Open banner above the coffee shop flapped in the breeze. Cassidy opened the door and looked over her shoulder to make sure I was still behind her before striding to the counter and ordering some complicated iced skinny something. I ordered a small black coffee and could barely sip it without the cream and sugar I always put in.

She chose a table in the back of the store, and we sat down. She didn't say anything for several minutes, so I did. "You have something you want to tell me?"

She nodded and wrapped her hands around her cup without looking at me. "I know you were wondering why I came to the viewing, and I would have come to the funeral if I could have, but I had to work. So anyway, the truth is—."

"Whatever you have to tell me, Cassidy, I don't want to know."

She had just enough millennial in her to be so engrossed with herself, she continued. "I loved your husband."

My heart plummeted to my stomach and beat like a full brass band. I tried to look calm and took a sip of coffee to keep from bolting. Pain radiated from her; fat tears rolled down her young cheeks and plopped into her fancy drink. "I just loved him."

She hurt, and she needed some sort of absolution from me. But I did not feel anything resembling charitable.

"Carrie." I ground out the wrong name like it didn't matter like she didn't matter, and she didn't bother to correct me. "Rhys is dead. He's not coming back. Nothing you can do or say is going to change that." I pushed back from the table and tossed the drink I didn't want into the trash. "So, whatever happened between the two of you, please, just keep it to yourself."

The barista ducked through double doors for cover like a bartender in one of those old westerns just before a shootout, leaving Cassidy and I alone in the shop. "But that's what I wanted to tell you," she blurted. "What I need to tell you. Please."

She got up from the table and stood about a foot from me. Eyes downcast like a child, ashamed of what she'd done, of what she and Rhys had done. Had she broken up with him? Was that what sent him to therapy? The good news, if there was any, was that she looked more like a broken woman than a perky airbrushed model.

"He was funny and charming and—." God, she was going to say hot. But for a long beat, she said nothing. "Anyway, I met Rhys when I was nineteen."

"You are fucking kidding me."

"I knew he had a family. We spent a lot of time together. He was just, I don't know—perfect. He was my--." Sobbing, her stark grief made her seem younger and closer to Emma's age. Bits and pieces of words were painfully earnest and redundant; she loved him. So much more than I did before he died, and she still loved him.

"I have to go." I tried to sound like a grownup, but my voice quivered with heartbreak. I needed to get out of there. I need my iPad. I needed chocolate and Amazon with same-day delivery of anything and everything I damned well pleased.

As I stood to leave, she grabbed my arm. "Please. Let me finish."

"Why would I want to sit here and listen to you cry for my dead husband? Why?"

"Because I knew what you were thinking at the viewing, that Rhys and I—." She closed her eyes; a steady stream of tears traversed high cheekbones. She would have made a better widow than me. She loved him.

"He was my dad," she wailed, "He was my Dad."

I plopped back down and watched her crying jag wax and wane until she could continue.

"When were you born?" I barely got the words out.

"December 4, 1992."

The year our garden variety rough patch ended with a fight and Rhys staying out all night. I'd been sick with worry and doubt, and then he'd walked through the door, looking like hell, and promised to love me forever. And things were so much better; we waited four more years to have kids.

"My mom met him at a bar uptown, and they slept together. The next morning, he told her he'd made a terrible mistake, and he was married. Mom was barely twenty and straight-laced. Even though she didn't know Rhys was married, she was appalled she'd slept with a married man and never told him she was pregnant with me. She never asked Rhys for a single thing, but I did.

"I contacted him when I was nineteen and told him who I was and that I wanted to meet him. It took him a few days to get over the shock of having another daughter, but he agreed to meet and asked me to take a blood test. When the test said he was my father, he was good about it. Je didn't deny it, but he didn't want to have a relationship."

"He gave you money." I thought back to the secret account and the withdrawals. Six for just under ten thousand dollars, and then the biggie for thirty thousand.

"He paid for my college and grad school but never contacted me. Then, two years ago, when Mom died of breast cancer, he saw the obituary in the paper and contacted me."

"A lot of money."

"He wanted to help me buy a house, but that's not what I wanted."

"What did you want?"

"I wanted my dad." She sounded like a little child, half sobbing, half pleading her case. "I just wanted him to be my dad. And after he bought the house for me, he was. Sort of. I got to see and know him better, and then he ended up on my floor at the hospital, and we--. I don't know. We liked each other and had so much in common. If he had lived, I think he would have loved me one day.

"I regret not contacting him sooner. I regret not having more time with him." She swiped at her nose and didn't meet my eyes. "And if I let you go on believing something sexual happened between us when it didn't, I know I'd regret that too."

While I had every right to be pissed off at Rhys and this pretty young thing, when she shoved her head into the crook of my neck and wrapped arms that would never jiggle around me, I held her until she stopped sobbing.

# Chapter Thirty-One

All the standard-issue gardens and precision-cut lawns in my neighborhood made my yard look shabby, another reminder that Rhys was the grass guru. The winter rye he'd planted and nurtured was tall and droopy. I pulled into my side of the garage. Although, technically, both sides were mine since Rhys was dead, and I'd donated his truck to the Brain Aneurysm

Foundation. They were ecstatic because they were near the bottom of the charity barrel, which was ridiculous since somewhere in America, someone's brain erupts every eighteen minutes.

I killed the engine and then headed through the mudroom into the kitchen, tossing one of the seven-ounce bars of chocolate Trader Joe's goodness on the table and stowing the others away in the cabinet. When I was a kid, Mom used to ration our Halloween and Easter candy, claiming we'd get sick if we ate too much in a single sitting. It was definitely high time to put that fun fact to the test.

I broke off a chunk, closed my eyes, and savored the first piece. At the same time, I sorted through the myriad of enticing offers in my email, which, until I got better, used to be the equivalent of turning a junkie loose in a drugstore. Or maybe I wasn't better because my finger trembled a little as I deleted offers for daily ads that promised unprecedentedly low prices! After seeing the same offer seventeen times in the last few months, they were obviously giving the stuff away.

Before I could start on a second piece of chocolate, my cell phone rang.

"Hello, favorite son," a creature of habit who calls his mother every Monday at 6:00 pm, no matter what. I was super impressed and flattered until I learned he had an app on his phone that reminded him and dialed my number for him. Still, I got a little jazzed from the obligatory phone calls he could just as easily have canceled.

Jordan snorted. "Hi, Mom. How are you?" Even though I'd just put him on a plane eleven hours ago, his inflection on the Monday check-in call was the same since Rhys died, hopeful, a little on edge until I gave him the response he needed, regardless of the truth.

"As good as I was when I dropped you off at the airport this morning. How'd your audition go?"

"It's bad luck to ask; I'll tell you when something happens, but I'm glad you're okay." I smiled and listened to him go on about his day. "I was at the gym and ran into some of the guys you met. They all asked about you and made it clear they liked you better than me. Frankly, I think they're all using me for my mom." He told me about his favorite barista getting fired for missing work for an audition and then nailing the audition and getting a small part in a new Broadway show. There was excitement in his voice and little jealousy and hope that that kind of luck was contagious.

"I booked something. It's off-Broadway," he said. "Just a short run experimental play, three weeks. It's a shitty script, but my part is really good."

"Jordan, that's fantastic. When is it? Julia and Willa, and I will come to see you. Maybe Emma will come too." I popped a stray crumb of chocolate into my mouth. "I'll spring for front-row seats. God, I'm so proud of you!"

"Um." Silence.

"Um, what?"

"Don't take this wrong, Mom, but I don't want you to see the show, especially with Emma and the aunts."

"You don't want anyone to come, not even me?"

"Look. It's not a big part."

"I don't care how big the part is. You're my son. This is your first really big break."

"And I'm naked."

I wasn't quite sure what stage mother etiquette was in this case. I tried to sound cool and nonchalant, but I could only say, "Okay."

"Or almost naked. I have to hold an encyclopedia over my junk, but it keeps falling down for comic relief, so no. God, no, I don't want my mother, my sister, or my aunts in the audience."

Though I was disappointed, I didn't really want to see that either. "Are you sure?"

"Yes, but you can come to New York when the show opens, all of you. I have a friend in *Hamilton* who can get you tickets. You'll have to pay for them, but they'll be great seats, and we can all go out afterward and celebrate." He paused and sucked in a breath. "God, I'm getting ahead of myself. My show has to actually open and stay open, but if it doesn't, you'll still have me and Lin-Manuel Miranda, his musical, not him. And please don't be mad, but I told Emma first."

"She actually talked to you? I called and left messages and texted her a couple of times today." When Julia stopped for gas and pee breaks. "But I haven't heard a word from her."

"She's fine."

"And you know this because? Every time I talk to her, she's too busy with work or really busy planning the wedding." Which made me feel like I was shirking my MOB duties, even worse my mom duties. But then Emma always knew exactly what she wanted, and if she needed my help, she'd ask for it. Except for that first and only cemetery visit. That was the first time in a very long time I felt like my daughter really needed me, but it didn't last long.

"She's fine," he clipped.

"Look, honey, I'm a mom, so that gives me a license to worry about both of you. Besides, you know I'd never ask you to rat on her."

"Bullshit," he says coolly. "Seventh grade."

"She was smoking."

"She didn't inhale." I wasn't sure if that was God's honest truth or a jab at the semi-truths I'd told my kids about my teenage years. "Besides, this is different. She's not thirteen, and she was just so withdrawn yesterday."

"I know, but if you know something, if there's some way I can help her--."

"She's grieving. And if you're so worried about how she is, why don't you ask Cam."

"That feels like I'm going behind her back."

"Well, you are."

"You're right. I'm just feeling a little crazy here because she's hurting. I don't know what to do about it, and it makes me feel like I'm losing her, Jordan. I can't lose another person I love, especially not my kid; I just can't."

"All right." He blew out a breath and mumbled something about how he should have run away and joined the Power Rangers when he was eight. "She's not okay, but she's working on it. Yesterday was hard for her; it was hard for all of us. She really has been busy with work. She started counseling a couple of weeks ago and has thrown herself into that. Maybe we're all crazy because I'm seeing one too because Dad is—he's—-gone. I can't even say that without thinking it's someone else's line from a really bad Lifetime movie, but Dad is gone, and now Grandma."

"Oh, baby." I caught my tears before they dripped onto my keyboard.

"I know I was lucky to have him for a dad. I have too many friends who grew up with shitty fathers who tried to beat the gay out of them or kicked them out of the house when they were just kids. Guys, who even ten or fifteen years later, aren't accepted by one or both parents and probably never will be. I'm grateful Dad wasn't like that. I'm so grateful he always loved me for who I am.

It makes me feel lucky, but, at the same time, it makes the loss feel so damn big sometimes that I can't breathe. And then I do, and it all comes back again."

"You want me to come up there?" No answer, only the sounds of the city as he walked to the train. "I can be on the next plane out if you want."

"And have you Doctor Phil me?" The always playful sarcasm in his recovery made my heart sing. "Not even a little bit. Besides, I'm going to be crazy for the next three months getting ready for this play."

I straightened several small, framed photos on the desk and up righted one of a dog we had when the kids were little. Molly was lying on her side, exhausted from feeding and caring for twelve chocolate and yellow lab puppies. Emma and Jordan each had a puppy and were grinning like fools. At the same time, poor Molly telegraphed so much mom anxiety I felt it fifteen years later. Or maybe that was my anxiety. "You promise you're okay? Emma's okay?"

"You and Dad did a good job, so stop worrying." He ignored my But—. "Emma and I know how to live a good life and take care of ourselves. You taught us that; it's our turn to do the rest."

# Chapter Thirty-Two

Jordan's words weren't harsh, but hearing them made me feel like I was on that damned Ferris wheel again, going down, down, down. Only this time, I was naked and alone.

My heart galloped with confusion. What was I supposed to do now? My kids had always been my life. I'd worried over them since they were babies and wasn't entirely sure I knew how to stop, or if

I even wanted to stop. In my head, I got that they were older now and they didn't need me as much, but then who was I? What was I? A retired school teacher? A widow? A mom whose job had been downsized? Was that all I was at fifty-five?

In the olden days, those midlife questions were enough to make a woman abandon her family and everything she knew and launch herself into the world to find answers. Luckily, I had Google, but before I could type in my search, there was an email from White House Black Market, and more heart galloping, but the good kind. WHBM was practically giving away their new spring lineup. My brain knew flirty, fun spring dresses wouldn't solve my problems, making it almost impossible to click on the special BOGO offer. But, lucky for me, the email below it made me feel like I'd won the lottery, and it appeared I had won the lottery. And, miracle of all miracles, on a Monday.

Due to a cancellation and the fact that I'd emailed or called them every day for the past two months, McCrady's new tasting-menu-only restaurant that was impossible to get into, at least for the next year, had one spot at the table promptly at 6:30. Yikes! Tonight.

"No." I told myself and opened a new tab to ask Google what a full-time widow and part-time mother was supposed to do with herself. Maybe I should make an appointment with a therapist, my own Misty so I wouldn't have to worry about keeping my story straight. But it was McCrady's, one of the best restaurants in Charleston.

Mom would—. And just like that, I heard her voice in my head with the disclaimer she always used when she was tending to my broken heart. "Good Lowcountry food won't always solve all your problems, Masie, but it sure as hell can't hurt."

I printed out the menu and called to give McCrady's my profuse thanks and my credit card number. I felt like an emotional mess, but by God, I would savor the taste of fifteen fabulous creations by James Beard award-winning chef Sean Brock. I dashed upstairs to get dressed.

Thirty years of marriage had me feeling guilty for being so jazzed about going to a restaurant Rhys would have balked at just because of the $75 a plate price tag, $160 if I opted for the wine pairings. I slipped on a dress that was a little short, a cross between a bona fide LBD from the wishful section of my closet and something out of Widows Wear Daily, and to my amazement, it fit. The black peep-toe heels that killed my feet would be fine since I'd be seated and eating for three solid hours.

I smoothed out the skirt that was almost snug because I hadn't been to the gym in over a week. The part of my brain where my mother will live as long as I do said, "It's too tight; take it off." But the girl on fire, who didn't know who the hell she was, said, "Yes!" It felt good to look good, not for my mother or some guy, but for me.

I was halfway down the stairs when someone knocked twice and then pushed open the front door. "Masie?" Willa called before she saw me gliding down the stairs. "Wow. Look at you, all dolled up to go to your grief group."

"Crap." My heel caught on the runner, and I nearly plummeted the rest of the way down the stairs. "I forgot."

"Which is why I'm here to take you. Is that the bag you're carrying?" I glanced at my black leather everyday purse I thought would be a good idea because my little black satin one looked too dressy.

"Yes. Look, Willa--."

Already she was rolling her eyes and moaning, "God."

"I know I told you I'd go to that stupid group three times, but I really have had enough grief. I should get a pass. Besides, we just buried Mom yesterday. "

"Besides, nothing. You know what happens when you don't take care of your shit." Why did I ever tell her what crotchety old Mrs. Kinsey said? She raised her shades and looked me dead in the eyes. "You. Promised."

"I know I did." Even though I'd completely forgotten I'd promised Willa I'd attend counseling and that damned grief group until I was magically healed. "But that new tasting menu place McCrady's opened had a last minute cancellation. And--."

"We made a deal, Maisie." Hands on hips, feet spread like she was getting ready for target practice with the berretta Tank gave her for Christmas.

"God, Willa, they're having eggplant jerky and quail egg tarts, and I've really grown to love those little eggs." I gave her the menu I'd printed out so she could see for herself that I had a golden ticket to a once-in-a-lifetime culinary event every Wednesday through Sunday. If you're lucky enough to get a reservation. "When will I ever have a chance to have eggplant jerky again?"

She looked over the menu, took out her phone, and texted someone before looking at me with that same smile she always had when we were kids, and she pulled a Tom Sawyer and conned me into doing her chores. "You need to get going," she said, checking her look in the foyer mirror. "You don't want to be late."

"Thank you for understanding," I gushed. "I swear, I'll go next week and, hell, forever to make up for this."

"No, sweetie, you're going to your meeting. You're going to bring something back to prove you went, like a program or a hand stamp or a chip like they give out at AA. But you'll have to drive yourself. I'm going to McCrady's."

Sitting in the parking lot at the Lutheran church gymnasium, I felt stupid for letting Willa guilt me into being there. I looked stupid all dressed up in black like I was going to the symphony or a fancy Spoleto event or a funeral do-over. The hemline was much shorter than I'd normally wear, and maybe it really was a little black dress.

I tried to yank the hem down, but it went barely went passed midthigh.

What was I thinking? This was a club till-dawn dress, not something a newly widowed and downsized mother of two should wear. The diamonds Rhys had slipped on my finger when he proposed sparkled against the black fabric. My teeth clenched at the memory of Cassidy's confession and Rhys's infidelity.

Why hadn't I taken the ring off before now? Would I ever take it off? Rhys took his wedding ring off when he went to the gym and when he banged Cassidy's mother. He probably had a whole gym full of women glancing at his left hand to see if he was taken. If he'd noticed. Of course, he'd noticed. Nothing got by him. He was a detective, for God's sake, and read people for a living. He would have been keenly aware of every look, every nuance, and he probably got a charge out of the attention. And, who knew, maybe Cassidy's mother wasn't his first.

I closed my eyes because it hurt to slip the gold band over my knuckles, which were bigger than when I was twenty-three. It just hurt. The rings made a clunking sound in the cup holder; at the same time, my phone pinged with a text from Willa. The eggplant jerky is divine. Ordered some to go for you. Now be a good girl and get your ass in that meeting.

The clock on the dashboard said I'd be a little late, but I would do this because I promised Willa and because I could feel the retail monster inside of me begging to be fed. I grabbed my bag and looked at my hand that was naked, almost childlike, then sent her a quick text. Hating you a little bit. Bon appetit.

I'd been so caught up in thinking about Rhys the empty parking lot was now full. A sleek black Mercedes sedan pulled in so close I couldn't get out of the car. I started to say something to the inept driver but then looked down at the yellow line that screamed I was the inept one, and the huge late model Cadillac on my right had taken advantage of the extra-large space, effectively hemming me in. I sucked in my stomach and opened the door, making the tiniest mark on the black sedan.

I licked my thumb, rubbed the spot, and was reasonably sure it would buff out before looking around for the owner as if praying I wouldn't see the owner. But there he was, the Paul Newman guy, with his sports coat slung over his shoulder, smiling at me.

"Sorry." My face flushed.

He offered the full Monty of all smiles and shook his head. "That's what I get for being late. He extended his hand. "I'm Hayden. And you're Maisie. Right?" I nodded and must have looked a little confused. "I saw you at a meeting. James and Rutledge and Big G and I always meet for a drink to catch up afterward, and they filled me in on you."

I blushed again and wished to heaven and hell I could turn it off. This man would think I was flirting with him, which I definitely was not. And sure enough, he glanced at my left hand that was naked, so naked, I wanted to squeeze myself back into the car and retrieve my rings from the cup holder. "Don't worry. It was all good, and Rutledge loved your shoes."

I looked down to see the peep toes were covered with parking lot dust, and the skirt of my dress looked like I used it to polish Hayden's car. "Nice to meet you," I clipped, grateful I'd never see this guy again since he only came twice a year, and I would have done my time long before then. "We'd better get inside." I swatted the dust off of my dress.

"Then let's go," he said, still smiling even after I dinged his car.

Walking beside him seemed as weird as walking ahead or behind him. My heels clicked on the sidewalk as I picked up the pace and reached for the door first.

Before I could open it, he said my name. Inside, Misty was wrangling everyone into their seats, giving the group an extra few minutes to catch up, and to wait for Hayden no doubt. But he was beside me, looking gorgeous and chagrined.

"What?" I snapped and opened the door.

"Your," he stammered to keep from laughing and motioned to my backside. "Bottom." I let the door close and craned my neck around. I couldn't see what he was talking about under the bright light above the entrance. "The dust," he said, pointing.

Rather than go into the meeting, he watched me hack away at the dust and perform my best impression of a giraffe to see if it was gone. But my neck wasn't long enough, and I had to look at him for approval unless I wanted to go inside with this man looking like he pushed me up against the car for God knows what.

"There's this—one spot. In the middle." I whacked at it and looked at him. "All good." His smile was warm and there was something genuine about him that reminded me of Mom.

"Thanks." My tone softened because she'd raised me to care about how I looked in public. "Even after I scratched your car, you saved me."

"I probably deserve some kind of reward," he teased, moving closer. "Join me for a drink or coffee after the meeting?"

My cheeks were on fire while he looked at me like this was the most normal thing in the world, a ringless guy asking a ringless girl out for a drink. He glanced at my left hand again to confirm this was all okay, and I wasn't sure. Was it okay? If his wife died a few months ago, it probably would be. But if the CrossFit couple or some other acquaintance saw me enjoying the company of another man, they'd peg me somewhere between a hussy and a whore.

As beautiful as Paul Newman was, and God, those blue eyes were really something this close, I was too much of a mess right now. But when I'd figured out who I was, when I'd taken care of my shit to my own satisfaction?

"Another time?" I offered, and he didn't make that slightly puzzled look Rhys always did when he turned on the charm and didn't get his way. Instead, Hayden opened one of the double doors and waited for me to walk in. "Coffee after the next time we end up at the same meeting?"

"Okay then. Same time next year," he said.

I laughed and was surprised at the pang of disappointment from having to wait so long.

When we strolled through the door, the Tweedle twins waved me over. Dottie patted the seat next to her and gave me a little wink, which I was sure had nothing to do with her saving me a seat.

"A year is pretty far off." Hayden said. "Can I sit beside you?"

I said yes, but could barely hear myself over the crowd until silence slashed through the room. I whispered hello to the twins, but their faces were fixed on someone in the circle of chairs, presumably Misty.

Hayden leaned in close and whispered, "You're not really going to make me wait, are you?" It felt dangerously delicious to look at him and his potent blue eyes, the way a thrill ride can feel too high, too fast.

Even the new me didn't do thrill rides, but I got it now, what Rhys must have felt when he walked into the bar, the night he picked up Cassidy's mother in the bar. I wonder how long he had to flirt with her before she realized he was giving the old tires a kick, before he offered dinner or sex? Or maybe he was never a tomcat, and it really was just that one time. On the other hand, maybe he just enjoyed the flirting, the attention, which to be honest, and I may very well go to hell for it, I was enjoying, too.

"So maybe coffee tonight?" Hayden whispered. The corners of my mouth turned up, and I looked down at my hands folded in my lap. They still look naked, but not childlike, and there was a part of me that wanted to keep the banter going because the flirting felt a little wrong but really good.

"Okay," I whispered.

"Mom?" A woman screeched. I looked up to see my daughter's eyes darting between Hayden and me. "What are you doing here?"

"Emma?" Oh, God. What was I doing?

"Okay," Misty said, drawing out the word. She thumbed through a clipboard similar to the one I filled out my first time here. "Emma Carver. Oh, dear, I didn't know—." She said and then glared at me. "And Maisie."

"What? What?" The inquiring Tweedle twins demanded, and strictly forbidden cross-talk roared like wildfire at the implication that something was very wrong.

Emma wouldn't even look at me. She grabbed her purse and started to leave, but Misty said something to her. She stood stock still and nodded slightly, looking down at her shoes that didn't match her bag or her outfit. Her hair was pulled back in a ponytail, which wasn't unusual, but the hives on her neck were unusually bad, like the ones she got when a classmate died of leukemia or when she was in the fifth grade and was being bullied by a teacher. Or the ones when her father died.

But she'd told me she was okay. She'd sworn it on my mother's grave. But maybe we're all just kidding ourselves that we can walk through death and be okay.

"All right," Misty shouted over the noise, and the sea of voices quieted on command. She handed out a written exercise to everyone except Emma and me and made no mention of the situation at hand. "Please complete the worksheet as thoughtfully and as honestly as you can. Maisie and Emma, follow me."

I didn't have to follow Misty Marrs. I could have walked right out of that gym and gone home, but Emma turned on her heels and stayed close to Misty. Emma whispered something to her dad's therapist and then glared at me over her shoulder, giving me no choice but to scurry after them like a petulant child. Misty checked several unlabeled doors until she found one that was unlocked. She flipped on the light, and we all filed into what appeared to be a cramped janitor's closet.

She closed the door and positioned herself between Emma and me like a referee. "You're Rhys Carver's daughter," she began in her slightly exasperated therapist's voice. Emma nodded, and her face crumpled. I reached out to touch her, but she jerked away and crowded her body against the shelf lined with gallon jugs of industrial strength cleaners promising gleaming floors and streak-free windows. "And you." She didn't look like she wanted to kill me anymore, and seemed more flustered than angry. "You're his wife? You came to my office because you'd lost your dad."

"Oh, my God," Emma gasped, "Don't tell me Grandpa has died too."

"That was your reason for coming to my office," Misty said.

"Emma, Grandpa is fine." There was no time to explain that I had lost my dad, that I'd been erased from his memory. And it felt so much like death, until I actually experienced the death of my husband, the death of my mother.

"Maisie?" she prodded.

"My father does have Alzheimer's, but he's not dead." I felt so stupid I'd lied to this woman and had lied to myself that I could somehow know my husband's secrets, that I needed to know them, that I deserved to know them because I didn't. But not knowing made me feel like I'd failed with Rhys like I'd failed myself, and the truth is we can't know anything for sure about someone unless they trust us enough to say the words. And my husband chose to spend his last words asking for a divorce.

But knowing why he wanted to dissolve our marriage wouldn't change anything. Knowing why wouldn't bring him back. Knowing why wouldn't make any of the crazy stupid things I'd done since he died okay.

"Yes," I whispered and then cleared my throat. "I am Rhys Carver's wife."

"Okay, Emma, you were referred to the group by your therapist," Misty said, taking off one of her mile-high pumps and rubbing her foot before slipping it back on "And you--." Misty began, but I cut her off.

"Emma, honey, look at me." But she couldn't or wouldn't.

"Please, answer the question, Masie." Misty's authoritative tone demanded a confession, but I hadn't even heard the question.

"Emma, I know this looks bad," I began while Emma looked down at her shoes, anywhere but at me. "I had a lot of questions after your dad died." And there it was again, that pulsing, throbbing urge to lift the window between this world and the next and scream, What were you thinking, Rhys Carver? Why did you ask me for a divorce, and what in the hell were you grieving?

"We're going to discuss this," Misty said, "like we'd discuss any other issue in the group."

"Oh, zip it, Misty." I shouldn't have snapped at her or grabbed Emma's arm again, but I did.

"Look at me." My authoritative voice trumped the hell out of Misty's, and my daughter finally looked at me. Tears spilled down her cheeks. I could see the full weight of Rhys' death. He'd broken her heart. He'd broken my baby's heart.

I brushed her tears away. In a flash, she was in my arms sobbing. "I've got you, sweetheart." She pressed her face against my neck like she did when she was little. I rubbed her back and glanced at Misty in apology for snapping at her.

She nodded and handed me a wad of toilet tissue from a roll on the shelf. "Do you want me to leave?" she whispered. Emma turned her face toward Misty and nodded.

"Don't go." I traced the outline of a heart on Emma's back like I did when she was a newborn, asleep on my shoulder. I knew how to mother and how to comfort, but this was bigger than all of that. "Please. We need all the help we can get."

"All right," Misty said quietly.

"I'm sorry, Misty. I didn't know Rhys was seeing you until after he died, and I found his appointment cards." The words I should have said from the beginning spilled out with more tears. "So, in a way, he referred me."

Misty let out a mirthless laugh. "Well, that's definitely a first."

"If he had just died, I don't think I would have done so many crazy things like lie to you, to the group. It's just that one minute, I was standing by his hospital bed thinking how much I wanted to make our marriage better, stronger. But before I could tell him any of that he said--."

Emma's eyes bore into me, hungry for anything about her dad. And, in that moment, I wanted to tell her everything, about the divorce, about his affair, about Cassidy so she could see that I was the better parent. I was the one who'd kept her vows, who'd carried the marriage, but that wasn't true. I'd never cheated with an actual person, but I had flirted hard with a future without my husband, so hard that I was ready to leave him.

"What did he say, Mom?" Emma swiped at tears, eyes wide like I could reconnect her to her father with his last words. And I could do that, be the hero, the one left standing. But we'd both failed.

"I couldn't make out what he said." The truth lifted the weight I'd been carrying. "I wish I could have heard him over the machines, but I didn't, and then he was just—gone."

"I see, Maisie." Misty said softly. "I understand your motivation, but I can't continue to treat you privately."

"That's okay." I made good use of the toilet tissue and handed Emma another wad. Somehow the truth, even if it wasn't the whole truth, made Emma seem calmer, better, but, as my mother would so gently point out, her smoky baby blues turned raccoon eyes needed a little touch-up.

I would tell her the rest of the story and Jordan, too, not about Rhys asking for a divorce, but about Cassidy. Who knew? One day they might want to have a relationship with their half-sister.

"I am so sorry I lied to you, Misty. Even though you really helped me, I never intended to see you again. I was just looking for answers in the wrong place and the wrong way." Take care of your shit, Maisie. "I know I still have a lot of work to do. I'd appreciate a referral to another therapist and maybe another group."

"I can do that, but both of you can stay in this group if you want. Since I don't treat either of you privately, there's no rule against family members being in the same group, and you might find it beneficial."

"I'd like that," I said. "But I'm a little worried the group will feel betrayed that I lied to them about my dad."

"'You let me take care of that." Misty closed the door behind her, and it was just me and Emma and the convoluted smell of bleach and Pine-Sol in the musty closet.

"You really didn't hear what Dad said before he died?" Emma asked.

"No." It was the truth. "I couldn't hear him over the machines, and then he was gone." She nodded and started to say something, but I cut her off. "And then I sort of lost my mind. I just lost it, and I let you down when I couldn't go to your dad's grave—, I'm so sorry, Emma."

"Was he pensive, Mom? No, that's not the right word. Uncomfortable?"

"Yes. How did you know?" Even when she was little, she was wise beyond her years. She would make an amazing judge someday and an amazing mother and wife. And she'd figure out a way to do it all, to be everything she wanted to be, including happy.

"I think I know Dad's last words."

She couldn't.

"It was the reason he was seeing Misty." She squeezed my hand to soften the blow. "He was going to ask you for a divorce because he knew you weren't happy. He knew you wouldn't ask for yourself, so he was giving you what you wanted." Her voice shook because she'd wanted to protect me the same way I'd wanted to protect her.

"How do you know this?" A stupid question, the two of them had always been close. But this close?

"Dad told me about a month before he died and made me promise not to tell you. He hoped things between the two of you would get better. But he started seeing Misty because I think he knew he'd already lost you, Mom. He was grieving you."

I sputtered and dissolved into tears. Rhys, the man I believed I didn't deserve because I wasn't pretty enough, or sexy enough, or just— enough, loved me, and grieved the loss of what we had. And we did have love, early on, we did love each other. Until it got lost in the minutia of work and kids and life, we had love.

"Knowing about the divorce has been eating me up inside. I wanted to tell you that day in the graveyard, but I was so angry at you. And angry at Dad, too, for telling me before he told you. I think it took him retiring before he realized how far apart you'd grown, but he loved you, Mom. He really loved you."

"And I loved him too," I said because it was the truth. Even if it wasn't the kind of love that lasted a lifetime, the kind of love that made a marriage work. I loved him.

# Chapter Thirty-Three

The truth was lighter than air. It picked Emma and me up and carried us out of the closet, past the group and Misty, who was wrapping up a discussion on Finding Your Authentic Self in the Midst of Grief. Together, we floated out of the double doors and into the night. A stand of sweet bay magnolias bordering the parking lot fluttered in the cool breeze, their fragrance sweet, at least to me. Emma hacked like she always did around, especially fragrant trees and women who overdo perfume, only she was laughing too.

What a beautiful sound, minus the hacking, an absolutely beautiful sound. "Go home and take some Benadryl," I said as she pulled a half-full water bottle out of her huge bag and downed it like a shot. She burped before dissolving into laughter again. "Your brother would be so proud."

"Yeah, and he'd get a kick out of the closeted secret metaphor. I should tell him now." She took out her phone and then stopped. "If that's okay with you."

"I'm tired of secrets," I proclaimed, although there was still Cassidy. But we'd all been through a lot, and the weight of that one didn't feel so heavy tonight.

Emma glanced at her phone and then back at me. "Can I ask you something?"

I nodded, not completely sure how a world without secrets worked.

"Who was that man?"

My face blushed hard, and my hand skimmed across my backside like it was still dusty. "What man?"

She rolled her eyes. "The one you were flirting with."

"I was not flirting." Oh, my God, Emma noticed. What if she thought I was-- what? Interested in him? Human?

The no-secrets rule didn't mean I had to share every detail of my life. There was no need to tell her about the dust on my dress or Hayden asking me out for a drink or coffee, which I am sure he meant in a non-sexual context. Besides, it would be weird for Emma, but mostly for me, and she would ask a million questions about a silly little encounter.

But it felt like a secret. "I met him in the parking lot. He asked me out for coffee."

She laughed that I was so embarrassed. Good God, my child was asking about me flirting with some random man? Of course, I was embarrassed.

She opened her car door and stopped. "You should go, Mom. When you're ready. He's cute."

On the drive home, my phone pinged with a text from Willa; I checked it at the next red light. In case you need me, I'm in Nirvana, and I'm never coming back. The light was still red, so I texted. The food's that good? Her answer was immediate. A holy experience. I'll swing by with your eggplant jerky and gloat later. Gotta run now. Only three more courses until dessert!

A few minutes later, I pulled into the garage. The riding lawnmower I gave Rhys for our anniversary a couple of months after we bought this house was parked where his truck used to be. I got out of the car and ran my hand across the rusted old handlebar where the five-hundred-dollar price tag had been twenty-three years ago. Rhys had fussed at me for buying it, but he didn't tell me to take it back. Took me forever to pay it off, but he'd loved it so much that it was worth it.

With our lot being just shy of 2 acres, he'd been killing himself with the push mower and was thrilled with the riding one. Emma named it Baby when she was little. It wasn't exactly a term of endearment. Whenever Baby got finicky and didn't want to start, Rhys would turn the key and growl, "Come on, baby."

Decades later, Cam came into our lives and teased Rhys mercilessly about Baby, kicking the tires with his thumbs in his pockets and making smartass remarks like, "How many miles do you have on this hunk of junk?"

But Rhys proclaimed Cam good son-in-law material after he helped out with Baby's most recent overhaul a couple of years ago. Lately, Baby had been a bit of a diva, and who could blame her after being fussed over for so long. If she didn't want to start, there was no amount of tinkering and swearing that would get her to budge. I'd gotten so tired of hearing Rhys grouse, of course not directly at Baby, and tried to get him to buy one of the newer models that worked all the time and vacuumed leaves and had those huge grass catchers you hardly ever have to empty, but Rhys wouldn't hear of it.

The lawn guy I'd broken down and hired after Rhys died had one of the newer models that zipped around the yard and was done in less than an hour. I'd had the garage door up the first time he came. He took one look at Baby sitting in the corner, recognized her as a well-loved semi-antique machine, and asked if he could take her for a spin. When he was done, he parked her where Rhys's truck was, looked at her longingly, and then headed back to his truck with his spiffy newish mower, which must have seemed like a dud after riding Baby.

Maybe he felt how much Rhys loved that old thing, and tonight I felt just how much my husband had loved me.

The last time I saw him in the hospital, I'd been desperate to make our marriage work, but it wasn't love that made me want to fix us. The loss of all those years we spent together just going through the motions slammed into me, and for the first time, I felt the loss of the love I'd let go.

My Dick Clark husband, the one I always felt like I wasn't quite good enough for, had loved me enough to let me go.

I was good with that, really good, but Baby was lonely and rusty, and I'd never love her the way Rhys did. I took my phone out of my bag and sent Cam a text. I know you and Emma said no wedding gifts, but would you like Rhys' mower? He fired back immediately, Baby? Are you sure? I smiled and texted back; Rhys would want you to have her. The three little dots danced on the screen, and then his message appeared, Apart from my bride, she'll be my absolute favorite wedding present.

I headed inside and then upstairs to my bedroom. It was only 7:30, but I changed into my pajamas anyway. Willa tricked me into going with her to Whole Foods yesterday, two grocery stores in two days a new record for me since Rhys died. I pulled out some stuff out of the refrigerator and made a salad that wasn't bad. In fact, it was pretty good, not Charleston restaurant quality, but it would do.

I clicked on the downstairs TV that hadn't been used in I don't know how long. The channel was still set on Rhys's favorite, the Gameshow Network. Family Feud was on, like it always was, and even if James Brown was alive, Steve Harvey would still be the hardest-working man in show business. The show was mindless fun, and my salad tasted better with every bite. By the mid-point of the show, I was scraping the bowl for the last bite that was pretty damn close to Charleston good. And Steve Harvey had worn out the fact that the Wong family was black and their opponents, the Johnson family, were Asian.

Last question to find out who wins the game, Steve said, "Name something a doctor might pull out of a person."

Shirley, the tiny Asian lady who'd given the worst possible answers, topped herself when she slammed her buzzer first and shouted something nobody, including Steve, understood. He asked her to repeat herself. She spoke slowly, "A gerbil." I slapped my hand over my mouth to keep from spewing my food, and Shirley added, "I heard about that one time. It was very bad."

The doorbell rang as I was rummaging around in the cabinet, trying to remember where I'd hidden the chocolate I'd bought at

Trader Joe's when the Johnson family blew their shot at twenty thousand dollars. They kind of deserved to lose for choosing Shirley to play in the Fast Money round. I waited for Steve to share the top answers before I answered the door and felt a little proud I had four out of five.

Willa and I would be beasts on this show and could field an awesome team. Emma, the warrior when it comes to any competition, Jordan for comic relief. Cam was super smart; we could draft him to be our fifth. Or Julia, the recesses of my brain sang.

Willa gave the Uber driver a little wave as I opened the door. She glided into the house and was positively glowing from spectacular food and the wine paring she'd obviously sprung for. The neat take-out box dangling from her finger made me salivate.

"I give you eggplant jerky," she announced with great ceremony.

I opened the box to find what I assumed was the aforementioned yummy appetizer, only to find the garnish and a smear of sauce. "You ate my jerky?"

Willa giggled and pretended to act insulted. "It was a tasting menu, hence the tiny portions."

"There's nothing here except the sauce." She tried to look guilty but then collapsed in drunken laughter on my couch. "Wait a minute. You would have been here hours ago if the portions were this small."

"Well, you try eating for three solid hours with 21 other foodies and then try to quit cold turkey. But I did leave you a speck, and the garnish is beautiful and tasty."

I moved the orchid blossom around until I found a tiny chip of what I presumed was eggplant jerky goodness and popped it into my mouth. "Wow," I said. She nodded and grinned like she'd single-handedly saved my soul. "Wow."

"I know. Can't stay long. I just wanted to come by and see for myself how you are with Jordan leaving. And, of course, Julia." I ignored the inflection that usually led to a bitch fest about our sister. "Honestly, I wasn't at all surprised that she left this morning, but I was disappointed. Dad's going to need all of us, and, well, damn it."

Her face flushed with surprise that I'd missed my cue to join the party and bash our sister. I knew Willa was still hurt by Julia's absence, what I used to think of as abandonment. It would have been easy to fix that, but it was not my truth to tell. Besides, I wanted a new party, a different party.

"Let's have a girls' night," I gushed. "I'll get the Ben and Jerry's while you call Tank and tell him I really really need you, and you'll be home first thing in the tomorrow."

"Do you?" She laughed as she took her phone out of her bag and was tipsy enough to let the Julia thing go. "Really need me?"

"Always," I said, hoping to God nobody, including me, had eaten the ice cream because Willa was too tipsy to drive to the grocery store, and I really didn't want to get dressed again. "And you'll stay?"

"Deal. But I want my own spoon," Willa called after me. "My own quart if you've got it."

I opened the good cabernet I'd picked up at Whole Foods and set it on a tray with two glasses before rummaging around the freezer through what my children called vintage meat or anything frozen that had passed the sell-by date. There was only a partially eaten quart of coffee ice cream, not Willa's favorite flavor, but then she got McCrady's.

I took two spoons out of the drawer and headed back to the living room just in time to hear her end her conversation with Tank. "Night, love." The warm, teasing tone she reserved just for him always put a stupid grin on my face.

"What?" she demanded with an equally stupid grin.

"You're just so cute when you talk to him, like you're fifteen, laying on the floor in the hallway in the house we grew up in, the phone cord stretched as far as it'll go, twirling it around your finger. Even after what, thirty-five years, you and Tank are adorable."

She smirked and grabbed the ice cream out of my hand. "Shut up and give me my spoon."

I obeyed and claimed my side of the carton of creamy brown goodness. "At our age, I'd say that's pretty amazing."

"It is at any age." She blushed again.

"Since I only got a speck of the jerky, I'll have to take your word on that," I said. "But I'm proud of you and Tank; you got it right. So did Julia and John, Mom and Dad, and, if I was a gambler, I'd bet the house on Cam and Emma."

"And you, dear sister?" She tossed the spoon in the carton. "What about you?"

I'd lived such a long time in the absence of happiness that I'd forgotten what it was like for someone to love me for who I am. To feel their touch, their smile, the intense energy of being with the one person who fits perfectly with me, who sees the parts of me that were broken and rejected. Really sees them and loves me, despite those things, because of those things. That is what will make me whole again. Even if the only person loving me that way is on the other side of the mirror, the grand and glorious happily ever after is mine for the taking.

# THE END

# ACKNOWLEDGEMENTS

Thanks so much for reading *I Should Have Said Something*. While I have two sisters and a father with dementia, the story is a work of fiction, and any similarities between the book and real life are entirely coincidental.

A huge thank you to Andrea Katz, who has loved this story from the beginning. Your encouragement means the world to me and has kept me going, especially when the words wouldn't come. Big thanks also to Shari Bartholomew and her sweet husband for using their medical expertise to help me get the medical stuff right. Thanks to everyone from the park rangers to funeral home employees for answering my questions about the logistics concerning Masie's mom's death.

Thanks to Stephanie Evanovich, Donna Ciriello, and Ron Block, who talked me into getting a small tattoo on one wild and wonderful book lovers' weekend. Our little bonding activity helped me understand the why behind all of Julia's ink. Lastly, thanks to all the readers who pinged me over the last few years to ask when my next book was coming out. This one's for you.

# ABOUT THE AUTHOR

Kim Boykin is a long-time women's fiction and contemporary romance author. Her debut nonfiction book, *Man Shopping: The 50+ Woman's Guide to Online Dating*, marks a new chapter in her writing career.

As a certified dating coach, Kim uses her gifts and talents to help women navigate the dating world. Kim Boykin Coaching is your ultimate resource for dating coaching, consults on your online dating profile, profile writing services, and more. As a certified coach with over 10 years of professional writing experience, she's been in your shoes and understands the challenges of dating after 50. That's why she offers personalized consultations, coaching sessions, and profile writing services to help you cultivate the confidence and skills you need to find companionship, love, and happiness.

Her approach is rooted in authenticity, positivity, and a deep understanding of what it takes to find love after 50. Everyone deserves to find happiness and fulfillment in their relationships, and she's committed to helping you achieve just that. Whether you're new to the dating scene or have been out of the game for a while, she's here to support you every step of the way.

At Kim Boykin Coaching, her goal is to help you succeed in your dating journey, and she's dedicated to supporting you in any way she can. Contact her today to learn more about how she can help you find love and happiness.

# OTHER BOOKS BY
# KIM BOYKIN

## Women's Fiction:

*The Wisdom of Hair*

*Palmetto Moon*

*A Peach of a Pair*

*Echoes of Mercy*

*I Should Have Said Something*

## Contemporary Romance Novellas

*Sweet Home Carolina*

*Caught Up In You*

*Just In Time For Christmas*

*Flirting With Forever*

*She's the One*

*Steal Me, Cowboy*